IMPACT

An absolutely gripping crime mystery with a massive twist

MARK MILLS

JOFFE
BOOKS

Joffe Books, London
www.joffebooks.com

First published in Great Britain in 2022

This paperback edition was first published
in Great Britain in 2022

Cover art by Nick Castle

ISBN: 978-1-80405-214-3

PROLOGUE

A pinprick of light, blinding bright, drills into her eye, her brain. She can hear the drill, its singing note dropping to a dull whine as it meets resistance.

'Ma'am, what's your name?'

Oh God, she thinks. *The dentist! I'm under with gas and air, but I'm coming out of it before he's finished working away at me.*

'Ma'am, can you tell me your name?'

It's not like they're friends, but after two porcelain implants, he could at least remember her name.

'The money you've had off me . . .' she slurs.

'Ma'am?'

More drilling. It's not her head that hurts, though. Her body is a symphony of shooting pains, like she's been dropped from a great height onto something hard. A belly-flop from the three-meter board.

Her dad is poolside in a moment, hoicking her vertically from the water by the wrists. They call it a 'Polaris,' but she can't remember why. *My clever baby girl*, he says. *You just invented a whole new dive . . . the Flopsy Pancake!* He's grinning and smoothing back her wild hair and rubbing her tummy, and she's doing her best not to cry with shame in front of him.

'Flopsy,' she says.

'Ma'am?'

'My name.'

But it isn't. Her dad calls her that. Only him. No one else.

'Florence,' she says.

'Florence what?'

She searches desperately for her dad — he'll know — but he's gone. Vanished. Got on a plane with a bunch of promises he intended to keep but couldn't. Not his fault, not his fault . . .

'Listen to me, Florence, you've been in a car accident, but we're going to get you out of there.'

What is this man talking about?

Someone else shouts: 'Fuck's sake, Dale, can't you smell the gas? Kill the angle-grinder for Chrissakes!'

The drilling stops, and an unseen hand twists a dimmer switch on the lights now flashing blue and red at the periphery of her vision.

Oblivion, black as bitumen, rushes up to wrap her in its arms.

ONE

Lyndon Winslow was woken from his doze by a low murmuring that suggested a gathering of some size and significance was taking place behind the paneled door leading to his study, where the two nurses who tended to him on rotation had set up shop. He called them Ratched and Klebb, but only for his own amusement, never to their faces.

He caught a brief snatch of Olivia's shrill and uniquely irritating voice. Not only had it defeated the best efforts of three speech therapists when she was younger, it seemed if anything to have grown more grating over the years. Olivia had driven out to Canaan, Connecticut, yesterday morning with her husband, Chester, and their two sullen boys, overweight for ones so young and quite charmless, like their father.

Lyndon opened his eyes and gazed around the library. It had been his private refuge, his *sanctum sanctorum*, for a good part of his life, and it was the room in which he would breathe his last. He had ordered that the bed and the medical equipment be set up between two of the double-height windows that flooded the room with light, although the vast space had been designed in such a way that the sun's rays would never strike the precious tomes that climbed the walls

3

on three sides, almost to the ceiling. The highest shelves were served by a steel walkway accessed by a pair of spiral staircases. The floor was of French parquet, reclaimed from an *hôtel particulier* in Paris, and the two long oak tables that ran down the center of the room, bought at Christie's in London, had purportedly been made for the Chapter House at Ely Cathedral during the reign of King James I.

As one who had spent much of his life peddling half-truths to the greedy and gullible, Lyndon doubted the provenance.

His books were safe — already gifted to the Smithsonian — but who would want the tables after he was gone? None of his three living children, that was for sure. Only Valentine had recognized the beauty of their lines, their proportions. He could picture his son now on first seeing them *in situ*, running his long fingers over the wood, admiring the grain and the age-soaked patina, inventing absurd little histories for the many scars that had accrued over the centuries, every dent, scratch and stain: a patch of tiny incisions ascribed to a game of stab the cockroach, a favorite pastime of young monks back in the seventeenth century; a shallow gouge where a serving wench had fended off the amorous advances of the Bishop of Ely with a silver goblet . . .

That was the same weekend that Valentine had dropped his bombshell — calmly, kindly — when the two of them were out walking on the ridge before Sunday lunch.

Valentine. His oldest boy. His firstborn child. The only one of his offspring who could make him laugh. Gone.

His eyes no longer lubricated themselves — that was a service provided by Ratched and Klebb — but he felt the faintest prick of a tear, a straining at the corner of his right eye.

Hearing the door handle turn, he closed his eyes once more. Maybe he would feign sleep, maybe he wouldn't.

He heard a good number of people enter the library and make their way toward his bed. Klebb was among them; he had come to know the distinctive squeak of her ugly, rubber-soled shoes against the parquet.

4

'Pa, are you awake?' William, the eldest of his remaining children, the team leader.

'Daddy?' squawked Olivia.

'Lyndon, it's important.'

The voice threw him. Victor's Saturday-morning golf game was a fixture set in stone.

Lyndon opened his eyes and looked at his attorney. Victor was at the foot of the bed, the others gathered around him. They were all there: his children and their spouses, and even Joe, William and Heather's only child, bookishly handsome.

'Shouldn't you be playing golf?' Lyndon asked.

'Something's come up,' Victor replied.

'It's Florence,' said Ralph, his youngest.

William interrupted before he could go on, snatching back the baton. 'She's been in an accident . . . a car crash, last night. Don't worry, she's all right, just a bit knocked about. She's in the hospital in Torrington.'

'Thank God.'

Lyndon's relief was real, palpable.

'The other driver wasn't so lucky,' Victor intoned grimly.

'Dead?'

'I'm afraid so, and it's still not clear whose fault it was.'

'Or whether she was over the limit,' Olivia added, pointedly.

They all knew that Florence had sought solace in drink following Valentine's death; only Lyndon knew that she had kicked the habit and been happily sober for two years now.

Victor drew closer. 'If she was intoxicated, then we're looking at felony homicide by a motor vehicle, which means a mandatory prison sentence.' He hesitated. 'And even if she wasn't DUI but they deem her culpable — speeding, negligence, whatever — she'll be charged with misdemeanor homicide, which also carries mandatory imprisonment.'

'To say nothing of the scandal,' put in Heather.

Lyndon fixed his daughter-in-law with a gimlet eye. So did Joe.

'Mom, you're kidding, right?'

Heather bristled. 'Well, it's true, isn't it? She still carries the family name.'

'A man is dead and you're worrying about our family's reputation?' said Joe, incredulously.

'You trade on it, too,' Heather shot back. 'Don't pretend you don't.'

'What about *his* family, what they're going through?'

'That's their affair.'

'Joe . . .' chided William, silencing his son before he could reply.

'No, quite right, Joe,' said Lyndon. 'Who wouldn't stop to think for a moment what his death meant to those who loved him?'

He glanced pointedly at Heather. He didn't care what she thought of him; he never had. He'd known her for what she was the moment he first met her: a mean-spirited woman sure of her beauty and with a keen eye to her own advancement.

He turned to Victor. 'Get her the best possible lawyer, and do it quickly, before they try to tie her in knots or, worse, before she incriminates herself. Not one of your lot. Someone from away, from the city.'

'The city?'

'A woman, preferably.'

'It won't be easy, not at the weekend.'

'I don't pay you for easy, Victor. And as soon as Florence is fit to be discharged from hospital, I want her here with us. Understood?'

'I'll get straight on it.' Victor turned and left.

'No expense spared,' Lyndon called after him. 'Send the plane for the lawyer if you have to.'

His family stared down at him. They seemed unwilling to draw closer, as though the cancer slowly consuming his body were somehow infectious. He knew what they were thinking; they were wondering why he had invited Florence up to the family home, having shunned her for years. He was happy to let them stew in their ignorance and even to stir the pot a bit.

'Which of you was the last to see her?' he asked.

A few glances were exchanged before William replied. 'We've lost touch with her.'

'Us too,' said Olivia, with a glance at Chester.

'Although I did speak to her a couple of days ago, when I heard she was coming for the weekend,' added William.

'We went to one of her fundraisers last Christmas,' Ralph confessed, almost guiltily. It was nothing that Lyndon didn't know already.

'I had lunch with her a few weeks ago,' said Joe. This drew a startled look from his mother, which Joe returned with a shrug. 'She called and invited me to lunch.'

'What was she after?' demanded Heather.

'Information,' Joe replied teasingly. 'She wanted to know how we all were.' Joe approached around the side of the bed. 'Are you in pain, Grandpa?'

Lyndon raised his right hand by way of reply, revealing the switch that allowed him to regulate the dose of morphine.

Joe bent down and planted a kiss on his cheek. 'Got to dash . . . tennis match at the club.'

'Keep your racquet head high on the backswing.'

Joe grinned. 'Now where have I heard that before?'

Joe had set the standard; the others now dutifully trooped past and kissed him on the cheek before leaving the room. Ralph's petite wife, Connie, was the last in line. She had been a ballet dancer of some renown before a rupture of the Achilles tendon had effectively put an end to her career. She now worked as a garden designer, having retrained.

'How's the business going?' Lyndon asked.

'Oh, you know . . . up and down, feast and famine.'

'This place could do with an overhaul, some fresh ideas.'

'Hey, the plans are drawn up and ready to go.'

Lyndon smiled. 'You're a wicked little thing, Connie.'

She kissed him on the cheek. 'Can't help it. Always was.'

'Poor Ralph, you must run rings around him.'

'You underestimate him.'

'Can't help it,' said Lyndon. 'Always did.'

TWO

Florence woke again, not for the first time since the accident, but now there was silence and she was still, not hurtling down corridors on a gurney while people barked urgent orders around her.

She was lying on her back, staring at a blue-and-white checkerboard ceiling. She felt very little pain, just a tightness in her neck as she turned her head to take in her surroundings.

It was day now, and a nurse was checking the bank of machines beside the bed, recording the readings on a clipboard. Her black hair, smooth as satin, was worn in a short bob. Florence's gaze strayed past her to the door, which was slightly ajar. She could see the legs of a man seated on a chair outside in the corridor.

'Who's the man at the door?'

It surprised her that her voice worked; she wasn't sure it would.

The nurse scribbled away on her clipboard. 'He's a policeman.'

Like in the movies, when a cop is assigned to guard the hospital room following an unsuccessful attempt on someone's life. Only, that wasn't the case now, she suspected. Something told her he was there to keep her in, not others out.

'What happened to the other driver?' she asked.

The nurse finally turned. Her name badge read: GLORIA.

'I don't know anything about that.'

Florence could see from her eyes that she was lying.

'Did I kill him?' she asked.

Or maybe it was a woman. Or worse. An awful thought crashed over her: that it was a family, a whole family, obliterated. She saw children singing songs in the back seat of the car and she felt suddenly sick, breathless, the bile rising. They were all dead, and yet she was alive, apparently unharmed.

'Oh God . . .' she muttered.

Was it her fault? Did she run a stop sign? Was she traveling too fast? She couldn't remember. She remembered that their song had come on, the playlist on shuffle, the playlist she called 'Soppy Shit.' She'd known the song was coming, just not right then, right at that moment.

Did she take her eyes off the road? Did she look down at her phone? She must have. Why else hadn't she seen the other car? The boondocks of northern Connecticut. A deserted country road at night. How hard could it be? No other lights. No distractions other than the trees and hedgerows hurtling by hypnotically on both sides, and the headlights scything the darkness up ahead.

It wasn't there, and then it was: a brief blur racing in from the left, out of the night, before the world went black.

Seeing that she was distressed, Gloria approached the bed. 'Listen, Florence . . . is it okay if I call you Florence?'

'Yes.'

'You didn't kill anyone. You were in a car accident. It's not the same thing.'

She bestowed the kindest, warmest smile and then stroked her forehead. Florence leaned into the small, delicate hand, wanting to make it stay there, make it stick.

'But someone died, didn't they?'

Gloria glanced toward the door then dropped her voice almost to a whisper. 'I can tell you this . . . your blood alcohol level was well within the legal limit. As for the rest, it's best you talk to Ray Hoskin about that. Ray's the chief of police up in Canaan. A good man. You'll like him. He looked in on you earlier. He'll be back. Now let's get you comfortable.'

Gloria thumbed a button and a motor whirred, raising the head of the bed. She adjusted Florence's pillow.

'You were lucky. A few scratches and some bruising, that's all they could find. You may have some concussion, but there's no bleeding on the brain, not according to the PET scan.' She held up a plastic beaker of water in a mock toast. 'Here's to the guy who invented airbags, right?'

Gloria tilted the beaker toward Florence's lips. She savored the lukewarm liquid; her mouth felt as dry as parched leather.

'Are you hungry?' Gloria asked.

'Starving. But I don't feel like eating, not right now.'

'Your accent . . .' Not quite a question.

'I'm British,' said Florence. 'Well, both. American, too, through my husband.'

'I'm sure he'll be here soon.'

'Unlikely. He's dead.'

'Oh my—' Gloria's hand shot to her mouth. It was such an endearing little gesture that Florence found herself smiling.

'It's okay, it was a long time ago.' Almost three years, but it was beginning to feel like an episode from another age, one that she could finally wrestle with and even overcome. 'There are other people I have to tell, though. They're expecting me.'

'I think that's been dealt with,' said Gloria. 'Winslow is a name that counts for something round these parts. Turn left down the corridor and you come to the Winslow Wing.'

Of course you do. She should have guessed.

THREE

Dylan heard the muffled ping of an incoming text, but his eyes didn't stray from the road ahead to the glove box.

Probably Evie, and probably still angry with him. He could picture her on the couch, long legs tucked beneath her, furiously thumbing her phone: *And this . . . And then that . . . And to cap it all . . .*

He couldn't blame her — he'd made her a promise — but it was hardly his fault that Max had called in sick with food poisoning. With any luck it would be a straightforward assessment: a quick howdy-do with the local cops, some measurements and a bunch of photos, then home within a couple of hours.

Ping went his phone in the glove box.

Definitely Evie.

* * *

The intersection was closed, cordoned off. An apple-cheeked state trooper with a sorry excuse for a moustache flagged him down at the plastic barrier.

'Sorry, sir, but you're going to have to turn around.'

'Dylan Bodine, accident reconstruction. I'm not in uniform, got called in at short notice.'

'Can I see some ID?'

Dylan hit the horn twice and waved at Chief Hoskin, who was shooting the breeze with one of the flatbed drivers waiting to load up the wrecked cars. The chief waved back.

'That do?' Dylan asked.

'Sure. Sorry.'

'You new?'

'Second week, sir. Trooper Phipps.'

'Welcome to the middle of nowhere, Phipps.'

* * *

Dylan parked up beside Chief Hoskin's patrol car.

'Good of you to show,' said the chief dryly.

Dylan grabbed his phone from the glove box and got out of the car. 'Not my fault. Max Jenner's sick.'

'You only just figured that?'

'Be nice to me. It's my day off and Evie wants my head on a stake.' Dylan popped the trunk and shouldered his bag.

'She still making those maps of hers?'

'It's called art, Ray.'

'Sure it is . . . and my wife calls her farts wind-chimes.'

'Yeah, but Thelma hasn't got a show opening tonight at a gallery in Westport, which is where I'm supposed to be headed as we speak.'

'Sounds to me like these two klutzes did you a favor.'

The chief nodded over his shoulder toward the wreckage.

'Jesus,' said Dylan, taking a moment to properly survey the scene of devastation. 'One dead, right?'

'The guy driving the Prius.'

'That's a Prius?'

'Flat-packed, like IKEA. There's more on the driver . . . news just in.'

'Later,' said Dylan.

He liked to approach an accident scene clean, unbiased. Everything he needed to know was already laid out before him, enshrined in the two heaps of twisted matter that had once been motor vehicles, and in the bits that had flown off them, and in the marks their tires had left on the metaled surface of the road. It was physics, pure and simple, Newtonian: the collision of two bodies traveling at speed. All you required were the magical laws and equations to unlock the mystery, to turn back time.

The chief grunted. 'Go do your mumbo jumbo, but be quick about it. The locals want their road back.'

Dylan ducked under the tape and shrugged off his shoulder bag. Shards of glass were strewn all around, glinting like scattered diamonds in the sunlight, and a faint smell of gas carried on the warm breeze. He sensed immediately that something about the scene was *wrong* but pushed the thought from his mind, focusing on the basics for now.

A gray compact SUV, what looked to be a Buick Encore, had been traveling north. Visibility was good, the road straight and relatively level, bordered by trees that thinned out shy of the intersection where the accident had occurred. On the left, a narrow country lane dropped down the slope toward the road and then climbed away once more on the right. Unless the Prius had been spun right around by the impact — and there were no signs of that — its driver had overshot the stop sign on the left, careened across the path of the Buick and been broadsided.

The Buick had struck the Prius with such force that it had ridden up and over the other vehicle, flipping it over and shearing away a large part of its roof, which now lay like a crumpled candy wrapper in the road. The Buick stood near the right-hand shoulder some distance away, badly misshapen yet strangely upright, facing back the way it had come. The debris pattern suggested that it had rolled twice before finally coming to a halt.

Dylan made a complete tour of the site. Taking the camera from his bag, he then made another, shooting the scene from all angles, before photographing in detail the surface of the road at the exact point of impact.

Chief Hoskin wandered up. 'What do you reckon?'

Dylan spelled out his interpretation of events. It was the only logical conclusion to be drawn from the evidence on display, but he was still troubled.

'You got everything you want?' The chief was clearly eager to pull the trigger on the cleanup.

'Everything but the skid marks, Ray. Where are the skid marks?'

The chief pointed. 'There?'

'Those are lateral tracks from the Prius when it was T-boned, but the driver didn't hit his brakes, not even for a moment, just flew straight over the road like it was his right of way.'

'Distracted?'

'Could be,' said Dylan. 'Maybe checking his phone.'

'If he'd had one, which he didn't. And no ID, no wallet on him, nothing to say who he was.'

'You've run the plates?'

'That's the news just in. It was reported stolen in Burlington, Vermont, first thing yesterday.'

Dylan absorbed the news. Despite the heat, he felt a slight shiver run through him. A stolen car, a John Doe, a fatal accident. Too many false notes.

He pinched the sweat from his eyes. 'Okay, let's say you're right, our car thief is distracted — changing radio stations, whatever — misses the stop sign. It works, but only if the guy driving the Buick was distracted at exactly the same moment, because he didn't brake either.'

'She. Young black woman, cute as you like . . . a real hottie.'

Dylan winced. 'Can't say that, Ray. You've done the course. It's called objectification.'

'Shit, yeah, sorry. Shoot the dinosaur.' He looked genuinely contrite, even embarrassed.

'This woman driving the Buick, why didn't she brake? She must have seen something, the Prius's headlights coming at her from the left. People brake, even briefly, it's what they do . . . instinct. There's always a trace. Not here, though. Nothing I can see.'

The only other time he had found no traces of braking was a head-on between two kids playing a game of 'chicken' that went wrong. The aftermath of that collision was an image he would never be able to scrub from his memory.

'Have you spoken to our only witness?' Dylan asked.

'I went by the hospital first thing, but she was still doped up. I'm heading back there as soon as accident reconstruction have finished dicking around and this lot is cleared away.'

'Five minutes,' said Dylan. 'I just need to take some measurements.'

As soon as he had, the flatbeds moved in, along with the Day-Gloed crew from the Department of Transportation, wielding their brooms and spades and black trash bags.

The thought only occurred to Dylan as he was strolling back to his car. It landed with a thump out of nowhere, and he hoped he was wrong; if he was right, it would raise more questions than it answered.

'Hold it!' he called to the team making to hoist the Prius away.

The door had been cut away in order to extract the dead driver. He expected blood, but there was very little of it, he noted, as he crawled inside the overturned vehicle. The dashboard was remarkably intact, and an airbag hung limply from the center of the steering wheel. He didn't know the instrument layout of a Prius, but he found the switch easily enough.

Unless it had somehow been twisted through 180 degrees by the force of the collision, the car's headlights had been off at the moment of impact.

* * *

Chief Hoskin was striding around in an agitated fashion while talking on his phone. Dylan waited for him to finish the call.

'Problems?'

'Don't have kids,' came back the chief's cryptic reply.

'Mind if I tag along when you go to the hospital?'

'What about Westport?'

'Evie will understand,' Dylan lied.

Judging from her many texts, it might mean the end of their relationship, but he needed to know the answer. And besides, he was growing sick of her threats. There were times when he wished she *would* follow through on them, for both their sakes, but also many more times when he prayed she wouldn't.

The chief narrowed his eyes suspiciously. 'You got an itch needs scratching?'

Dylan told him about the Prius's headlights being off.

The chief nodded a couple of times, processing the information. 'It's beginning to stink.'

'It sure is,' said Dylan.

'Time to call in the cavalry?'

Dylan had had enough dealings with the detective bureau over the years to know that it was effectively closed for business at weekends.

'Let's go see what she has to say first.'

FOUR

There were two of them. The older one was wearing a police uniform, the shirt straining against his belly. The other was considerably younger — late twenties, at a guess. Tall and trim, he was dressed in jeans, sneakers and a faded Pink Floyd T-shirt: a thin beam of white light refracted through a pyramid into rainbow colors. Dark Side of the Moon.

Florence saw her father's vinyl collection. She saw her father.

'I'm Ray Hoskin, chief of police in Canaan. And this is Sergeant Bodine.'

Pink Floyd ambled over to the bed and extended his hand, blue eyes steady as still water. 'I'm an accident reconstructionist.'

His grip was firm yet gentle, and Florence was instantly wary. She had lost a chunk of her early twenties to guys like him: good-looking, loose-limbed, laconic types.

'That's a job?'

'Not really, but don't tell the police department.'

They both pulled up chairs and settled into them.

'How are you feeling, Mrs. Winslow?' asked the police chief.

'Battered.'

'Battered's good, given what you've been through,' said Pink Floyd. 'You went up and over the other vehicle and rolled twice. I expected leg casts, pulleys . . . a neck brace, at least.'

'Sorry to disappoint.'

He smiled, teeth white and neat.

'Who was in the other car?' she asked.

They weren't expecting that, and they traded a quick glance.

'A man,' said the police chief gravely. 'I'm sorry to say he didn't make it.'

She had prepared herself for this — she had played the scene through in her mind and she had coped — but now that she was living the inescapable truth of a human life snuffed out, she fell apart, her body shaking uncontrollably, her chest tightening, the tears beginning to flow.

Pink Floyd was beside her in a moment. 'Hey . . .' He laid a consoling hand on her forearm, and when that didn't work, he stooped low and slipped an arm around her shoulders, holding her tight.

'Hey, it's okay,' he said.

But it wasn't, and she clung to him. Hard. If she let go, she would fall into the abyss and never come back.

'It was his fault, not yours, his fault entirely. Isn't that right, Ray?'

'Sure is, Mrs. Winslow. Dyl here checked it over. The guy ran a stop sign. Could just as easily have been you dead, not him.'

It helped, but not by much, and it was a while before her sobbing subsided.

'Nails,' said Pink Floyd softly, his lips inches from her ear.

'Oh God, I'm sorry.' She retracted her claws, releasing him.

He perched on the edge of her bed.

'Who was he?'

Even as she asked the question, she realized she would never be able to shake him off. The dead man would darken her days and haunt her nights forever.

'Just some guy, not from around here,' said the police chief.

'Did he really run a stop sign?'

'Uh-huh. You didn't stand a chance. A split second later and he'd have caught you full-on on the driver's side.'

A split second later. *What if?* she wondered.

'Mrs. Winslow, there's a couple of things we couldn't make sense of—'

'Ray . . .' interrupted Pink Floyd, before turning to her: 'Something on your mind?'

'The song . . .'

'What song?' he asked.

'"Cheek to Cheek." It was our song, my husband's and mine.'

'Tell me about it.'

'It came on . . . just then, just before. I was upset. I braked.' She didn't tell him it was because the tears in her eyes were clouding her vision; he'd think she was a soppy Susan who spent most of her time crying.

'Then what?'

'Then nothing.'

She pictured it now: her foot going to the brake, and then the blackness, almost as though the two events were connected.

'Sounds to me like that song might just have saved your life.'

She was thinking it, too: that if not Valentine himself, then at least the thought of him had somehow interceded to protect her.

The police chief leaned forward in his chair. 'Mrs. Winslow, you say, "Then nothing." You didn't see anything? No headlights, even?'

She thought on it. 'No. I don't know. I don't think so.' It was weird; she hadn't considered it before now.

'When we found your phone, it had an auxiliary cable attached. You were listening to the music via your phone?'

'Yes.'

'Could it be that you, I don't know, reached for the phone, took your eyes off the road?'

An alarm bell rang.

'We're not trying to catch you out,' said Pink Floyd, still seated beside her on the hospital bed. 'There's nothing you could have done to prevent the accident, not given the speed he was going.'

'You can tell?'

'We'll be able to calculate it from the tire marks, but I've seen enough to know already he was traveling at quite a clip. I'm guessing you were up near the speed limit, too. Actually, that's something you can help us with.'

'Oh?'

'Your phone. It'll have a fair amount of information stored on it, stuff we could use, like the exact time of the crash.'

The alarm bell got louder. 'What's in it for me?'

'Peace of mind?' said Pink Floyd. 'I don't think you were speeding, but you can prove it, put this behind you, move on, knowing you were completely blameless.'

She wasn't a fast driver — she never had been; it used to irritate Valentine — and anything that lightened the load of the awful guilt she was feeling right now could only be a good thing.

'Okay.'

The police chief levered himself to his feet. 'That's great, Mrs. Winslow. We appreciate it.' He pulled a sheet of paper from his pocket. 'We're going to need your written consent. You know how it is these days . . . data protection and all that jazz.'

He handed her the sheet of paper and a ballpoint pen.

She stared at the printed text, its bland legalese swimming before her eyes.

Pink Floyd pointed. 'Here at the bottom.' He gave her a reassuring smile. 'It's just a formality.'

She was about to do it when an urgent voice filled the room.

'Don't sign that!'

They all turned.

A woman stood at the door, looking chicly corporate in a navy-blue pencil skirt and a white silk blouse. Her auburn hair was pulled back off her face in a ponytail, and a tan, leather bag was hooked over her shoulder. She strode briskly over.

'Let me see that.'

'And who the hell might you be?' said the police chief moving to block her path.

'Alice Arnold, Ms. Winslow's attorney.'

It was the first that Florence had heard of it.

Alice Arnold pushed past the police chief, took up the sheet of paper and scanned it quickly.

'Oh, very cute.' She tore the paper in two and then turned. 'While we're on the subject, my client will be requiring the immediate return of her cell phone.'

She held out her hand.

'It's not here,' said the police chief.

'Then I suggest you make a call . . . make it come here.'

The police chief glared at her.

Pink Floyd's expression was somewhat different: more guarded, and also mildly amused.

FIVE

Dylan knew something was up, because Evie had stopped returning his texts and his calls.

The note was waiting for him on the kitchen table, propped (purposely?) against the vase of arum lilies he had bought for her yesterday.

BETH HAS OFFERED TO DRIVE ME TO WESTPORT. MAYBE SEE YOU THERE.

No kiss, of course, just in case he failed to pick up on the passive-aggressive tone of the words themselves. He sensed Beth's self-serving hand in the phrasing. Unassisted, Evie would have gone for something more along the lines of:

DEAR ASSHOLE, WAITED AS LONG AS I COULD.

He could picture the two of them tearing into him as they journeyed south. Beth, unlucky in love and hopelessly in awe of her best girlfriend, always searching for ways to level their prospects and thereby shore up their childhood bond. Evie was smart, easily smart enough to pick apart the sick dynamic; they had often joked together about Dylan's vital role as punchbag in the preservation of Evie and Beth's friendship.

'You don't mind, do you, Badger? It's so simple. Whenever she's unhappy, all I have to do is crap on you. Just think of the pleasure it brings her . . . *you* bring her.'

Easy enough to accept when things were good between them, but no comfort at all when their relationship was suffering, as it had been for the past few months, for reasons he couldn't quite pinpoint.

When pushed, which she didn't like to be, Evie ascribed her remoteness to her upcoming show, for which she had been working absurdly hard in her studio. A gallery in Westport, the satellite of a serious operation in New York, had taken a gamble on her, and to her mind it was now or never, do or die, provincial obscurity versus metropolitan acclaim. Maybe she was right; at the grand old age of twenty-nine, maybe this really was her last roll of the dice. If so, then she had chosen a cruel world for herself, one that he had blithely assumed was more long-sighted, more meritocratic.

What did he know? Only that Evie was anxious and needy, and that when she had required him to be present — close by, at her side — he had failed her.

He fired off a text: *Hot on your heels. Will explain all but not tonight . . . YOUR NIGHT! Can't wait. Love you as only badgers can. XX*

He went to the fridge and poured himself a glass of the gloopy green sludge that Evie mixed up every morning. He thought about showering and packing first, but when it came to it, he scrolled through the contacts on his phone and called Captain Dyson. Better to alert him right away, even if — as Dylan knew — the chief of the detective bureau would not appreciate being disturbed on the weekend.

Sure enough, when it came, the reply was curt and to the point.

'This better be good.'

'It's Dylan.'

'I can see that.'

'I'm flattered I'm in your phone, Greg.'

'Don't be . . . so's Charlene from accounts.'

SIX

Lyndon took in the view from the terrace: the grand sweep of clipped lawn giving way, apparently seamlessly, to wild pasture where cows were grazing, lazily swinging their tails.

The effect had been lifted almost wholesale from Rousham, the country house north of Oxford that he had come to know and love when studying in England after his time at Harvard. A magical year. The most perfect year of his life. That was a judgment he could now make with absolute certitude, now that his life was all but over. 1973 would never be surpassed, could no longer be surpassed. It was there at Oxford University, while studying for his Master in History, that he had first met Deborah, a junior research fellow in Psychology at Queen's College, by way of the University of Wisconsin–Madison.

Two Yanks abroad and in the throes of young love while England was falling apart around their ears: the rampant inflation, the striking miners, the three-day working week and the electricity blackouts. The whiff of anarchy in the air had, if anything, bound them more closely together. And, frankly, nothing they were facing came close to the dark cloud of conscription that Lyndon had been living under for two years: the dread prospect of a tour of duty in Vietnam when his number came up in the draft lottery. It hadn't, though, and from August of that year — a month before he arrived in Oxford — conscription had been abolished.

He knew of many who had dodged the draft, pulling strings to secure positions for themselves in the National Guard or moving to Canada, but their father, a veteran of the war in Europe, had made it perfectly plain to his two sons that he would strike them from his life should they look to shirk their duty as citizens. Poor Freddie had paid for this principle with his life, and for all Lyndon's high-minded statements on the matter, he had never forgiven his father for the death of his adored elder brother. Indeed, he had grown to hate him with a quiet yet consuming vengeance.

His morose musings were interrupted by the sound of footsteps. Bevan appeared from the house accompanied by a young woman, the city lawyer whom Victor had found for Florence.

'Ms. Arnold, sir.'

'Thank you, Bevan.'

She offered her hand. 'Mr. Winslow.'

'Please, Lyndon. I hope the room is to your satisfaction.'

'Thank you, yes. A bit pokey, but I'll cope.'

Good radar. One look and she had sized him up as someone who could handle a bit of over-familiar irony. He gestured toward a teak garden chair. 'Please.'

She settled down and admired the view, the shadows lengthening with the westering sun.

'That's some backyard.'

'There's a ha-ha running between the lawn and the pasture.'

'A ha-ha?'

'It's an eighteenth-century device, a concealed ditch that serves as a sort of fence. The cows can't in fact wander onto the lawn.'

'They look happy enough where they are.'

'Yes, they do, don't they?' And every single one of them would outlive him, he reflected. 'Thank you for stepping in to help at such short notice.'

'It was this or a week in Montauk with my partner and his children, not forgetting his ex-wife and her new family.'

'Interesting.'

'Let's just say I fought off two colleagues to get this job.'

Lyndon smiled and gestured toward the drinks cart. 'Help yourself. I'll have a gin and tonic, please.' He read the look in her eye. 'I can assure you, cirrhosis of the liver is the least of my worries.'

He was curious to see how she reacted. He had opened the door to the subject, but few seemed willing to talk about the disease that was killing him, even his nearest and dearest.

'Is it cancer?' she asked, moving to the drinks cart.

'No one said?'

'Only that you were rather poorly.'

'How very Victorian of them. Yes, cancer, pancreatic, although it's gone walkabout since then. I don't have long.'

'You seem very . . . calm.'

'That'll be the morphine.'

'My grandfather was on morphine at the end. He still died cursing his misfortune.'

'Not my way, it's true,' said Lyndon. 'I've always been too much of a realist, a pragmatist.'

'Two ice cubes?' she asked.

'Perfect.'

And it was: on the strong side.

He liked Alice Arnold. She had a way about her, an appealing mix of poise and recklessness.

'If this were a job interview, I'd know by now I was going to hire you.'

She looked mildly surprised by the statement. 'Too late, I'm already on the payroll.'

He laughed. 'All right, let's hear what I'm getting for my money.'

The news from Torrington was good, better than he could have hoped for. Florence was fine, still in shock but miraculously unharmed, aside from a concussion and a few bruises. The doctors wished to keep her under observation until Monday, but they were happy for her to receive visitors as of tomorrow. More importantly, the police had already formed a view that the other driver was to blame, overshooting a stop sign before colliding with Florence's car. That said, they weren't willing to formally exonerate her until the data gathered at the scene by the accident reconstruction expert had been properly analyzed. There was still a possibility of some kind of negligence on Florence's part, which the police might choose to follow through on.

'Are you happy to remain here until we know exactly where they stand?' Lyndon asked.

'Of course.'

'I'm sure we can stretch it to a week, knocking Montauk on the head.' It was a pleasing thought, having her around for company after the house emptied tomorrow.

'You won't find me complaining.' Her smile wavered then faded. 'There's something else . . .' She trailed off.

'Yes?'

'A feeling, I'm not sure.' She took a delicate sip of the Campari cocktail she had mixed for herself. 'The police were keen to get access to her phone, which I nixed.'

'Her phone?'

'And I couldn't get anything out of them about the other driver.'

'All of which means?'

She thought on it. 'Probably nothing.'

SEVEN

'It's me.'

'Had a feeling it might be. You calling from a public phone?'

'Take a wild guess.'

'Hey, there's no need for that.'

'Seriously? You think? What went wrong?'

'Dunno, not yet, I'm working on it.'

'Well, I do. Your man is dead and she's alive . . . very alive.'

'Yeah, I heard that. Look, I told you I was subcontracting the job.'

'To an expert.'

'That's right. The guy's a pro . . . well, was.'

'I don't care. My deal was with you, and you failed to deliver.'

'Hey, I'll deliver.'

'Tick tock.'

'I'm on it. Don't worry.'

'Why aren't I comforted by that?'

'Listen, shit happens in this game. You just have to roll with it.'

'This is me rolling with it. You have my money — a considerable amount of my money — and I have nothing to show for it.'

'You're safe. That's something.'

'Am I? Am I really?

'I wasn't kidding. The guy was a specialist, stuff you can't imagine. He'll have covered his tracks. Who wouldn't in his game? Relax, sleep easy. I'll get this done.'

'All right. Okay. I'll get you what I can from my end.'

'There you go. That's more like it. Friends again.'

EIGHT

Dylan was at his computer, modeling the accident in 3D, but distractedly.

He was still reeling from the success of Evie's exhibition on Saturday night. They both were. It was the first time that the Fish Factory had sold out a show at a private view — every available painting snapped up before the general opening. Annie, the gallery's manager, had sensed a buzz building, but no one had anticipated the scrum of collectors, art consultants and dealers who had fought over Evie's giant monochrome canvases. Within twenty minutes of the doors opening, Annie had been forced to send her assistant out for more wine, and you could no longer hear the thrum of traffic from the Connecticut Turnpike, which cut a concrete streak through the sky nearby.

Evie Horn had found her voice, and the art world had been quick to recognize it. The touching story behind her bold new change of direction had clearly played a part; much had been made of it in the catalog and in the moving speech that Annie had delivered to the packed gallery. As the only child of divorced parents, Evie had often accompanied her father to work during the school holidays. He had been a government surveyor with the Office of Construction in Thomaston, and Evie would hit the road with him and help carry his gear and hold the surveying rod. Her love of landscape was rooted in those early forays around the northern reaches of the state with her father, and although she had sought to convey it at first through a more representational form of painting — sweeping slabs of color applied with a broad brush — she had decided eighteen months ago to return to her roots, to her father and his craft, as a way of honoring his life, his recent passing.

Armed with the theodolite that Dylan had bought her for her birthday, she had gone out over a number of weeks and painstakingly produced a contour map of her favorite place in the Litchfield Hills, a spot where two steep valleys converged. Once the technical work was done, she then took the map and meticulously copied it onto a huge white canvas, hand-painting the looping black lines, which at that scale took on the appearance of ripples, whorls and eddies stirring the surface of a lazy river.

The paintings were hypnotically beautiful objects in their own right, but they could also be read, the lines converging where the gradient steepened, before drawing apart once more. The more you stared, the more the landscape seemed to rise off the surface, coming to life in your head, until you could almost feel yourself striding across it, straining up a slope or stumbling down another.

The phone on Dylan's desk rang.

'Dyl, it's Greg.'

'I'm almost done.'

'You got a moment?'

'Now?'

'My office.'

The detective bureau was housed on the second floor of Torrington police headquarters, an old and imposing brick pile rising four-square halfway along Main Street. It had once been the North School, and for some reason many of the windows had been sealed up when the building had been renovated to house the various police departments, which made for a world awash with electric light.

31

Greg's office was a windowless box. It could just as well have been night outside, not a gloriously sunny Monday morning.

Greg already had company.

'You know Detective Fuller.'

'Sure,' said Dylan. But only to nod at, as he did now. 'Hi.' She nodded back at him.

Carrie Fuller had arrived from Philadelphia a couple of years ago, raising the grand total of female detectives in the Torrington Bureau to two, and also raising the average age of her fellow investigators by a fair bit. Some wag in the Canine Unit had promptly christened her 'Roots,' because she'd been growing out her gray hair at the time. Famously, she had told him she was cool with that, so long as he didn't mind her calling him 'Dog Fucker.' The 'Roots' nickname didn't stick.

Dylan hadn't had much to do with her; she tended to work the tougher cases, narcotics and sexual crimes. As for her hair, she now wore it short in a silver side parting that wouldn't have suited many in the way it did her. The big green eyes and the high cheekbones helped.

'Why don't you tell Carrie what you told me?' said Greg.

'And anything else that comes to mind,' she added.

Dylan took his time, recounting his examination of the accident scene in tedious, chronological detail. The first time that Carrie Fuller stopped him, it was to ask about the angle at which the lane the Prius had shot out of met the main road. The second time was to ask if there was any chance the Prius had in fact been stationary in the middle of the road, possibly stalled, when the other car struck it.

'I wondered that, too, but the angle of the tire marks at the point of impact suggested it was moving perpendicular to the Buick's path. The calculations I made this morning confirm it.'

'Any idea of its speed?' she asked.

'Close to sixty miles per hour. Fifty for the Buick.'

'Go on.'

He told her about his sudden hunch and the discovery that the Prius's headlights had been switched off.

'Ray Hoskin was impressed by that,' she said.

'You know Ray?'

'Everyone knows Ray . . . he's hard to miss. What if one of the cops first on the scene turned the headlights off?'

'They didn't. I've talked to both.'

'Tell me about the hospital,' she said. 'Seems it was your idea to get the Winslow woman's phone off her.'

She had obviously had a thorough chat with Ray.

'It didn't work out.'

'Why?'

'Her attorney showed up.'

'I mean, why were you after her phone? What were you hoping to get from it?'

'Didn't Ray say?'

'I'd like to hear it from you,' Carrie Fuller replied evenly.

Dylan glanced at Greg, who remained expressionless, a silent observer, as he had been from the first.

'I don't know. Given everything we'd seen, I thought it could be useful to you guys . . . you know, down the line.'

Greg finally came to life, leaning forward in his chair. 'What do you think?' he asked Carrie Fuller. 'Foul play?'

She looked skeptical. 'Bits and pieces that don't add up to squat.'

'A stolen car?' said Dylan. 'A John Doe at the wheel?'

She shrugged. 'People steal cars and crash them. It happens.'

'No phone on him? No wallet? No ID?'

'Could be any number of reasons for that. You ever watch CSI? Ever heard of MMO? Motive, means, opportunity. We've got no motive, a few scraps when it comes to the means, and nothing on the opportunity.'

Dylan was growing to dislike Detective Carrie Fuller. He certainly didn't appreciate her patronizing tone.

'What do we know about the woman?' she asked.

'Florence Winslow, British by birth, daughter-in-law to Lyndon Winslow through the old man's eldest son, Valentine. She was heading to join the family for the weekend. They've got a big spread up near Canaan. What else? She's a widow. Valentine died a few years back — sepsis — while they were traveling in South America. Colombia. Very sudden, very tragic. She now runs a charity based in New York that raises awareness of the disease.'

'I'm guessing you didn't hear that from her,' said Carrie.

'I got it off the internet yesterday.'

'Nothing better to do on a Sunday?'

Maybe 'dislike' didn't quite cover it.

'Anything else?' asked Greg.

'Not much. Old man Winslow is about to croak from cancer.'

'A deathbed farewell?' Carrie asked.

'Looks that way.'

'You don't sound convinced.'

Dylan knew that whatever he said now would only arm her for a further assault. 'It's probably nothing . . .'

'Let's hear it, anyway,' said Greg.

'The old man hasn't seen her in years, not since he cut them off, her and Valentine.'

'Why would he do that?' asked Carrie.

'Valentine turned his back on the money, the family business, decided he'd had enough. Walked away from it all. Wanted a simpler life with his new wife. Daddy reacted by disinheriting him.'

'You get that off the internet, too?' asked Carrie Fuller.

'Off a guy I know who works at the country club near Canaan.'

Greg glanced at Carrie. 'What did I tell you?'

'You're right, he's not as stupid as he looks.' She turned back to Dylan. 'You want to take a ride with me?'

'Not really.'

'Good, 'cause I've got an errand to run after, so we'll go in convoy.'

34

NINE

The polite suburban sprawl northwest of Torrington soon gave way to gentle hills, blanketed with trees and studded with small farmsteads. Dylan led the way, turning north at Goshen onto the 63, the hills building around them, the forests thickening. It was a pleasant drive through unthreatening wilderness, the same route that Florence Winslow had taken on Friday night, although Route 7 from Kent, to the west, would have made more sense when coming from New York. So what was she doing on the 63? It hadn't occurred to him before now, and he made a mental note to follow it up.

They pulled in and parked their cars on the wide grass shoulder just south of the intersection. There were no remaining traces of the accident, nothing to suggest that a man had lost his life here three nights ago. All was peaceful. The wind teased the treetops, and they could hear birdsong.

Dylan painted a picture of the grim scene for Carrie, pointing out where both vehicles had ended up.

'Let's go with your theory,' she said. 'He was out to get her.'

'Not my theory.'

'Whatever. Indulge me. Put yourself in his shoes.'

They set off up the side road on the left that the Prius had shot out of. The narrow lane climbed gently up the slope away from the junction, flanked by high hedgerows.

'What are you thinking?' Carrie asked.

'We keep walking. He needs a run-up, needs to pick up a head of steam.'

It wasn't much, a slight widening of the lane some fifty yards farther on: two shallow scoops out of the facing banks, so that a couple of cars could pass each other.

'Here,' said Dylan.

Beyond the hedgerow on their right, an overgrown pasture dropped away toward a thin belt of trees that trimmed the main road south of the intersection. A red pickup passed by, heading north. It was visible through the trees.

'He can see her coming all the way,' said Carrie. 'Even easier at night, what with the headlights.'

'Yeah, but how does he know it's her?'

'Exactly,' said Carrie.

'There's a tracking device in her car.'

'Only, he's got no phone.'

'Right. So he must have been following her. He overtook her, got ahead of her, set himself up. He has to hurry, has to spin the car around, but it's doable.'

'It works.'

'No, not sure it does,' said Dylan. He took a moment to follow through the flaw in the thinking. 'Only if he'd scouted the place beforehand.'

Carrie looked intrigued. 'Go on.'

He spread his hands. 'It's obvious to us in daylight it's a great spot to pick. For him, at night, how does he know he's not going to be unsighted, unable to judge his run at her? What, he overtakes her and just happens to choose a side road that perfectly suits his purpose?'

'He got lucky,' Carrie suggested.

'Not so lucky that he didn't die.' Dylan hesitated. 'That's the other thing bothering me.'

'Don't hold back.'

'What if he hadn't died? What if it had gone to plan? He catches her on the driver's side, takes her out. He's shaken up but okay. Job done. And if she's still alive, he finishes her off. Then what? What's he going to do? Flee the scene on foot?'

'Good point,' she said. 'Not much of a plan.'

'He had an accomplice, another car to get him safe away.'

Carrie thought on it. 'So why doesn't the accomplice finish the job? It's a fuck-up, yeah, but Florence Winslow is right there. How hard is it to snuff her out?'

'He freaks out, just takes off. Or she.'

'Right, or she,' said Carrie. 'Still, too convenient.'

'You didn't see the crash site; it was a horror show.'

'You're reaching.'

'Maybe. But if I'm right, someone out there knows what really happened here. You just have to find them.'

'That all?' said Carrie with an amused grunt.

* * *

She waited until they were back at the cars before coming out with it.

'How do you feel about working with me on this?'

Dylan wasn't sure if he'd heard her right.

'Not my idea . . . Greg's. He's had his eye on you for a while, wants someone to blood you, bring you on.'

It was the first that Dylan had heard of it, and at that moment a truck thundered past, catching them in its backwash. He waited for the silence to return.

'I like what I do.'

'Mr. Ambitious, eh?'

'From the woman who left the big city for the back of beyond?'

He had seen Carrie Fuller smirk before now, but he'd never seen her smile. 'You'll never know why if you don't say "yes." This is my last case.' She caught his look. 'That's right — fifty-five in a month. I'm retiring.'

'You're okay with the idea?' he asked.

'Can't wait.'

'I mean, working with me?'

She nodded. 'I am now. I've always been big picture, you're more nuts and bolts.'

'Is that a compliment?'

'I could learn a lot from you.'

'I doubt it.'

'I just did. You see things I don't, and vice versa.'

'What do *you* see?' asked Dylan.

'I see a dead man who didn't just know where she was coming from, but where she was going.' She cast a glance at the intersection. 'It's a puzzle in search of a solution. Who knows, we might even have some fun along the way.'

Dylan thought about Evie's success on Saturday, and what it meant for them going forward, and what his promotion — for that's what it was — would mean to her.

'Okay,' he said. 'Why not?'

'It'll mean ditching that very smart uniform of yours. A lot of people are in it for the uniform.'

'Not me. And I can still wear it at home when no one's looking.'

Carrie offered her hand. 'Welcome to Team Fuller.'

'Message received.'

'You learn quick,' she said. 'Now let's go take a look at those two cars.'

'I thought you had an errand to run.'

'That was it — a trip to the pound. Wasn't sure then you'd be coming too.'

TEN

Florence could clearly recall her first visit to the house. She remembered the long driveway winding through parkland and Valentine pointing out an oak tree that he'd fallen out of when he was a boy, fracturing his leg in two places, ruining his summer in the process. Most of all, though, she remembered her trepidation, because she had been about to meet his family for the very first time, and for all Valentine's assurances to the contrary, she was convinced they wouldn't approve of her. Why should they? She had learned early in life that distrust of the other was an ugly impulse not easily mastered, and she was everything they weren't — a foreigner, dirt-poor and black.

Now, though, it wasn't Valentine driving, but a burly man called Bevan; and Alice, her attorney, was beside her in the back seat; and they were in a Range Rover, not Valentine's crappy old Golf with the velour seats. Years had passed, and nothing was the same, aside from the nerves she was feeling as the house finally swung into view.

It appeared bigger than she remembered it, grander. Had the columned entrance been there last time? Possibly. She was pretty sure the abstract steel sculpture rising in angled slabs from the circular lawn out front was a new addition.

Why was she here? All she knew was that Lyndon had called her two weeks ago and told her he was dying and that he wished to see her before he did. She could have said no — it had been tempting — but then she'd asked herself a simple question: What would Valentine do? He would go — unquestioningly, in spite of everything — and seeing as he couldn't, she should, for him.

It struck her that she was here, as she had always been, by association with Valentine, never quite in her own right: a curiosity, an outsider, an intruder into their privileged world. The fact that she was now a victim helped in some small way. It had brought the best out of the family when they'd all come by the hospital yesterday — the full complement of brothers- and sisters-in-law, along with Joe. They had showered her with sympathy and marveled over her good fortune. She was lucky to be alive. Everyone said it. A matter of mere moments. A split second here or there.

One song, their song — Fred and Ginger — enough to make a difference.

Not so for Valentine. One silly stumble on their hike in the hills, one rusty nail in a gatepost. A scratch. A nothing scratch, but the wrong kind of bugs inside him, silently finding a home. And when they had finally shown themselves back in Medellín, the antibiotics had proved powerless against the infection.

'Fly him out, fly him out now!' had come the call from back home. Finally. Eventually. Too late.

She had lost her husband — the man whose children she was ready to carry inside her — and yet because of it, many had survived when they would not have otherwise. She knew that for a fact, and it was a salve of sorts. The truth was, though, there were times when she would happily have traded all of them for Valentine.

The Range Rover drew to a halt at the front steps, and they all got out of the vehicle. Bevan grabbed her suitcase from the trunk.

'Thanks for picking me up,' she said.

'No worries,' he replied, which made her think that behind the American accent lay an Australian.

She was surprised to see Heather appear from the house and hurry down the front steps, brisk and beautiful and smelling of citrus.

'It's so great to see you on your feet.'

'Only just,' said Florence. 'It's like learning to walk again.'

'You poor thing. Here, take my arm.'

It was bony but toned, an arm that spoke of a rigorous fitness regime, of personal trainers and free weights that Florence would struggle to lift off the floor, let alone above her head.

Yesterday, Heather had definitely given the impression that she was heading back to the city with the others. Apparently not. Apparently, Heather could read her mind.

'I couldn't leave, not now, what with it being so close to the end.' Heather stopped in the entrance hall and turned to Florence. 'You should prepare yourself. He's not the man you used to know. So very . . . thin.'

Maybe she was being cruel, but it almost sounded like Heather was jealous.

* * *

They all accompanied her upstairs, past the giant Donald Judd painting on the landing, where the wide stone staircase divided and turned back on itself. Valentine had loved that painting with a passion. Memorably, she had once seen it bring tears to his eyes.

Bevan stayed just long enough to deposit the suitcase in her bedroom. Heather played hotelier, pulling open closets and talking her through the operation of the futuristic steam shower in the en-suite. Alice lingered, expressing an interest in talking to Florence. It was Heather's cue to leave them alone, which she finally did, reluctantly, judging from her expression.

Alice opened the doors to the balcony that overlooked the parterre at the side of the house: geometric beds of roses trimmed with box hedges and separated by gravel pathways.

'Are you happy to be here?' she asked. 'I mean, are you okay with it?'

'Why *am* I here?'

'Lyndon wants to speak to you.'

'About what?'

'Your guess is better than mine.'

This was her first exposure to the family, Alice explained. She wasn't part of the usual team of lawyers and advisers and general fixers that Lyndon had always surrounded himself with, the cohort of slick operators who had stepped in to act as intermediaries when things had turned sour with Valentine, and Lyndon had refused to have any more direct communication with them both.

'Listen, Florence, Lyndon may be picking up the tab for my services, but as far as I'm concerned, *you* are my client. I'm here to protect you, to serve your best interests. I just want you to know that.'

The words were a comfort. Alice must have sensed her unease or possibly experienced some of it herself over the past couple of days. The Winslows presented a formidable front; it was easy to feel cowed by their fierce sense of family, by the finance house that bound them together in work, and by the amount of time they chose to spend together when not in their neighboring offices, making their millions.

'Where did he find you?' Florence asked.

'His own attorney did. We're a small outfit. You won't have heard of us. We stay in the shadows, which is where most of our clients like to remain. We solve problems, discreetly.'

'You've done this sort of thing before?'

'A car accident? No, not exactly. But the law is the law, and we're used to dealing with the police, who sometimes have their own reasons for behaving as they do. We police the police. That's what my father says. He's my boss.'

Alice couldn't promise anything, but her instincts told her that the matter of responsibility for the crash would quickly be resolved, and favorably so. 'They're no fools, though, especially the young guy.'

'The Pink Floyd T-shirt?'

'Right, the ugly one. He worked quite a number on you with that phone nonsense. I just wonder why.'

Florence shrugged. 'I don't know.'

'They're holding something back. We'll know what it is soon enough. Until we do and I've dealt with it, I won't be going anywhere.'

Lyndon was resting right now, but she could see him later. To the exasperation of the nurses who cared for him, he insisted on being removed from his bed in the library and wheeled out to the terrace for a cocktail at six o'clock every evening.

'It takes it out of him, but he won't have it any other way.'

It sounded like the Lyndon she used to know.

'I'll let you unpack,' said Alice.

'Thank you.'

Alice turned at the door. 'You'll be just fine. I mean, look at you. In your position, I'd be a complete mess.'

'I doubt it somehow.'

'Don't be fooled by my capable air. I needed three days off work when my cat died.'

ELEVEN

They didn't require a warrant for an inventory search of the cars involved in the collision; Dylan knew that already, just as he knew that the wiry, balding man who happened to be on duty at the auto pound when they arrived — twenty years in the job and counting — took an almost sadistic pleasure in extracting payment from those who'd had their vehicles towed for parking infractions.

Carrie, new to the place, explained the purpose of their visit and flashed her badge.

'Spoil your day, did we, Bernie?' Dylan asked.

'There'll be others through soon enough.'

Bernie wasn't joking, and the maniacal glint in his eye suggested that the poor souls would be made to suffer terribly for Dylan's glib comment.

Both cars were parked in a separate section at the back of the pound, beyond a low breeze-block building. Nearby, a fence of vertical steel struts topped with razor wire climbed to some fifteen feet or more.

'You squeamish?' asked Carrie.

'Not particularly.'

'Then you can take the Prius.'

She pulled some surgical gloves and evidence bags from her knapsack and handed them to Dylan.

'A first sweep, anything that seems important. Anything else, shoot with your phone so we can check it with the owner, see if it's hers or not. Forensics will do the real work, if it comes to it.'

'If it comes to it?'

Carrie tilted her head at him. 'We can't call them in based on a few wild theories. We need hard evidence. Go and find us some.'

* * *

Dylan started with the trunk and soon established that the Prius's owner — a hospital pharmacist in Burlington, Vermont — was a keen tennis player, as well as being on the small side. The tennis bag contained three identical Wilson racquets, a couple of tubes of unopened balls, and a pair of size 5 Nike tennis shoes. Beneath the deck board in the trunk he found the jack, a wheel nut wrench and a tire puncture repair kit, which included a small air compressor. Despite the current condition of the vehicle, the impression was of an owner who kept her car fastidiously clean and clear of clutter. An examination of the rest of the vehicle confirmed it. The console box between the front seats contained a Linen & Sky air freshener, still in its packet, and all he could find in the glove box were a small LED torch and the vehicle's user manual.

A thought occurred to him, and he flipped through the manual until he found the relevant page. He went and joined Carrie, who was in the back of the Buick, searching beneath the seats, which could only mean one thing.

'Looking for a tracking device?' Dylan asked.

'If there's one here, it's got to be inside. I've checked the wheel arches and undercarriage.'

'Inside would mean someone getting their hands on her car key.'

'Or someone she gave a ride to, someone she knew. Or valet parking. Whatever, it would throw up some leads. You?'

'Nothing yet. Can I grab the key to the Prius?'

'In my bag. Why?'

'Just a thought.'

The Prius had suffered structural damage, but the electrics were still functioning. Dylan followed the instructions in the manual to navigate the options on the multi-functional display. It took him a while to find what he was looking for. The pre-collision system had been set to OFF, disabling automatic braking. It was possible the Prius's owner was responsible, but if she wasn't, it pointed to a certain malicious intent on the part of the man who had stolen her car. It suggested that John Doe had known exactly what he was going to do with it.

'Good thinking,' said Carrie, when he broke the news to her. She was now busying herself in the trunk of the Buick, prizing away the plastic side panels with a screwdriver. She soon gave up.

'If there's one here, I can't find it.'

'Can we scan for it?'

'First thing I did.' She pulled a device from her knapsack. It looked like a first-generation cell phone, with a stumpy antenna sticking out of the top. 'Bug detector. Trouble is, most trackers only transmit when the vehicle's in motion, to preserve battery life.'

Dylan patted the roof of the Buick. 'So we put it on a flatbed and take it for a ride.'

Carrie shrugged. 'I guess we do.'

'I'll go break the good news to Bernie.'

* * *

Neither of them held out much hope, but Carrie's gizmo picked up a signal within a block of the pound.

'Bingo,' she said. 'With bells on.'

The sound emitted by her detector was in fact more like a low drone. It rose in pitch as they edged their way cautiously around the steel platform toward the front of the car. Dylan hauled up the crumpled hood. The engine compartment definitely appeared to be the source of the signal.

'I already checked it,' said Carrie.

They poked around some more but found nothing. Dylan tapped on the rear window of the driver's cab and gave a thumbs-up.

All became clear when the mechanic back at the pound raised the Buick on his hydraulic lift and removed the skid plate from the underside of the engine. A black box tumbled to the concrete floor at his feet as the plate came away. He stooped to pick it up.

'No touching,' said Carrie.

She used a pencil to flick the box into an evidence bag, which she held up to the light.

'Waterproof box with a magnetic attachment. No prizes for guessing what's inside. It must have come loose in the accident, dropped to the bottom.' She turned to the mechanic. 'Is it possible to open the hood without popping it from the inside?'

'This guy managed it,' joked the mechanic, nodding up at the Buick.

'Very good,' said Carrie flatly.

'Sure, if you know what you're looking for. You can get to the latch through the front grille.'

* * *

They left it for the lab technician back at Headquarters to open the waterproof box and remove the tracking device. Disappointingly, both tested negative for prints when dusted. Carrie asked the technician to get her everything he could on the device, then they headed upstairs to break the news to Greg. He was away from his office, out on business.

Carrie dumped herself in one of his chairs anyway and indicated for Dylan to do likewise.

'What now?' he asked.

47

'We get her in — the Winslow woman. We'll have to go through her attorney.'

Dylan pulled his wallet from his hip pocket and produced the business card that the attorney had given him at the hospital. He handed it to Carrie.

'Alice Arnold. What's she like?'

'Daunting.'

'Age?'

'Early thirties?'

Carrie handed him back the card. 'You make the call.'

'It'll have more clout coming from you.'

'Which is what we don't want. Keep it vague, no mention of the tracker for now.'

Dylan thought on it. 'How about I say we just need to go over a couple of things with her and her client, formalities, before giving the all-clear?'

'Maybe throw in some paperwork that needs signing, documents her insurance company is going to need from us, that sort of thing.'

'Got it. Nothing alarming for now.'

'Mind if I listen in?'

'No.'

He tapped Alice Arnold's number into his phone and was about to press dial when a thought stalled his thumb.

'Worst-case scenario, this was an attempt on Florence Winslow's life, right?'

'Uh-huh,' said Carrie.

'Which means someone out there still wants her dead.'

'Unless that someone is already dead. Could be John Doe was a guy with a grudge, maybe a jilted boyfriend.'

'Say he isn't . . . then she's a sitting duck, right now, as we speak.'

'We've no grounds to take her into protective custody. Maybe she was the one who fitted the tracker to her own car.'

'I'm just saying—'

'I know what you're saying, but there's only so much we can do right now. And yes, if you stick at this game, stuff will happen, stuff that shouldn't, stuff you'll blame yourself for . . . things you missed, warning signs ignored.' She hesitated, and Dylan could see in her eyes that her mind had turned briefly to some memory or other.

'Lecture over,' said Carrie. 'It's good that you care. Most don't. Now make that call.'

TWELVE

'Hello, Lyndon.'

It wasn't the timbre of her voice, or even her expression; it was the look in her large, dark eyes that betrayed her feelings: a look of profound sorrow at seeing him there, seated in his chair on the terrace. No trace of pity or revulsion, both of which he had grown accustomed to lately.

'Florence.' He held out his hand toward her. She took it. 'How are you, my dear, after your ordeal?'

'Sore. A bit wobbly still.'

He could have done it then, blurted it out, but it wouldn't have been fair on her. And in truth, he wanted to stretch out the anticipation for himself, to enjoy the knowing. It was, he realized, the only thing he had left to look forward to.

'I've missed you.'

'Lyndon—'

'It's true, even if all the evidence suggests otherwise.'

'It certainly does,' she replied, releasing his hand. A just rebuttal, he told himself, but then she knelt down beside his wheelchair and hugged him. It was such an unexpected gesture that he remained frozen for a moment, his hands hovering, before finally settling like birds on her back.

'We missed you, too,' she said.

He searched for some words but couldn't find them. He just hugged her harder, as though he were hugging Valentine, too.

When they finally released each other, she said with a wry smile, 'Just so we're clear, this doesn't mean you're forgiven.'

'I would never expect it, not after the way I treated you.'

She rose to her feet. 'Do you mind if we don't talk about it? I've worked hard to put all that behind me . . . successfully, I think. There's no point in dredging it up. I don't suppose you were thinking straight at the time, and you're a proud man, not someone to go back on a decision once he's made it.'

He stared at her. 'My God, what happened to the callow young girl I used to know?'

'Nothing much good, but I'm still here.'

'Still here, and doing good.'

'Tut-tut . . . doing *well*,' she said, correcting his grammar.

'Doing good,' he insisted. 'I was talking about the charity. I want to hear all about it, but not before you've poured us a couple of drinks. Mine's a gin and tonic.'

'Alice said.'

She moved to the drinks cart.

'You like her?' he asked.

'It's hard not to. And thanks for sorting out that side of things.'

'Is it sorted?'

'As good as. I'm in the clear, apparently. The police called earlier. We just have to go in tomorrow and sign some papers.'

She seemed to be taking the death of the other driver remarkably well, but he didn't suppose she was, not deep down. Unless the slings and arrows of outrageous fortune had numbed her soul over the intervening years, it would be eating her up.

'What a thing to happen. It seems you were very lucky.'

'It's weirder than that,' she said, handing him his gin and tonic.

'You're not having one?'

He felt bad asking it, but he was curious to see how she would respond.

'I got on the wrong side of alcohol a while back. I don't touch it anymore.'

'That must be tough.'

'It was. Maybe it will be again . . . not right now, though.'

Lyndon watched as she poured herself a glass of soda water with a slice of lime, and he wondered how he could ever have doubted Valentine's decision. He felt a sudden stab of pain in his side, just below his ribcage, and although he knew it was the cancer, it felt for a moment as though it were his conscience reprimanding him for what he knew in his bones to be the real reason he had cast her as the enemy, the usurper of Valentine's affections and loyalties.

He hit the button in his hand; the pain receded, ebbing away in tiny waves.

He had always imagined himself dying a happy man, but in that moment he despised himself more than he had in all his life.

* * *

He listened to her story of the song coming on just before the crash and the tears that had caused her to brake suddenly, thereby saving her life, and he wanted to believe what she wanted him to believe, and for a moment he almost did. But Valentine was gone — as he would be, too, before long — soaked up into the nothingness. No, if Valentine lived on, it was only through Florence's actions, the charity she had set up in his name.

'So tell me . . . how is the battle against sepsis going?'

He didn't need to hear the answer. He knew that sepsis was a silent scourge and that many hundreds of thousands of people died of the disease every year in the United States alone, most of them quite unnecessarily.

'It's all about education, early diagnosis. We're doing what we can, along with many other charities.'

'You've saved lives?' Lyndon asked.

'Some. Not enough. Never enough.'

'Is it a question of money?'

Florence took a sip of her soda. 'I'm not here with a begging bowl, Lyndon. Anyhow, we're a lot luckier than most. We receive two hundred thousand dollars every year from an anonymous donor . . . first of January, like clockwork.'

'Probably a tax deduction thing. We advise many high net-worth clients on such matters.'

'Is it you?' she asked.

'No.'

'Say that again.'

'No,' he insisted.

'Thank you, Lyndon,' she said softly.

He shrugged. 'Don't mention it. Like I say, it's a tax deduction thing. I'm not sure I don't even turn a profit.'

'I doubt it.'

It was the perfect opportunity to raise the subject, and he might well have, if at that moment Heather hadn't come striding from the house, almost as though she had read his mind and was looking to thwart him.

'Is it okay if we join the party?' she asked with forced jollity. 'Alice is on her way.'

It could wait until tomorrow. And if he died in the night, Florence could hear it from Victor. It amounted to the same thing. In the final analysis, it was just money he wouldn't be needing where he was headed.

'Well?' asked Heather, put out that her question had been ignored.

'What a lucky man I am . . . Lyndon and the Three Graces.'

He took a sip of his drink, the memories crowding in on him. Canova's sculpture in the Victoria and Albert Museum in London; their first family trip to Europe; all six of them together, staring up at the masterpiece.

Zeus's three daughters in a group hug, enshrined in gleaming white marble.

THIRTEEN

Evie was in the shower when Dylan returned to their small clapboard house in Hotchkiss Place.

'Hi!' she called from upstairs, hearing the front door slam shut. 'Two minutes!'

It had been Evie's idea, soon after she had moved in with him, to knock through and create an open-plan living/dining area on the first floor. They had done most of the work themselves, although they had required the services of a plumber and an electrician to help install the galley kitchen that now ran the length of the back wall.

Dylan dumped the bottle of champagne on the countertop, grabbed two glasses from the cupboard, then flipped through his mail. Buried in the nonsense was a letter from his mother, and he could tell from the thickness of it that she had included the usual batch of photos. He tore open the envelope. Sure enough, the photos cataloged his parents' latest adventures in Florida: brandishing garishly colored cocktails on the balcony of their waterfront condo in Bonita Springs; on their boat with their wraparound shades and their perma-tans; his father standing on a beach, holding a big fish; his mother holding the same fish close to her face, lips pouted as though to kiss it; his mother cradling his graduation photo while looking terribly sad with a comically downturned mouth like a clown.

They had moved to Florida two years ago, ostensibly for his mother's arthritis, but had somehow stumbled on a whole new lease of life. He knew from his rare visits that the photos weren't staged to stir envy. They were genuinely happy — possibly happier than they had ever been — and they would be genuinely happy for him when he called them later and told them his news about being bumped up to the detective bureau.

He had just finished reading his mother's letter when Evie appeared at the foot of the stairs in linen shorts and a navy V-neck. Her wet hair was combed back off her face. She flopped down beside him on the couch and kissed him on the lips.

'Heavy day?' she asked.

'You can tell?'

Her eyes alighted on the bottle of champagne and the two glasses standing on the counter.

'I'm not sure I can. Haven't we done enough celebrating?'

'This one's for me.'

She tilted her head at him. 'Oh?'

'They want me to be a detective. I kind of am one already, as of this morning.' That was overselling it; the detective bureau had asked him to help out on a case, with a view to seeing how he performed. He was on probation, no more than that. 'Well, not officially, not yet.'

Evie threw her arms around his neck. 'Oh Badger, I'm so proud of you. Tell me what happened. No, wait—'

She went to get the champagne, and as he watched her tearing off the foil top, he couldn't help thinking that there was a time not so long ago when news of the sort he'd just shared would have had her squealing and running around the room like a crazed child, bouncing on the furniture.

He joined her at the counter once she'd popped the cork. 'I can't wait to hear.' She filled the flutes, and they clinked glasses. 'Detective Badger,' she said, by way of a toast.

They both savored a sip. 'Tell me, tell me all. What do they have you doing? It's that car crash, isn't it?'

'That's the thing . . . I can't say. I'm not allowed to.'

Carrie had been very clear on that. She had asked him if he was in a relationship and had stressed that all talk of work was off-limits at home. 'It's no bad thing for those we live with,' she had said. 'Ours is a dirty business. Like they say . . . no one wants to see how sausage is made.'

Evie took a slug of champagne. 'At least tell me *how* it happened.' She sounded a little riled.

'The chief of the detective bureau called me in. Turns out he's had his eye on me for a bit.'

'Well, of course . . . my brainy Badger.'

'I've been partnered with a woman.'

Evie narrowed her eyes. 'Anything I should worry about?'

'Only if you think I've got mother issues. She's fifty-four.'

'Hmmm . . . not exactly Stabler and Benson.'

Evie was a big fan of *Law & Order: Special Victims Unit*.

'Fuller and Bodine,' he said.

'Hey, not bad. Has a ring to it.'

'Not for long . . . she's about to retire.'

Evie kissed him on the lips again. 'I'm so proud of you.'

'Goodbye to this.' Dylan pulled at the shirt collar of his police uniform.

'Need someone to help you take it off for the last time?' Her lips curled into a smile as she took another sip of champagne.

'Are you hitting on me?'

'Just curious. I've never fucked a detective before.'

'I'm not, not yet.'

'I've never fucked an almost-detective, either.'

* * *

They decided to treat themselves to a meal out at the Ritz Crystal Room on Main Street, their favorite place to eat (except when they had a pizza craving). The small upstairs restaurant — a former speakeasy — was elegant, quirky and intimate: the perfect venue for celebrating a special occasion, which this most definitely was.

It was a ten-minute stroll from the house, and they were halfway there when Evie broke the news to him about New York.

'Annie called this afternoon. I've had a summons from the main gallery.'

News of her sell-out show was spreading fast. A number of newspapers and magazines, including *Vanity Fair*, had requested interviews.

'I have to do it, Badger. You know me, I don't want to, but I have to.'

'Of course you do. When?'

'Tomorrow. There's a drinks party at six I'm meant to be at. They're going to put me up in a hotel for a few days.'

She had to be at the drinks. One of the gallery's most important clients was in New York, but only for one night, and there was talk of a commission.

'A Civil War battlefield in Virginia, near to where he lives. Maybe more battlefields after that.'

'What if they're flat?' he asked.

'Nothing is flat.'

'Glass is flat.'

'Not if you're a microbe.'

'Fair enough, it's the fucking Rockies if you're a microbe.'

They walked on a bit in awkward silence before Evie squeezed his hand and said, 'I'm sorry, I'm not trying to steal your thunder.'

'That's not what I was thinking.'

'What *were* you thinking?'

Should he say it? Would it sound weak and insecure if he did? In the end, he didn't have to decide.

'You're worried about us,' said Evie. 'You don't have to be.'

'No? It's not like we've been at our best these past few months.'

'That's just the pressure of the show. It's over.'

'Tell me you're not feeling even more pressure right now.'

Evie hesitated. 'It's a different kind of pressure. The look-at-me bullshit doesn't come naturally.'

'And I love you for it. But this is big, Evie. You've always dreamed of elsewhere, and elsewhere just came looking for you.'

She looked at him askance. 'That's beautifully put.'

'Damn, it was, wasn't it?'

She stopped in her tracks, took his face in her hands, and kissed him hard on the mouth.

'You think I'm going to throw away four years just like that?'

'No.'

'Damn right I'm not.'

They walked on, hand in hand.

Not just like that, thought Dylan. *Not without a struggle that would leave her feeling completely wretched.*

FOURTEEN

Tuesday was Bevan's day off, so it was Alice who drove them in the Range Rover to the meeting with the police. Heather didn't see them off; she was still sulking after Alice had turned down her offer to accompany them.

'Hey, we'll hit them with the Three Graces routine. Who can hold out against that, right?'

This awkward appeal to a spirit of sisterhood had been made in the kitchen, Heather still wet from her morning swim. Alice had done her best to let her down gently, but it was never going to be enough for a woman accustomed to getting her own way. Heather had flounced off upstairs in her terry robe and her Gucci pool slides.

'She's a handful, that one,' said Alice, as soon as they were on the road.

'She means well.'

'You think? Some of those things she said last night over dinner. Does she have any idea how she comes across?'

'What do you mean?'

'She sees other women in one of two ways . . . as competition or too insignificant to bother with. No prizes for guessing where we fit.'

* * *

Alice drove with caution, saying she was unused to being behind the wheel of such a large vehicle. She took a circuitous route to Torrington, one that avoided the scene of the accident, Florence noted.

A part of her wanted to revisit the intersection where she'd almost lost her life, to see it in the daylight, to make sense of what had happened and maybe find some kind of solace. The dead man, still nameless and faceless, had invaded her dreams last night, when she hadn't been lying awake for long, lonely hours in the darkness, thinking of him and those he had left behind — people whose lives would forever be colored by his violent death.

It hit her again, a tsunami of grief and guilt. She choked back a sudden sob.

'Hey,' said Alice, laying a hand on her thigh.

'It's not right. He's dead because of me. The song. I was distracted. If I hadn't been . . .'

Alice's hand moved from her thigh to her arm. Its grip was firm, purposeful.

'I understand, I do, but you have to try to park it for now. There can't be any talk like this when we get there . . . nothing like this. He was clearly to blame, they've said as much. He ran a stop sign and could have killed you. Think about that, only that.'

'I'm not sure I can.'

'Then keep your mouth shut, let me do the talking,' said Alice. 'That's what I'm paid for.'

* * *

Florence had dried her eyes and pulled herself together by the time they arrived at police headquarters, a large brick building that sat near a busy intersection in the middle of Torrington. There was plenty of parking at the side of it, and Alice pulled the Range Rover into one of the bays where a number of patrol cars were lined up.

They only had to wait a few minutes in the lobby before a tall woman with short, silver hair appeared from a door and approached them on Cuban-heeled ankle boots tucked into skinny jeans.

'Detective Carrie Fuller,' she said, shaking their hands in turn. Florence could sense Alice bristling beside her. One thing they weren't expecting was a detective.

'My client is here entirely of her own volition,' said Alice. 'You don't intend to question her under caution, I hope.'

'Not at all.'

'I mean it, if you Miranda her—'

'Just a friendly chat and some paperwork to go through.'

FIFTEEN

Carrie had asked Dylan to take the lead, and he was still trying to work out what his opening gambit should be when the three women entered the small interview room.

'Dylan Bodine. We met at the hospital.'

'We did,' said Alice Arnold, her wary eyes sliding over him to the table, where the GPS tracker sat sealed in a clear evidence bag.

'Good to see you vertical,' he said to Florence.

'Still feeling a bit bruised.'

'You're taller than I imagined.'

'I have a small head.'

Not so small. Pretty much perfect.

'Shall we?' said Carrie.

Dylan pulled out a couple of chairs for them. 'Please, take a seat. Water?' He twisted off the bottle cap before the replies came in. The water was poured, the four glasses filled.

'Forgive me,' said Alice Arnold, 'but I don't see any paperwork. All I see is that. What is that?' She pointed at the evidence bag.

Dylan held it up for Florence to examine. 'Have you seen this before?'

'No. What is it?'

'How long have you owned your car?'

'A year or so.'

'Exactly, please.'

'Ten months . . . ? Yes. Since last October.'

'How is this relevant?' said Alice Arnold.

'Patience,' said Carrie. 'We're here to help.'

'It's a 2018 model, right?' Dylan went on. 'So you bought it used?'

'From a dealership in Brooklyn.'

'Are you in a relationship? Or have you been during the past three months, say?'

'Oh, for goodness' sake,' said Alice. 'What has this got to do with anything?'

Dylan turned to her. 'It's very simple. This is a GPS tracking device, state of the art. We found it in Ms. Winslow's car. The specialists in tech tell us it has a maximum battery life of three to four months, from which we can conclude that someone put it there subsequent to her purchase of the vehicle. We're now trying to establish if a jealous lover may have planted it.'

'I ask again,' said Alice, undeterred, 'what has this got do with the accident?'

Carrie stepped in.

'Everything, potentially. You see, we can't establish the identity of the man who collided with your client's car because he had no wallet on him, no phone, nothing. We do know, however, that the Prius he was driving had been stolen the night before in Burlington, Vermont, and that before he slammed into your client, he deactivated the vehicle's anti-collision system. Oh, and for some reason he had also decided to turn the headlights off before driving into her, which he did without braking, although he must have seen her coming. That's what we've got so far. Toss in the tracking device and you can see why we thought we should . . . well, reach out to you both.'

In the silence that followed, Florence looked helplessly to her lawyer for guidance. The fight had gone out of Alice

Arnold. 'Where is this leading?' she asked, a slight waver in her voice.

'That's what we're trying to establish,' said Dylan. 'And we can't do it without your cooperation.'

'I haven't been in a relationship for over a year,' said Florence.

'How did it end?' he asked.

'It wasn't serious.'

'Amicably?'

'He ended it. I didn't put up a fight, if that's what you mean.'

'What *do* you mean?' said Alice Arnold.

Dylan hesitated. 'Ms. Winslow, can you think of anyone, anyone at all, who would want to kill you?'

SIXTEEN

It was such an absurd question, preposterous, the sort of thing that people asked other people on TV shows. But this was reality; Florence knew it was, because she saw her two real hands reach out and grip the top of a real table.

She felt Alice's feather-light touch on her forearm. 'I'm sure there's another plausible explanation.'

'But there *is* someone . . . someone I can think of.'

She took in their puzzled expressions and then the four walls of the small room, no bigger than a prison cell.

'You need some air?' asked Carrie Fuller.

Florence shook her head; she just a needed a bit more time to allow the memory back into her life. It had been overtaken by other events in recent years to the point that it had practically ceased to exist. Like some crazy incantation, Dylan's question had raised it from the dead.

'I'd like a word in private with my client,' said Alice.

'Later,' said Carrie Fuller. 'Go on, Ms. Winslow.'

And Florence did, because despite Alice's words of caution in the car about keeping her mouth shut, she couldn't, not about this, not after what she had just heard.

'My father was an academic, a history lecturer at the LSE . . . the London School of Economics. He was also an activist.'

'Was?' asked Carrie Fuller.

'He's dead. At least, we're pretty sure he is. No one knows for certain.' She hesitated. '*I'm* sure. It's been six years since he went missing. My mother still holds out hope, but that's her thing, not mine.'

'Go on,' said Carrie Fuller.

She explained that her father had been born in Rhodesia, in Africa, when a white minority still held sway over the country, and much of his childhood had been spent under the shadow of a guerrilla war that was being waged to overturn white rule.

'My father was dancing in the streets when Rhodesia became Zimbabwe in 1980. Then the atrocities began, the bloodletting.'

Matabeleland, where her father's family was from, saw the worst of the massacres, tens of thousands dead, murdered . . . friends of his. He was teaching at the university in Harare by then, and he spoke out against the new regime he'd initially embraced. When it became clear he would be silenced, that his life was in danger, he fled Zimbabwe for England, continuing the fight from London, writing academic papers and newspaper articles, lobbying politicians, anything he could do to keep alive the story of the genocide in Matabeleland and in particular the actions of a general in the 5th Brigade.

It required a force of will on her part to utter the name.

'Nelson Ngomo. My father knew him as a boy . . . even admired him. That boy became a monster, and my father went after him, wouldn't let go.'

He had pushed for years, seemingly in vain, until the International Criminal Court in The Hague finally sat up and took notice. Not long after, a clean-cut, young, black man, whom her father assumed at first to be a student, approached him in the university canteen in London and presented him with a message: *General Ngomo says to leave it alone, or die.*

'He didn't. He couldn't. It was his life by then.'

Her father had flown to Africa, not to Zimbabwe — he wasn't that stupid — but to neighboring Mozambique to meet with fellow sympathizers looking to topple President Mugabe's teetering reign of terror.

'Somewhere between the airport in Maputo and his hotel, he disappeared. We know he caught a taxi at the airport — there's CCTV footage — but it was a set-up. The taxi was a fake.'

She knew she had been rambling on, speaking as much for herself as for them, to set things straight in her own head, but she was still surprised when Carrie Fuller asked almost impatiently, 'I'm sorry, it's a terrible story, but how exactly does it fit?'

'The young man in the canteen . . . he said my father would be killed and his bloodline wiped out. That means me. I'm his only child.'

Carrie Fuller nodded a couple of times. 'Do you mind? We need to . . .' She glanced at Dylan.

'Go ahead,' said Alice.

The two of them left the room.

'Sorry,' said Florence feebly. 'I had to tell them.'

'Of course you did.' Alice reached across and squeezed her hand. 'Of course you did.'

SEVENTEEN

'I don't buy it,' said Carrie, drawing to a halt in the corridor outside.

'I don't think she's selling,' said Dylan.

'Don't be so sure. Look, I get it, she's fucking gorgeous, she bats those big eyes of hers at you . . . the temptation is to believe everything she says. Resist. Skepticism . . . the first rule, the *only* rule. We're looking at the tip of the iceberg here. Who knows what really lies beneath? A hundred bucks says it isn't this General Ngomo. Her father's killer finally following through on his threat against her six years later? A car crash made to look like an accident, coordinated from Africa? You think? I don't.'

'Is this what you call big picture?'

'Big picture's a feeling, and I'm not feeling it.'

'What if you're wrong?'

Carrie shrugged. 'Most of being right is being wrong first.'

'You dragged me outside to tell me that?'

'No, to tell you I'll take it from here.'

When they returned to the interview room, Carrie's request that Florence take a look at John Doe's body didn't go down well with Alice Arnold.

'Is that really necessary? Can't you show her a photo or something?'

'It's not the same. How many photos do you know where you hardly recognize yourself?'

'Most of them,' said Alice. 'Who's that woman with the facial lines, because I sure as hell don't have any.'

Carrie smiled. 'Right.' She turned to Florence. 'It would really help us. It's just we've got a no-show so far from the databases on both his photo and DNA.'

Florence shook her head. 'I can't do it.'

Dylan leaned forward. 'I can guess how you've been feeling, but you can stop now. You're not responsible for his death, Florence. This man was out to get you, kill you. Try to think of him as the enemy.'

It was a few seconds before she replied. 'How is he looking?'

'Presentable,' said Carrie.

She didn't add that John Doe had been scalped in the accident, but stitched back together.

Florence finally nodded her assent. 'Okay.'

* * *

The state morgue was in Farmington, a forty-minute drive to the east. Carrie had a couple of calls to make, so Dylan took the wheel of the Chevy. He leaned across her and tucked his phone away in the glove box before firing the engine.

'Temptation,' he said, catching her questioning look. 'I see what happens when people give in to it, even for a second.'

Florence and Alice sat silently in the back for much of the journey, barely exchanging a word or even a look. The few times that Dylan caught sight of Florence in the rear-view mirror, she was staring out of the window at the world whipping by outside. How could she remain so still, so calm, after what she had just learned from them, just shared with them? An attempt on her life, quite possibly staged by the man behind her father's disappearance. She was probably in a state of shock.

Another quick glance. This time she caught his eye in the mirror. There was nothing vacant in her look, and the wan smile she gave him seemed to carry in it a mix of vulnerability and resolve. No, not in shock, just made of sterner stuff than he was.

The Office of the Chief Medical Examiner lay on a leafy road near the University of Connecticut's health center and medical school. It was a large, modern facility spread over three floors. The associate medical examiner, Dr. Vaughan, a petite woman with a brisk manner who had greeted Dylan and Carrie yesterday, led them all through to the mortuary, where John Doe's body was waiting for them, lying on a gurney and draped in a blue sheet.

'Sure you're okay?' Dylan asked.

Florence nodded, and Dr. Vaughan raised the end of the sheet. Dylan was aware of Carrie closely scrutinizing Florence, who didn't flinch as she peered down at the pallid face of the dead man, taking her time. He was in his early thirties, at a guess, his chin dusted with stubble, his lank, blond hair receding into a widow's peak. The stitches ran in a straight line around his crown, like a zipper.

Florence shook her head.

'Are you sure?' said Carrie. 'He measures in at . . .' She turned to Dr. Vaughan.

'Six feet one and a half inches.'

'So, kind of tall.'

'I've never seen him before,' said Florence. 'I'm sure of it.'

The grim business dealt with, a mortuary assistant then escorted Florence and Alice back to the main waiting area.

'Did you make any headway on the tattoo?' Carrie asked Dr. Vaughan. John Doe had a tattoo on the inside of his left forearm that had been removed by laser.

'We tried ultraviolet and negative imaging, but it's impossible to say what it used to be.'

Toxicology was done off-site, but on Carrie's request it had been rushed through. She scanned the results in the dossier.

'THC and alprazolam . . .'

'But not in sufficient quantities to impair his motor functions to any great degree,' said Dr. Vaughan.

'A small joint to chill out, then a tab or two of Xanax to hold his nerves steady.'

'Looks that way. Did you get anything from his clothes?'

'Forensics are on it,' said Carrie. 'Nothing yet, only that the jeans were vintage Levi's worth a crazy amount.'

Carrie proposed that Dylan also take the wheel on the drive back to Torrington.

'I like the way you drive,' she said, which sounded suspiciously like his mother praising him for his excellent lawn-mowing the first time she'd let him loose in the backyard. Anything not to do it herself ever again.

'Thank you for that, Florence,' said Carrie, twisting in the front passenger seat. 'It's never pleasant, but we needed to be sure.'

'What happens now?' asked Alice Arnold.

'That's for you to decide.'

'I'm not going into hiding,' said Florence. 'That's how the Ngomos of the world win.'

'Unless it wasn't him,' suggested Dylan.

It was the merest of glances, but the fleeting look from Carrie was a clear warning to keep quiet. *Team Fuller*, he told himself. *It's not your place.*

'It has to be him,' said Florence. 'There's no one else. I run a charity, for God's sake. I'm a good person. I don't have enemies. Only him.'

'And he's still out there,' said Carrie.

'You're never going to find him, arrest him, even if you *can* show he's behind it. He's in Africa, I'm here, and I'm not going to let him shrink my life back to nothing. My father didn't.'

'And look what happened to him,' put in Alice. 'I'm sorry, but it's true.'

'He went down fighting for what he believed in . . . for what was right. I used to curse him for it. Now I understand.'

Dylan snatched a brief look at Florence in the rear-view mirror. She was staring out of the window, jaw set.

'I strongly advise that you don't return to New York,' said Carrie. 'And we'd like you nearby. Can you stay at the Winslow place?'

It was Alice who replied. 'I don't see why not.'

'What's security like there?'

'The first floor is alarmed at night. And there's a big guy called Bevan.'

'You should think about some extra protection.'

'You can't provide it?' Alice asked.

'Not round the clock,' said Carrie. 'Private is best. I'm guessing money isn't an issue for the Winslows.'

They were passing through Burlington when Alice asked, 'What about your other lines of inquiry?'

'We can't exclude the possibility of an accomplice,' Carrie replied.

This was an understatement; they were sure of it now. The discovery of the tracker in Florence's car changed things; it suggested that John Doe had indeed had a phone on him, which in turn suggested that an accomplice must have recovered it from the wrecked Prius after the crash. But if they'd had the presence of mind to do that, to say nothing of the strong stomach required, why hadn't they also finished off Florence before leaving the scene?

'Material evidence?' Alice asked.

'Not much, mostly speculative, but tall oaks from little acorns grow.'

'How very comforting.'

'I hope so,' Carrie replied tightly, 'because it took a fair bit of work in a short bit of time to get to where we're at.'

'I'm sorry,' said Alice. 'You've done a great job.'

'Thank our driver . . . he was the one who first read the runes.'

'I wish I'd been wrong,' said Dylan.

'Better to know the truth,' came Florence's voice from behind him.

'For sure,' concurred Carrie.

* * *

Back in Torrington, numbers were exchanged and stored in phones. Carrie stressed the importance of staying in touch. Florence was not to go out on her own, even for a stroll round the grounds. In fact, it would be best if someone kept her company at all times.

'Even at night?' Alice asked.

'That's up to you. They wanted it to look like an accident, which takes time, planning, but that doesn't mean they're not ready to change tack.'

'You're scaring me,' said Florence.

'I hope so . . . if it keeps you safe.'

The two women were getting into the Range Rover when Carrie said to Florence, as if in afterthought, 'Oh, one more thing . . . how long is it since you last saw your father-in-law? We heard you and your husband had a falling-out with him.'

'Yes, but we're friends again.'

'How long?'

'Almost four years,' said Florence.

'And he was the one to offer the olive branch?'

'Yes.'

'Any other peace offerings?'

Florence frowned. 'What do you mean?'

'She means money,' said Alice Arnold.

Florence turned back to Carrie. 'He wanted to apologize for his behavior. It's more than enough.'

Carrie nodded. 'Sorry for probing; it goes with the job.'

They watched as the Range Rover pulled out of the police headquarters parking lot and was swallowed up in the traffic on Main Street.

'What was that about?' asked Dylan.

'Money. It's usually about money.'

'Not this time.'

'We'll see.'

They headed for the entrance of the building.

'You don't think it's Ngomo, but you want them to believe it?' Dylan asked.

'No, I want the person or people responsible to think *we* believe it. You got any plans over the next couple of days?'

Evie would already be on the train to New York, not back till Friday evening. 'No. Why?'

'Ever been to Burlington, Vermont?'

'The stolen Prius?'

'Our only lead.'

'Not much of one.'

'Keep the faith,' said Carrie. 'There'll be others along soon enough.'

EIGHTEEN

Alice was keen to break the news to Lyndon the moment they returned to the house. Florence wasn't convinced that he needed to know. It would only upset him, and it wasn't like there was anything he could do about it, not in his state. He was happy that she'd come to visit, delighted even, and he could now die knowing that he'd patched up the damage of the past. The more she talked it through with Alice, the clearer it became to her that she wanted to shield Lyndon from the grim news of the attempt on her life.

'You need extra protection,' said Alice. 'I'm not sure we can hide it from him.'

'We can try.' Effectively confined to the library, Lyndon could be kept from the truth.

Alice eyed her coolly. 'I'll run it past Penfold, see what he says.'

Victor Penfold was Lyndon's good friend and attorney, the man who had brought Alice in to help, the man who held the purse strings as Lyndon neared his end.

'He may sign off on it,' said Alice. 'I'm not promising anything.'

Florence asked that Heather also be kept in the dark, at least for now. 'You know what she's like, she'll just take possession of it . . . It'll become all about her.'

'Yes, let's not give her that pleasure.'

Florence had told Lyndon that she'd fill him in on the meeting with the police the moment they were back.

'All we say for now is I'm in the clear, that they're not going to prosecute.'

'Fine,' Alice conceded.

When they stopped by the library, though, the nurse on duty informed them that Lyndon had had a particularly tough morning and was now too medicated to receive visitors.

* * *

The letter was waiting for Florence on the dressing table in her bedroom. There were two words in a messy scrawl on the envelope. One read *FLORENCE*, the other *CONFIDENTIAL*. She tore it open.

My dear Florence,
Forgive the hieroglyphs. I wish I could blame the disease, but my handwriting has always been this atrocious.

This letter is an act of cowardice on my part. I have never been able to speak openly of my feelings. There was a time when I was better at it, before you knew me, when Deborah was still alive. She taught me so many valuable things, and she continued to push me until the day she died. Her death brought me low, far lower than people know. There were times when I struggled to swing my legs off the bed in the morning. Unlike you, who has always worn her feelings on her face, I am a grand dissimulator, and I don't suppose people thought of me as anything other than a grieving widower, understandably glum.

The only person aware of my depression was the idiot therapist I saw a few times, a woman fixated with the idea that

I was reliving the loss of my older brother in the Vietnam War, as though it somehow trumped the death of my wife, my love, my best friend, my guide.

I got over it eventually — the medication helped, I don't deny it — but I see now that I never fully recovered. I thought I was myself when Valentine came to me and said he wished to break off and forge his own way in the world. I told myself he was ungrateful, inconsiderate, irresponsible — traits he had shown from an early age. In truth, he had never been any of those things. I was terrified of losing him, terrified of another hole in my life, and in my panic I tried to close it off by shutting the two of you out. You saw how doggedly I stuck to my guns, but that wasn't me. It was a damaged man still struggling to pick a path through the pain.

I don't seek your forgiveness for the way that I behaved toward you both. Indeed, I'm happy to carry it with me into the abyss, which is where it belongs. I do want you to know, however, that I was not a well man, and certainly not equipped to accept my son's choices, which included you, I'm afraid.

Enough of the past. Now to the business that has a bearing on your future. I have watched you from afar, but closely, and I have seen how you have put over your life to honoring Valentine's memory through the charity you set up in his name. I know of the many wonderful things that you have achieved, I know how you have gone about them, and I know how difficult it has been at times. I'm ashamed to admit it, but I even know how little you pay yourself — the bare minimum, just enough to lead a meager life.

That is all about to change. In brief, I have chosen to reverse events. I disinherited Valentine, and now I am reinstating him, which means you, his wife, his widow. You shall receive his full and fair share of what I leave behind in my will.

It is a considerable amount of money, and I don't doubt you will do many wonderful things with it, just as he would have done.

Moreover, there is the question of the Winslow family fund, which holds the greater part of our collective wealth in trust. United States trust law is a notoriously complicated business, but in a nutshell, I am proposing this. The Winslow Trust will move all of its positions held in a variety of markets to purely ethical investments. Your mission, should you choose to accept it (Mr. Hunt), is to determine where the money goes. If you meet resistance, and you may, the trust will be wound up, the necessary taxes paid, and one half of the outstanding amount shall come to you, to do with as you see fit. I know you will spend it wisely. As I say, I have been watching you closely; I am aware of your work outside of the charity, your involvement with a number of other groups that are looking to move this troubled world of ours forward in ways that hopefully ensure its survival.

It would be easy to assume that these are the last-gasp wishes of a man looking to salve his soul as the Grim Reaper reaches out a bony hand. Maybe they are, but I don't believe that's the full truth of it. Rather, I see it like this. Had I taken Valentine seriously, had I not dismissed his serious concerns about the manner in which we ran our affairs and used our wealth, he would not have felt the need to walk away from the family. All I have done is ask myself how things would have turned out had I listened to him and acted as he suggested at the time. Well, this is it, I believe. This is where we would be by now, where he wanted us to be. It really is as simple as that. Valentine had a vision. It is for you to go out there and make it real.

I'm sure you can see now why I chose to write this letter. Could I have said even half of the above to your face? I suppose I have always been a man more drawn to the written *word than the spoken. Why else am I lying here in the library? So many different books, but all asking the same question: Why are we here? I suspect we are little more than dogs howling at the moon. I'll know soon enough.*

I trust, dear Florence, that things went well for you today with the police and that you were fully exonerated. If not, I daresay the formidable Alice will ensure that you are before too long.

With profound regret for all the suffering that a disturbed and foolish man has caused you over the years,
Lyndon

P.S. I only ask one two things of you: that you keep this from the rest of the family for now, and that you keep my name out of it when I'm gone. If I ever get to hear of 'The Lyndon Winslow Institute of Climate Whatever,' I'll come back and haunt you.

Florence pinched the tears from her eyes. It was too much to bear: first her father, brought rushing back into being by developments today, and now Valentine, called forth by his own father in a letter. The two most important men in her life, both gone. Dead.

Had she ever felt more alone? No, not just alone, but in unimaginable danger. It came back to her now, just how ghastly it had been when her father went missing and her mother had felt duty-bound to finally tell her of the threat that had also been made against her own life. She remembered the poisonous cocktail of grief and paranoia, the weeping while keeping one eye over her shoulder: every time she left the small house in Kennington, every glance from a stranger on the Underground, every bus she boarded. How long had it taken for the dread and the constant alertness to dissipate? A year? More? Had they ever stopped shadowing her? If they had, they were back now, more acute than ever. Her bruised and battered body ached with the truth of it.

She flopped onto the bed, expecting to bury her sobs in a pillow. More tears didn't come, though. She found herself thinking of Valentine, of the pained smile on his lips the last time she had seen him breathing without a ventilator, of the quiet courage in his eyes just before the doctors in Medellín induced the coma. They had marveled at his determination, somehow reading it off the machines, even believing for a while that he would pull through.

They were wrong. But he had fought hard for his life, and she would do the same. She would fight back, even strike back. She now had the resources to do so . . . the money promised her by Lyndon in his letter. She lay there for a long while with that thought, testing it, measuring it against the person she had become.

No, she would not be forced to live in trembling terror again. General Ngomo might be beyond the law, beyond the reach of the Carrie Fullers of the world, but there was nothing to stop *her* turning the tables on him and avenging her father in the process.

Only her conscience, but she knew she could live that.

* * *

She went in search of Alice, who was in the kitchen, chatting to Mary the cook.

They wandered outside to the terrace. 'I just spoke to Penfold,' said Alice. 'He was pretty shocked to hear it wasn't an accident, and he thinks you're right about keeping it from Lyndon if we can; it'll just distress him. He's giving Bevan the go-ahead to hire a couple of bodyguards on the quiet.'

Florence handed over the letter. 'It was in my room. It's from Lyndon.'

Alice took a seat at a table in the shade and read the letter through.

'My God, this is huge,' she finally said, looking up at Florence.

'I'm going to need a lawyer.'

'Don't you have one?'

'Not one like you.'

Alice eyed her for a moment. 'I'm touched.'

'Say yes.'

'On one condition. That you agree we bring this to the attention of Detective Fuller.'

'Detective Fuller?'

'It could have a bearing on what happened to you.'

Florence took a moment to grasp what Alice was intimating. 'That's ridiculous.'

Alice leaned forward in her chair. 'Florence, listen to me. We can't sit on this.' She held up the letter. 'I don't know the details of the legal documents that have been drawn up to see through Lyndon's wishes, but there may well be clauses in there that mean none of it happens if you predecease him. Do you have a will of your own?'

'Yes.'

Valentine's sudden and unexpected death had opened her eyes to the need.

'Who's the beneficiary?'

'My mother gets everything, not that there's much.'

'Well, there *is* now. Look at it this way . . . let's say you'd died in the crash; would Lyndon have wanted your mother to step into your shoes and receive all these benefits? He knows nothing about her. These changes are a reflection of his belief in you, not a woman he's never met before. Speaking as a lawyer, I would have ensured there was a clause rescinding the new will if you died before Lyndon.'

Alice's words made sense; it was what she wasn't saying that troubled her.

'You think one of the Winslows . . . ?'

'God knows . . . probably not . . . but I do know that Detective Fuller would expect us to share this with her. And as your attorney — if that's what I really am — I'd be remiss not to insist on it.'

Florence sensed movement out of the corner of her eye, at one of the upstairs windows. When she glanced up, there was no one there.

'What?' said Alice.

Florence dismissed the question with a small shake of the head. Probably just the reflection of a passing cloud against the glass.

'All right, go ahead and tell her, but Lyndon stays in the dark about the crash.'

'I can't promise that,' said Alice. 'It's not for us to decide, not anymore. That's Detective Fuller's call.'

NINETEEN

Chester had billed it to her as a dinner party for friends, but the moment he'd listed the names, Olivia had known it for what it really was: a chance to drum up backing from some wealthy acquaintances for his latest venture.

She had been forced to bail him out of the last one, a leasing scheme for superyachts that had gone belly-up after a year. It had set her back a small fortune, saving Chester from being sued by the investors for breach of his fiduciary duties as a director. His latest wheeze was Parisian property, as the French capital looked to take on London's mantel in the aftermath of Brexit. She had read the glossy promotional brochure. She had also banned it from the dinner table. Blinded by his own boyish enthusiasm, Chester was inclined to go in too hard with the sort of people who preferred a more measured approach, a softer sell.

Olivia didn't mind that he'd hijacked the evening for his own ends. They were pleasant enough people, and it was also a chance to show off what Connie had done with the long, narrow strip out the back of their West Village townhouse. The decking and gravel combo, inherited from the previous owners, was a soulless look that had never worked for her, despite the splashes of ochre and orange that flamed from the dwarf Japanese acers in fall. All gone, scooped up and carted off by a team of workmen, everything but the deep stone trough into which water now trickled from a fashionably crude and corroded copper pipe. The look that Connie had gone for — her defining look — was down-home Tuscan rustic: a mix of hard and soft, of weathered flagstones and shaggy borders billowing with tall grasses. Not forgetting the vine-threaded pergola at the end of the garden, beneath which dinner was currently being served at the slate-topped table.

The barbecue where Chester had flame-grilled the lamb cutlets earlier was a slender slab of pale travertine protruding like a tongue from the wall nearby. Keep it simple, it said. Less is more. Heat and meat. Despite our millions, we're peasants at heart. It was a fraudulent message but appealing to those who were weary with excess and had seen something of the world, as they all had.

The woman to Olivia's right was waxing lyrical about a yoga retreat she'd attended in southern India when Olivia's phone lit up near her elbow.

'I'm sorry, I have to take this. It's my brother.'

Everyone knew that their father's life was hanging by a thread — it had been touched on earlier — and yoga woman fashioned what was presumably meant to be a look of concerned compassion. Thanks to the heavy-handed Botox, she could just as well have been sucking on a slice of lemon.

Olivia briefly caught Chester's questioning look as she took up her glass of Brunello. She wandered off toward the house, answering the call as she went.

'Will?'

'Are you alone?'

'Give me a second.' She made sure she had drifted well out of earshot. 'Okay.'

'Victor just called me. It looks like Florence's accident wasn't an accident after all.'

'What do you mean?'

'That's what the cops are saying . . . an attempt on her life.'

'Are they sure?'

'Convinced enough to suggest Florence get some serious personal protection. There's more. She knows about the new will. Heather found a letter Pa wrote to Florence.'

'Lying around, was it?'

'Don't play the saint with me, Liv . . . not after everything.'

'What's that supposed to mean?'

'You know damn well what it means. And if you had anything to do with this—'

'How dare you!' Olivia hissed into her phone. 'You can't seriously think . . . ?'

'I had to ask.'

'No, you didn't, Will. No, you fucking didn't.'

'Some of the things you said about her that night you came round to ours . . .'

'What, now you're her number-one fan? You don't want her anywhere near this family; you never did.'

Olivia hadn't smoked in over five years, but she wanted a cigarette now — a clear and sudden craving. She took a moment to compose herself.

'Listen, we all agreed how we'd play it with Victor after Daddy is gone. I got on board with the plan. I'm still on board.'

She heard William let out a low sigh. 'We're going to feel some heat.'

'Not if we all keep our heads . . . keep our mouths shut. Best if you stress that to Heather.'

'Don't worry about Heather. She knows exactly what's at stake here.'

Olivia snuck a sip of Brunello and then took a seat on a low wall. The blocks of imported Sienese sandstone had been distressed at great expense, artificially weathered to suggest centuries of exposure to the elements.

'Let's go again from the top,' she said. 'Tell me everything Victor told you.'

TWENTY

Dylan had washed up after his solo supper and was sprawled on the couch watching *Saving Private Ryan* for the fifth or sixth time when Carrie called. She didn't bother with niceties.

'It's me. We have an in with the Winslows.'

'The Winslows?'

'This was always going to lead back to them. Alice Arnold called as I was driving home.'

She told him about the letter that Lyndon Winslow had written to Florence, burying the hatchet and welcoming her back into the family fold. 'Valentine was disinherited, but Florence now gets his slice of the pie when the old man goes.'

'How much?'

'No number. One that people like you and me can't relate to. The point is, it's money that would have gone to the other three kids. Millions, for sure, maybe tens of millions. And there's more.'

There certainly was. Lyndon's change of heart ran deep, extending to the Winslow Trust, whose collective assets were invested in the hedge fund they ran. 'He's empowered Florence to steer the fund's holdings in a more ethical direction. If she can't, the trust is wound up and she gets half of it . . . half the family's shared wealth. No number on that, either, but I'm guessing one whole lot of noughts.'

'Jesus,' he said quietly.

'We have a motive that holds water.'

'Only if someone else was in the loop about the changes to the will.'

'Which they clearly are.'

'I don't know.' He took a moment to think it through. 'This letter was the first Florence had heard of it?'

'Looks that way. Alice says she's in shock.'

'She's been at the house — what — three days now? And no one else thought to bring the subject up? Something that big? Sounds to me like the family don't know about the new will, not yet.'

'It's a good point,' Carrie conceded.

'Only Lyndon Winslow knows who he's told.'

Carrie was silent for moment. 'What do you say we pay him a visit, stop by the house tomorrow on our way to Vermont?'

'Can't do any harm.'

'Are you packed?'

'Yep.'

'Then you can go back to what you were doing.'

'Watching *Saving Private Ryan*.'

'I love that movie. I wept floods when Tom Hanks dies.'

'He dies?'

'Shit,' she groaned, 'you haven't seen it before?'

'Tom can't die. The heroes don't die in Hollywood movies.'

There was a pause before Carrie said, 'You're a terrible liar.'

'I know.'

'We need to work on that. See you tomorrow.'

She hung up before he could reply. Dylan stared at his phone, then dialed Evie's number. It went straight to voice-mail again.

He didn't leave a message this time.

TWENTY-ONE

It was almost nothing: a tug on a single thread deep in his unconscious. A smell. Or rather, a combination of smells woven together into a particular scent that triggered some primordial warning system in his brain. It told him that fast asleep was not a place to be right now.

He made no show of waking, keeping his eyes closed. His ears, however, searched for sounds of a presence in the library: a soft exhalation of air, the rustle of cloth, the slightest squeak of polished parquet underfoot.

Had he imagined it?

No, it still hung there around him, a faint odor of citrus tinged with vanilla and musk. He didn't know the name of the perfume worn by Heather, but he recognized it.

He opened his eyes and looked around him. There was no sign of her, yet he was convinced she had been there, and recently. The digital clock on the nightstand read twenty past two. Strange. What on earth had prompted her to pay him a visit in the dead of night?

There was a small camera on top of the respirator beside the bed that allowed the nurses to monitor him remotely from the study during the day. It was turned off at night, or he could have gotten Bevan to pull the digital footage from the computer. He could have observed Heather observing him.

He lay back. It had been a bad twenty-four hours. He had spent much of it poleaxed by pain and wiped out by the meds, drifting in and out of fitful consciousness. There had been no question of evening drinks on the terrace, and he still didn't know from Florence how things had gone with the police, let alone how she had reacted to his letter.

He would find out soon enough.

Tomorrow. If he made it.

He reached for the remote on the nightstand. The sound system was set up at night for his audiobooks, and he picked up where he had left off earlier with *Landmarks*, Robert Macfarlane's lyrical musings on language and landscape.

TWENTY-TWO

Dylan had put out the garbage, watered the houseplants, and was brewing a pot of coffee when the doorbell rang.

It was Carrie, ten minutes early.

'Ready to roll?' she asked, spotting his small suitcase beside the front door.

'You want a coffee first?'

'Sure, a quick one. Heather's got a yoga class at ten.'

Dylan closed the door behind her. 'Heather?'

'Heather Winslow, wife of William, the eldest son. Go make the coffee and I'll fill you in.'

Carrie cast an eye around her as she followed him toward the kitchen.

'Nice place you've got here. Who's the artist?'

Evie's colorful, early landscapes decked the walls.

'My girlfriend.'

'Does she have a name?'

'Evie.'

'Well, Evie sure can paint.'

Dylan grabbed the catalog of Evie's new show from the sideboard as he passed. 'This is what she does now.'

Carrie dropped into an armchair and began flipping through the catalog. 'These are interesting.'

'They're huge, better in the flesh. If you want a laugh, read the introduction.'

She did laugh, several times, before picking out a passage to read: '"There is an atavistic tension at the heart of Evie Horn's debut series of topographical landscapes that is as guileless as it is self-aware: the provocative delicacy of each individual line belies the coiled and sinuous strength of the whole. As if this teasing polarity weren't enough already, her shimmering monochrome canvases are philosophical explorations of the conundrum that has puzzled representational painters since time immemorial, to wit: how to convey three dimensions on a two-dimensional surface."'

'First *she'd* heard of it,' said Dylan wandering over with the tray.

'My God, who wrote this crap?' Carrie flipped back, searching for the name. 'Angus Lovelock.'

'He's not so bad. I met him at the private view last Saturday.'

'Oh? Did she sell any?'

'Only all of them.'

He didn't say that Angus Lovelock — fashionably malnourished and dressed entirely in black (aside from a white patent leather belt) — had stuck strangely close to Evie for most of the evening, and that only a fool would have been blind to the coded intimacy of their smiles and looks and whispered words.

Instead, he poured the coffee and said: 'Tell me about Heather Winslow.'

'She stayed on at the house when the others went back to the city on Sunday night. I wanted her out of the way when we stop by, asked Alice to sort it out.'

Alice hadn't needed to; Heather's morning yoga class at the country club had provided them with a window of opportunity. Time was tight, though, and they didn't linger over their coffees.

The Chevy was parked on the street in front of the house. Carrie popped the trunk, and Dylan loaded his suitcase.

'I feel like a cougar heading off on a dirty weekend with my toy boy.'

'I think Mrs. Beckstein might agree with you.'

'Who's Mrs. Beckstein?'

'Morning, Mrs. Beckstein,' Dylan called, raising a hand in greeting.

Their elderly, curtain-twitching neighbor who lived opposite was checking her mailbox, but aimlessly, only to get a closer look at the dubious happenings across the way, one sensed.

Carrie slammed the lid of the trunk and tossed Dylan the keys.

'Let's hit the road, big boy.'

She said it just loud enough to send poor Mrs. Beckstein scampering back up the pathway to her house.

'Oh, Christ,' Dylan groaned.

Carrie dropped into the passenger seat. 'Lighten up, we just made her day.'

'Her year, more like.'

* * *

The drive north to Canaan was an opportunity for Carrie to fill him in on what she had learned about the Winslows from Alice, information she had then topped up with a couple of hours at her computer last night. She had scribbled copious notes in a black A5 hardback, the handwritten text interspersed with all kinds of crazy doodles and arrows and diagrams, and even a pie chart, Dylan noted.

The Winslows were northwest Connecticut through and through. It wasn't a classic rags-to-riches tale, so much as one of riches-to-even-more-riches. Wealthy landowners from the earliest days of settlement, in the eighteenth century they had then found themselves sitting on one of the richest seams of high-grade iron ore in North America. Dylan knew the story; they'd all learned it in elementary school: the mines and the blast furnaces which, for a time, had turned this quiet corner of the state into a thriving industrial hub.

The Winslows had flourished. More importantly, they had gotten out before competition from the Midwest began to bite, offloading their assets and turning their sights on New York, on Wall Street. Once producers, they now became speculators, gambling on the efforts of others to extract meaningful rewards from what lay beneath their feet: metals, minerals, coal and oil. Mistakes had been made, some catastrophic, but all had been corrected many times over by Lyndon's grandfather, who had anticipated the Crash of 1929, betting against it. Joe Kennedy had done the same and turned his family into one of the great American dynasties. The Winslows, less keen on the limelight, had pushed along silently in the shadows, discreetly accumulating.

Carrie must have felt Dylan's attention drifting.

'Bored with my history lesson?'

'No, it's interesting.'

'It's more than that; it's context that's relevant. They're private people, private as hell. I had to hustle this stuff together; there's no Wikipedia entry out there. They've spent how long building up their reputation, their name? More than two hundred years? They're not going to give it up without a fight, and certainly not to folks like us. We're nothing to them. Don't forget that.'

She hadn't been able to discover much on Cherwell, the multi-billion-dollar hedge fund that Lyndon Winslow had built up, only that it was a family-run affair. There was a daughter, Olivia, and two sons — William and Ralph — all of whom worked for Cherwell. Olivia was married to Chester, a businessman; William to Heather; Ralph to a garden designer called Connie. Six potential suspects in all, plus two from the next generation who were old enough to have orchestrated something like this: William and Heather's only child, Joe, the editor of an online magazine; and Amber, daughter to Ralph and Connie, who had recently graduated *summa cum laude* from Yale Law School.

'As I see it, that's our cast of suspects for now.'

'And General Ngomo?'

'Did a bit of snooping there, too. He survived the regime change in Zimbabwe, but there's talk of early-onset Alzheimer's. Still not in the frame, not as I see it. Doesn't mean we can't use him, though.'

'How's that?'

'You tell me.'

She was testing him.

'As misdirection?'

'Right . . . to shield our real suspicions.'

* * *

The Winslow property came with a stone-built gatehouse set at the head of the driveway, just within the perimeter wall. A big guy with a buzz cut — all chest, arms and jaw — was busying himself out front, training a climbing rose to a trellis with a kind of attentive delicacy.

He turned at the sound of the car as Dylan pulled up.

'We're here to see Alice Arnold,' said Carrie.

His eyes roamed over the dun-colored Chevy, trying to find a fit between its bland mediocrity and the whizz-kid lawyer from the city.

'Thataway.' He nodded down the driveway.

'Bevan, right?' said Carrie.

'Uh-huh.'

'Thought so. Alice mentioned you. Big fella, she said . . . verbal diarrhea.'

A ghost of a smile played across Bevan's lips.

'That'll be me.'

TWENTY-THREE

Yesterday had been a day of pain for Lyndon, not the localized spasms he had grown accustomed to and been able to dull with a dose or two of morphine. This had been something different, less intense but more diffuse, a pain that had fizzed and arced like an electrical current through his body, from the top of his skull to the tips of his toes, leaving him juddering at times.

He knew what to expect — he had read widely and dispassionately on the subject — and he assumed that the cancer was in the process of leaping from his organs to his nerves. His body was putting up a fight, doing its best to repel the intruders. The rogue cells would have their way, though. From the nerves it was a short leap to the brain, and the end. Oddly, he felt considerably better today, almost as though the besiegers and the besieged had negotiated a temporary truce, now that the walls had been breached and the final outcome was inevitable.

He was enjoying this uneasy hiatus, lying with his eyes closed and listening to Bach's *St. Matthew Passion*, when he heard someone enter the library.

It was Florence. She was alone.

He turned down the volume, a feat his trembling fingers wouldn't have been able to perform yesterday.

'Hello, my dear. I'm sorry I couldn't make it for cocktails on the terrace yesterday; I wasn't feeling so good.'

'Yes, I heard.' She pulled up a chair. 'I read your letter. I don't know what to say.'

'You don't have to say anything.'

'I was very moved by it. It made me cry.'

'Well, it *is* an eye-watering sum of money we're talking about.'

She smiled weakly at the joke. She seemed very subdued, almost downcast.

'It's a lot to take on board, I understand. We can discuss it more another time, if you plan on staying around for a bit.'

'I don't have much choice,' she said.

So that was it; that's what explained her mood.

'Things didn't go so well with the police yesterday?'

'You *could* say that.' Before he could reply, she blurted: 'Lyndon, listen . . . the accident . . . they think it might have been an attempt on my life. In fact, they're pretty sure it was.'

He might have snorted in disbelief had her face not been set hard as iron, and his brain not already lurching toward a conclusion it couldn't begin to accommodate. It was all he could do to speak.

'Tell me.'

'You remember how my father died?'

'How could I not?' He had heard the story from Valentine and, to his shame, had never once raised the subject with her.

'The man responsible vowed to kill me too.'

This terrible revelation came to him carried on a warm wash of relief. There was, at least, an alternative explanation.

'You've told the police this?'

Florence nodded. 'I didn't want you to know. But then your letter . . .' She petered off. 'Alice insisted we share it with them.'

'Of course she did, I understand. What makes them think it was an attempt on your life?'

96

'It's best if you hear it from them. They've just got here. I wanted to explain first . . . in person.'

She was so calm, so composed.

'Who are they?'

'Detectives. A man and a woman. She's older. He's . . .'

'Younger?'

'Kind, thoughtful. I like him . . . both of them.'

'Go and tell our guests I'm ready for them.'

He wasn't, though. The moment Florence left the library, the old impulses came trooping in, the cautionary mantra he had heard chanted since childhood.

Outsiders, the uninvited, sought only to profit or destroy.

He closed his eyes and waited, certain now of one thing — his was not to be a peaceful death. Best to accept it and put aside all thoughts of a smooth exit.

* * *

They made for an odd couple, she surely nearing the end of her career, he considerably younger and far too handsome for his own good. Detectives, like spies, were supposed to be forgettable, nondescript, so they could move through the masses unnoticed. They both took seats next to his bed. Detective Fuller glanced around her.

'That's a lot of books. Have you read them all?'

He pointed high up to his right. 'Not that one there.'

She laughed, an honest chuckle, not looking to ingratiate herself.

'Where are you from, Detective Fuller?'

'Why do you ask?'

'Fuller is an old American name, one of the very oldest.'

'Well, I'm honest-to-God trash from West Virginia, with a bit of Lithuanian Jew thrown in.'

'The Winslows came over from England on the *Mayflower*. There were Fullers on the same boat . . . three of them, I believe.'

'You don't say? Well, my lot must have been scrubbing the decks while your lot were, fuck knows . . . fiddling with the sextant.'

It was his turn to laugh. He liked women with what Deborah used to call 'a potty mouth,' usually when apologizing for her own.

'No Bodines on the passenger manifest?' asked her partner.

'I'm afraid not.'

'Too bad.'

'Something tells me you'll get over it.'

Detective Bodine exuded a languorous air. It was hard to imagine anything ruffling his feathers. Florence had said he was kind, and Lyndon could imagine it. He also knew that men who looked like Detective Bodine didn't have to work quite so hard for women to ascribe positive qualities to them.

'I know why you're here. Florence explained, though not the reasons for your thinking.'

'I'll let my colleague spell it out, seeing as he was the one who first figured something was wrong.'

'I'm an accident investigator,' said Bodine.

'Not a detective?'

'Not officially, not yet.'

'We're trying him out for size,' said Detective Fuller.

Bodine smiled. 'Just a beginner.'

It was an unabashed admission, and he went on to give a detailed and, at times, technical account of the slow build-up of their suspicions, together with the supporting evidence. It was a convincing case, presented with clear-minded precision. It was also chilling to hear just how close Florence had come to being annihilated by the mystery driver of the other car. Her fate really had turned on a split second.

Detective Fuller took up the reins. 'We're on our way to Vermont to look into the circumstances of the Prius's theft, but we thought we should meet you first.'

'Of course, anything I can do to help.'

She shifted in her chair. 'Why don't we start with the changes to your will favoring Florence?'

'Not exactly favoring . . . reinstating her hereditary rights.'

'I'm sorry,' said Bodine, 'but we haven't read the letter, so I'm only going on what they told us, but surely the provision that Florence gets to oversee the ethical investments in the Winslow Trust, well, favors her over your own children.'

'Not financially, not unless they resist her efforts.'

'At which point the trust is dissolved and she gets half its value, to do with as she pleases.'

Lyndon felt his hackles rising. 'She's shown herself to be extremely responsible when it comes to the wise distribution of wealth.'

It was Detective Fuller's turn again. 'You don't have to explain yourself to us, Mr. Winslow. We're just wondering who else knew about these changes to your will. Did any of your children know?'

He had been waiting for this, and here it was.

'No, only my attorney.'

'Name?'

'Victor Penfold.'

She wrote it down in a black notebook. 'Does he stand to lose out, or even benefit, from the changes you got him to draw up?'

'No. And let's be clear . . . Victor is my oldest friend, my dearest friend. He is utterly scrupulous. I can vouch for him.'

Detective Fuller spread her hands in a placatory gesture. 'Please don't infer anything from these questions. We have to ask them. Is it possible that someone else — someone in Mr. Penfold's law firm, say — got wind of the alterations?'

'Anything is possible, Detective Fuller, but I demanded one hundred percent discretion from Victor, and that is what he gave me. He drew up the changes himself. He confirmed it to me.'

'Forgive my ignorance, but does something like this need to be witnessed by a third party?'

'No. And I don't think you're even one little bit ignorant, Detective Fuller.'

'Careful, Mr. Winslow, I flatter easily, I'll lose my thread.'

'I don't believe that, either.'

Another one, thought Lyndon. First Florence, then Alice, and now this . . . smart, strong women he would have liked to spend more time with, get to know better, but wouldn't. Had they always been there? Could he only see them now with his dying eyes?

Detective Fuller pressed her palms together. 'Well, I think that just about covers it.' She looked at Bodine.

'I reckon,' he said. 'Just one more thing. When were you planning to tell your children about the changes to your will?'

'I wasn't.'

It was a mistake. He should have lied.

'Quite a shock for them, no, finding out after you're dead?' said Bodine.

Lyndon smiled wryly. 'Quite a shock for me . . . someone using the d-word in my presence.'

'I'm sorry.'

'Don't be; I much prefer it to the ghastly euphemisms. Dead is what I almost am. You were saying?'

'How did you think they would react . . . your children?'

'They were my wishes; they would have respected them. They still will.'

'Me, I'd be pretty pissed,' said Detective Fuller. 'But I guess that's the deck-scrubber in me.'

'You mean the ignorant deck-scrubber who flatters easily?'

'Damn, we only just met and you've already got me down pat.'

She rose to her feet. He hadn't registered before quite how tall she was.

'We're going to need to speak to your attorney as soon as we're back. Until then, I'd appreciate it if you said nothing of this to him. Or anyone else, for that matter. We weren't here.'

'My daughter-in-law must have seen you arrive.'

'Heather? She's at yoga.'

So, a judiciously timed visit, and an indication of where their true suspicions lay.

'And the man responsible for the death of Florence's father . . . the threat he made against her life?'

'General Ngomo? Our strongest lead by a mile,' Detective Fuller replied, yet somehow with little conviction.

'What are you going to do to protect Florence?'

'We're not; you are. A couple more goons are being hired. One isn't enough.'

'I see you've met Bevan.'

'Fiddling with some roses at the gatehouse. Very Norman Rockwell. Is that where he lives?'

'Yes.'

'Is he trustworthy?' she asked.

'I'm not even going to dignify that with a response.'

'A simple yes or no will do.'

'I'd trust Bevan with my life . . . what little is left of it.'

'Ex-military?'

'That depends what you mean by military.'

'Intriguing.' She stepped forward and shook his hand. 'Thanks for your time, Mr. Winslow.'

Bodine followed suit.

'It was a pleasure to meet you, sir,' he said, with his firm grip and his matinee idol smile.

TWENTY-FOUR

'That was a masterclass,' said Dylan, the moment the library door closed behind them. 'Were you flirting with him?'

'He was flirting with me.'

'To quote him: I don't believe that, either.'

'You have a good ear. What else did you hear?'

'Defensiveness,' said Dylan.

'Tick.'

'Hesitancy.'

'For sure.'

'Honesty.'

'Up to a point.'

'I like him.'

'I don't trust him,' said Carrie.

'You think he's holding out on us?'

'Not that. I don't trust him not to get involved. Men like Lyndon Winslow are used to running the show. That's okay, though. He can help us while we're on the road.'

'Why would he want to do that? I thought they didn't give a shit about people like us.'

'He'd be doing it for himself . . . because he needs the answers, too.' Carrie stopped at the door that led into the main body of the house. 'Dollars to doughnuts we wouldn't be here right now if he hadn't changed his will. The question is, who else knew about the changes? And how?'

'That's two questions.'

'Two questions he's asking himself right now,' said Carrie, pushing through the door. 'Let's see what he turns up for us.'

* * *

As arranged, they stopped by the kitchen again, a large, bright space with its own dining area and a wall of French windows giving onto a flagged terrace, where Florence and Alice were now seated at a circular tin table beneath a sunshade.

They had a four-hour drive to Burlington ahead of them, and they stayed only briefly, just long enough for Carrie to fill them in on the meeting with Lyndon.

'He says no one in the family knows about the new will, and they won't until after he's gone. Let's keep it that way. Our secret.'

Florence's eyes were fixed on Carrie. 'You're not convinced, are you?'

'Our job is to keep an open mind. Your job is to stay safe and tell us of any developments here, however small. We'll be gone a night, maybe two.'

Florence and Alice saw them off at the front door.

'I meant to say yesterday,' said Florence, 'thanks for the way you were with me in the hospital. I was a mess.'

'Shock's a weird thing,' Dylan replied.

'It helped.'

'My pleasure.'

He was heading for the Chevy with Carrie when he remembered what had been niggling at the back of his mind.

'Last Friday, you were coming from New York, right? So why not take Route 7 from Kent, why go east to the 63?'

Florence hesitated, as though pondering it for the first time. 'William suggested it.'

'Heather's husband?'

'He called me to say hi, and how they were looking forward to seeing me again . . .' She trailed off, understanding now the reason for his interest, forming the connection.

'And he suggested the 63 over the 7?'

'Not exactly. He said they always go via Torrington on Friday nights because of the traffic. They drive it all the time.'

* * *

'How long have you been sitting on that?' Carrie asked as they made off down the driveway.

'It occurred to me the other day when we drove out to the intersection. I just assumed Satnav had rerouted her.'

'Apparently not. Good job you asked. William Winslow offers directions.'

'Doesn't make him guilty.'

'Doesn't exonerate him, either.'

There was no sign of Bevan at the gatehouse as they passed by and out of the estate. The big man and his green fingers were gone.

'Out of interest, how *were* you with her in the hospital?' Carrie asked.

'I don't know . . . sympathetic?'

'I'm no good at that stuff. Never was.'

'Bet you're lying, bet you're a big softie at heart.'

Carrie laughed at the idea. 'You'll find out soon enough.'

They headed north out of Canaan toward the state line, Dylan driving in silence, replaying the encounter with Lyndon Winslow in his head, picking it apart.

'Let it out,' said Carrie as they were passing through Sheffield.

He glanced across at her. 'What's that?'

'I can almost hear the cogs grinding.'

'It's kind of odd, don't you think? Assuming the old man was telling the truth.'

'About what?'

'About not having any plans to tell his children, leaving them to find out about the changes to his will after he was dead. I mean, I'd understand if he was going to sit them all down last weekend and talk it through. But he hadn't seen Florence in years, not since he cut her and Valentine out of his life. And now he's inviting her to stay? He must have known they'd be wondering what the hell she was doing there. It's like he was looking to . . .' He petered off.

'Go on,' said Carrie.

'I don't know . . . taunt them with her presence.'

Carrie sat with the thought a while before replying.

'You continue to surprise me, Mr. Bodine. Don't stop.'

* * *

They were through Massachusetts in no time and heading deep into Vermont, the forested hills rising around them, hemming in Route 7. They stopped for a late lunch at a farmer's market near Salem, the sort of place where you paid double for vegetables with the dirt still on.

It had a small restaurant attached. Carrie turned out to be a vegetarian.

'Since when?' Dylan asked.

'Since way back when . . . before you were born, probably.'

'I was born in 1991.'

'Christ, you're a baby. I got married that year. Divorced, too. Tommy Gallagher, an untamed Irishman with a big motorcycle and not much else going for him.'

'I can't see it,' said Dylan.

'Every girl has to have a bad boy at some time in her life. My mistake was thinking he was husband material. My mom warned me, but what did she know? She was, like, *forty years old*.' She smiled, remembering. 'Tommy Gallagher. It should have worked — we were in love with the same person.'

Dylan laughed, turning his attention back to the menu.

'I'm thinking of having the chicken stir-fry. You're not going to be offended, are you?'

'God, no . . . just curious. They're dinosaurs. All birds are. Just seems a little unfair that they survive tens of millions of years only to be eaten by one of the hairless monkeys . . . who, by the way, were amoeba grubbing around in the primordial slime when they were already up and at their thing.'

Dylan held up his hands in surrender. 'Okay, you win. I'll have the steak instead.'

He got an incoming from Evie soon after they'd ordered. He made his excuses and headed out front to take the call.

'Hey, what are you up to?' Evie asked.

'Waiting for my zucchini and eggplant gratin to arrive.'

'Huh?'

'Forget it. What about you? How's it going down there?'

'It's hell.'

It didn't sound like hell, but something close. She was taking a short break from the endless round of interviews and photo shoots. 'I'm lost, Badger. I'm talking out my ass.'

He knew it wasn't true; she would be talking with earnestness about her work while punctuating those heartfelt opinions with jokes and self-deprecation, which would show her to be the humble person she truly was. He told her as much.

'Listen, I've got to go. There's hair and make-up in five and Angus wants to brief me first on the interview.'

There had been no mention before of Angus Lovelock chaperoning her down there.

'Say hi to him from me.'

'Yeah, sure, of course, I will. Speak later. Love you.'

'Love you too.'

He didn't need to kill the call; she was already gone.

He stood and stared at the traffic thundering by.

A fork in the road had loomed out of the fog and separated them. No one really to blame. It stung like hell, but he couldn't be angry with her, not about this, not about her dream. He would never become the guy who held her back. That way lay resentment and certain ruin.

He returned inside and dumped himself back at the table. 'Sorry about that.'

Carrie scooped up some humous with a piece of home-made flatbread, both of which had arrived in his absence.

'I've been thinking about what you said, and you're right . . . I'm smelling bad blood between the Winslows. We need to drive this forward while we're on our little road trip. I know a guy in New York who can do some digging for us.'

'What kind of digging?' he asked.

'The sensitive kind — the Winslows, their hedge fund, anything else he can turn up. I get it that the old man feels bad for the way he treated Florence, Valentine too, wants to put things right, but what he's doing is a kick in the teeth to his kids, whichever way you slice it.'

TWENTY-FIVE

The South Burlington police department building was a boxy, two-story structure set in a leafy sector of the city, lost and anonymous in the maze of malls and low-slung warehouses that were its neighbors. Detective Lieutenant Ernesto Safran, commander of the investigation division, was expecting them; Carrie had called him yesterday and then put in a follow-up when they'd stopped for lunch. He was a good-natured, bull-necked man who greeted them warmly and then promptly introduced them to his fellow detectives.

Carrie's decision to seek his sanction before conducting an investigation on his turf had pleased him. 'Believe me, most don't. They just show up and help themselves.' She had also advised him that they would be carrying their weapons across state lines, not a requirement but a courtesy that had also gone down well. All this was, in fact, a piece of disingenuousness on Carrie's part.

'Swamp them with good manners and they'll leave us alone,' she had said in the car.

She wanted no outside involvement, and with this in mind, there was to be no mention of attempted murder or anything else that might pique the local detectives' interest and see them muscling in. No, they were simply here to interview Mrs. Chiltern, the owner of the stolen Prius, with a view to establishing the identity of the car thief who had perished in the accident. To reinforce the routine nature of their visit, Dylan was introduced as an accident reconstructionist, brought along for his technical expertise and nothing more. He was to sit and observe for now.

Detective Safran didn't stand a chance. Carrie turned the full weight of her charm on him, quizzing him about his work and his cases, comparing notes with her own in Torrington. He unquestioningly handed over the police report on the break-in at the Chilterns' house that had led to theft of the Prius, and he promised to distribute throughout the whole police department the photo of John Doe they'd brought with them.

'What if we need them later?' asked Dylan as they crossed the lot back to their car.

It was maybe hoping for too much, but if an arrest did have to be made, it could only be performed by an officer of Vermont law enforcement.

'Ernesto looks like the sort of guy who'll get over it.'

* * *

They had a couple of hours before their meeting with the Chilterns, time enough to check into their hotel and go over the police report. There was to be no bland motel on the outskirts of the city for them; Carrie had found an internet deal on two rooms at a downtown hotel that fell just within departmental budget limits. It was a grand old townhouse on a leafy street, with a big garden round the back and breakfast thrown in.

Dylan's room was painted tasteful tones of gray, and the four-poster bed stood on honeyed wooden boards. It was far more luxurious than any hotel room he'd ever stayed in with Evie, and he took a photo of it to send her. He deleted the photo. It would look like he was competing with the fancy hotel in Tribeca that the gallery had stuck her in.

Hey, look at me up here in Vermont! Not doing so badly myself, eh?
Pathetic.

* * *

They found a table in the back garden and went over the police
report with a fine-tooth comb. It was standard fare: a break-in
downstairs while the Chilterns were asleep upstairs. There were
big trees round the back of the house, and it had been a windy
night; they hadn't heard the utility room window being jim-
mied. The Prius's keys had been lifted from a bowl on a table
in the front hallway, which was where Mrs. Chiltern always
dropped them when she returned home at the end of her day
from the University of Vermont Medical Center, where she
worked as a pharmacist. There was no way of knowing when
the incident had occurred. None of the neighbors interviewed
had seen or heard a thing, and the perpetrator had clearly
worn gloves, because no fingerprints other than those of the
Chilterns and their cleaning lady had been found.

'Ah, a cleaning lady,' said Carrie.

'Too obvious, no?'

'We take what we can. This is our only way in . . .
through the back door.'

She had a point, and she spelled it out to him. If, for the
sake of argument, William Winslow lay behind the attempt
on Florence's life, what were they going to do? Slam him
up against a wall and beat a confession out of him? People
like the Winslows were so lawyered-up you practically had
to catch them in the act to get them sent down. What they
couldn't do, however, was scrub out the traces of their
involvement, however faint they were.

'People spoke to people, met people, money was handed
over. Phone calls were made. I figure phone calls are still
being made, those of the "what-the-fuck-happened?" variety.
If we're right about the accomplice, then they're still out
there, maybe freaking out, behaving erratically.' She took a
sip of her jasmine tea. 'No, forget about the Winslows for

now. We build a case the old-school way, coming at them from the other side, through the back door.'

* * *

The Chilterns lived in an affluent suburb of South Burlington. The houses were widely spaced and set well back from the tree-lined road, two factors that had played in the car thief's favor. The Chilterns' home was a large Cape-style property: cream-colored weatherboard topped by a shingle roof. A brand-new Lincoln sedan, possibly an insurance company courtesy replacement, was parked in the driveway in front of the double garage. Dylan pulled up behind it.

It hadn't occurred to him before. 'Perfect car to steal, a Prius. Hybrid. Would have slipped off in electric mode, silent as a shadow.'

Mrs. Chiltern was small and pert, with a sour mouth set in a pinched face. She greeted them frostily at the front door, until she saw that they had brought her tennis bag with them.

'Well, that's something, I suppose.' She was thrilled that her two racquets were still there. 'They're like old friends. My game would have suffered. They haven't made this model for years.'

'There's always eBay, I guess,' said Dylan.

Her look told him in no uncertain terms that she wasn't the sort to buy old, used gear off other people.

'I'll get some tea together. My husband will be back any moment. Make yourselves at home in the lounge.'

'Couldn't have happened to a nicer person,' muttered Carrie as they entered the bland yet impeccably furnished room.

If Mrs. Chiltern was charmless, her husband, who appeared at about the same time as the tea tray, was down-right offensive.

'Serves the fucker right, good riddance to him,' was his verdict. 'You got any idea what this is going to do to our premiums?'

'No, do tell,' said Carrie.

And being deaf to irony, Bernard Chiltern did just that, until his wife interrupted him. 'I told you we should have protected our no-claims bonus.'

'Shouldn't need to . . . not if scumbags like that were kept off the streets.' He glared at them, as though he held them personally responsible.

'Talking of which . . . one dead scumbag.'

Carrie shoved the photograph of John Doe under Mr. Chiltern's nose. He recoiled. 'Oh Jesus Christ, what the hell . . . ?'

'Those stitches? That's where he was scalped and they reattached the top of his head. I'm guessing they'd have done a better job if he'd been alive. Recognize him?'

'No.'

'Take your time.'

'No already!'

Carrie took the photo back and handed it to Mrs. Chiltern. She kept having to look away, sneaking little glimpses, before she could pronounce that John Doe was also unknown to her.

'Tell us about your cleaning lady,' said Carrie.

Mrs. Chiltern looked startled. 'You can't possibly think Maria was involved.'

Carrie heaved an exaggerated sigh. 'It has been known, I'm afraid.'

Dylan struggled to keep a straight face.

'I told you, didn't I?' said Mr. Chiltern to his wife. 'Something not quite right about her.'

'Don't be ridiculous, Bernard!'

'I knew it . . . first time I met her.'

'That's where we come in,' said Carrie. 'Even the act of asking a few questions can give you a sense of someone's guilt or innocence.'

While Mrs. Chiltern went off to call Maria, her husband showed them the utility room window, inside and out. It had been replaced, and the new one had bars on it. The police had found no footprints in the flowerbeds that bordered the large backyard, which would have suggested that the property had been approached from the rear. Carrie and Dylan made a thorough check, though, just to be sure. Mrs. Chiltern joined them in the garden. Maria was out of town, visiting her father at his retirement home up near Highgate. She would be back late.

'No problem,' said Carrie, 'we're staying the night in Burlington. If we could have her number, we'll take it from here.'

Their final stop before leaving was the hallway. The bowl from which the car keys had been filched stood on a console table about five or six feet from the front door. Above it was a hideous painting of a white stallion galloping through surf under a full moon. Carrie scanned the space then crouched by the front door and raised the brass letter flap.

'Am I wrong, or has this been tampered with?'

It was a safety letter flap with a ridge that limited the aperture, so that a hand couldn't be inserted. The ridge had been dented, bent out of shape.

'Well, I'll be damned . . .' said Mr. Chiltern.

Carrie said nothing more on the subject until she and Dylan were back in the Chevy.

'Conclusion?' she asked.

'Someone tried and failed to fish the keys from the bowl.'

'Which suggests?'

'It was someone who knew they were there.'

'Not necessarily, but give yourself a gold star anyway.'

TWENTY-SIX

Rowan was the rock in Florence's life. He had come on board in the early days, when the charity was little more than a registered name, with Florence hunched over her laptop at the kitchen table in her rat-hole of an apartment. It was Beth, an ex-girlfriend of Valentine's from his Harvard days, who had introduced her to Rowan, though not with a view to anything. It had simply been a dinner party at Beth's place: a good woman looking out for her, aware that she was suffering, struggling to cope. Since Valentine's death and working in the charity sector, she had learned that the world was full to brimming with kind and compassionate people, and yet for some reason it was the handful of assholes who seemed to get all the airtime.

Rowan had been an actuary for an insurance company and extremely bored, his husband, Carl, a currency trader for a German bank and extremely wealthy. Both of them must have been moved in some way by the story that came out that night, for a week or so later, Rowan had called her and offered his services *gratis*. Because he could afford to, he said, and because he wanted to do something more meaningful with his life.

Rowan now received a salary, and they no longer worked from Florence's apartment but a warren of tiny offices on the Lower East Side clustered above a Korean restaurant, the smells from which left them all in a near-permanent state of hunger. Rowan described himself as her 'right-hand man' (or sometimes her 'handmaiden'), but the truth of it was he knew considerably more about the machinery of the charity, more about everything, than she did. He had freed her up to perform, to play front-of-house.

On Friday afternoon she was supposed to be giving a talk to a group of young medics about the early warning signs of sepsis. If just one of them listened, it could mean a life saved. If she'd acted on instinct in Colombia and thrown Valentine into a cab and made hell-for-leather for the nearest hospital, he might still be alive today. She knew what she was talking about. She had suffered at the sharp end, as had the other people she'd drafted in to help drive home their point on Friday: that paramedics, ambulance crews and ER doctors were still not fully versed in the speedy diagnosis of the symptoms, and that because of it hundreds of thousands of people were dying quite needlessly from sepsis every year in the United States. That was more than were killed by opioid overdoses, breast cancer and AIDS-related illnesses combined.

'I can't do Friday,' she said to Rowan. 'But don't cancel. You do it.'

'Me?'

'You've heard my spiel a hundred times.'

'Try two hundred,' he replied dryly.

'Seriously, Row, you should think about it.'

'It's okay for you; some of us are stage shy.'

'Yeah, I remember your tabletop rendition of "I Will Survive" at your fortieth.'

'That wasn't me; I swear my drink was spiked!'

'Someone has to keep the show on the road while I'm out of action.'

'How are you doing, princess?' Rowan asked suddenly, with tenderness. 'I hate to think of you up there, all bashed about.'

'Don't, I just had a nice long swim. All my limbs are working again and I'm lazing by the pool with my book.'

'Ping me a photo so I can picture you,' he said.

'Only if you stand in for me on Friday.'

'Okay, okay, I'll do it, *Mein Führer.*'

She ended the call, feeling guilty. She and Rowan shared everything. There would be a shitstorm to face when he found out she hadn't come clean with him about the motive behind the crash, but he would forgive her eventually.

She was thinking about a final dip in the pool when Heather appeared from the house. She knew what was coming; she was just surprised it hadn't happened earlier.

'Hi,' said Florence.

Heather took a seat on the adjacent lounger and put on her most kindly and concerned expression. It wasn't a look that came naturally to her.

'Hey, you . . . I'm worried about you.'

'I'm okay.'

'Prove it. Dinner at the club with me, just the two of us. I know it's not your kind of place, but they do a mean octopus and chorizo salad.'

No, not her kind of place at all. The one time she had been there, with Valentine, she had counted four other black people, two of whom had been in uniform. It had been an act of defiance on Valentine's part, but she was the one who had suffered for his principles, squirming under the polite scrutiny of the other members. It had led to their first-ever argument.

'Not today. Thanks, though.'

'You seem very . . . subdued.'

'I killed a man, Heather.'

The bald truth of it seemed to surprise Heather at first.

'Do they know who he was?'

Was Heather fishing?

'Just some guy. They have to contact the next of kin first.'

Heather pushed her bug-eyed Prada shades up onto her head like a hairband, ending the charade.

'I don't appreciate being lied to, Florence. I know it wasn't a simple accident. I know what the police are saying. We all do. Victor told us.'

'I imagined he would have by now.'

Heather did a good job of looking flabbergasted. 'So, why didn't you tell me as soon as you knew?'

'I didn't want to worry you.'

'Someone tried to kill you and you didn't want to worry me?'

'I guess that's the sort of person I am.'

A facetious response, but Heather kept her cool.

'That's not how we work as a family. We share these things. Don't be afraid to reach out. We're here for you. *I'm* here for you.'

It was such a bald-faced lie that Florence almost let fly with the years of hoarded resentment. The most she'd ever had from any of them, other than Joe, was grudging acceptance.

'Thanks.'

When she offered nothing more, Heather leaned closer and said, 'I remember Valentine telling me the story of your father's disappearance. The police think the man responsible is also behind this?'

'Yes.'

'No wonder you've been acting so weird.'

'Have I?'

She thought she had managed to remain remarkably level under the circumstances. It was largely thanks to Alice, who had shadowed her everywhere and been so thoughtful, distracting her with amusing tales of her checkered love-life and the two young children who were so persistently vile to her, now that she was their father's new squeeze. It had only been a few days, but Alice already felt like an old friend.

'Are you sure you haven't got, I don't know . . . swelling on the brain or something?'

'They scanned it, Heather.'

'Doctors aren't gods. They miss things.'

'You sure know how to make a girl feel better.'

117

Heather got to her feet. The wounded pout screamed bad actress. 'I know when I'm not wanted.'

'Come on, I never said that.'

'You know, Florence, you've changed.' And not for the better, her expression suggested.

This time, it was a step too far.

'How can you say that? You never tried to get to know me before . . . you don't know me now.'

Heather looked genuinely shocked but recovered quickly. 'I'll put that down to the trauma of what you've been through.'

'Please don't. We both know it's the truth.'

Heather turned and headed for the house. And as Florence watched her stalk off, it struck her that she hadn't really changed. She was, in essence, the same person. All she had done just now was speak to Heather as a white woman would: on her own terms. That's what Heather had meant with her talk of change, even if she didn't know it.

Any developments, however small . . . Carrie Fuller had been very clear about that.

Florence reached for her phone.

TWENTY-SEVEN

Carrie had booked a restaurant in Burlington's bustling city center, a short walk from their hotel. She had opted for a navy-blue linen dress and low leather pumps, which left Dylan feeling woefully underdressed in a polo shirt and khaki combats when they met up in the hotel lobby.

'Florence called,' said Carrie, the moment they were on the move. 'Heather knows the truth about the crash, they all do now. They heard it from Penfold.'

'It was always going to come out.'

'Sure, but Florence says it felt like Heather was fishing for information.'

'The wife of the man who put her on the road where someone tried to call her.'

'Almost her exact words.'

'Doesn't prove anything.'

'It proves Lyndon's attorney is in contact with the children.'

'Innocent enough. He's a close family friend.'

'That's my point . . . just how close? What else has Victor Penfold shared with the Winslow kids?'

* * *

The restaurant specialized in fish and was discreetly aware of itself, with marble-topped tables and leather banquettes and crisp, white, linen napkins.

'This one's on me, not Torrington PD,' said Carrie. 'You can take me out when we've solved the case.'

'You think we will?'

Carrie eyed him. 'I wouldn't normally say this, but yeah, I do. Your first case and my last.'

They scanned their menus.

'Aren't fish dinosaurs?' he asked.

'Allow me a few double standards, smartass.'

Carrie ordered a bottle of French Chardonnay from the waitress.

'So, tell me about Evie.'

'What's to say?'

'I don't know. Are you going to get married?'

'I doubt it.'

'But you're not sure?'

'It takes two to tango.'

'She doesn't want to?'

'I'm guessing no.'

'You haven't talked about it?'

'Not for a bit.'

'Ah, but the subject has been raised?'

'A while back.'

'One more question, then I'll stop,' said Carrie. 'Just how uncomfortable are you feeling right now?'

'You have no idea.'

'Yes, I do . . . you're throttling your napkin.'

She was right; he was. He spread the napkin on his lap. 'Can we change the subject?'

'Sure, but conspiracy theories are off-limits, or I'll end up getting thrown out of here, probably arrested.'

Their waitress appeared with the wine, and by the time they had cooed over its quality and then turned their minds to ordering, the Evie moment seemed to have passed.

He was wrong.

120

'Back to Evie,' said Carrie.

'Jesus. Really?'

'I'm worried about you. After she called at lunch today, you stared at trucks for a whole minute. I saw you through the window.'

'It wasn't a whole minute.'

'But they *were* trucks.'

'True,' he conceded.

'Don't say if you don't want to, but I'm just an old woman who isn't going to tell anyone.'

She reached across the table and gave his hand a brief squeeze. It was such a surprising gesture, so kind and unexpected, that he started to talk: about Evie's sudden success, her hunger for recognition finally satisfied; his fear that their humdrum existence would no longer be enough for her; the overweening attentions of Angus Lovelock; even his strong suspicion that something had already happened between the two of them. And as the words poured out of him, he asked himself why he hadn't spoken to his friends about his feelings, and he realized it was because he couldn't face seeing it in their faces: the predictability of the outcome; their pained pity.

Carrie, at least, was someone who could give him a different perspective, a more positive one.

'I got to say, it's not looking good.'

'You think?'

'Sounds like she's had itchy feet for a while. And I'm not seeing it, the glossies the morning after some gala event: Evie Horn, rising star of the international art scene, and her partner . . . provincial detective Dylan Bodine.'

'Ouch.'

'Artists are like movie stars; they breed with each other. Sometimes you just have to cut a person loose.'

'If You Love Somebody, Let Them Go,' said Dylan sneeringly.

'Christ, that book was a piece of crap. My daughter sent it to me. I think it was her way of saying, "I love you, now fuck off out of my life."'

'You have a daughter? With Tommy the Irish bad boy?'

'Not him.'

'Who?'

'Another time. I'm not done with my interrogation.'

Dylan flattened a sip of the Chardonnay against his palate. It really was damn good.

'Kristin Scott Thomas,' he said.

'What about her?'

'Movie star, beautiful, talented, successful . . .'

'All of those things.'

'She's happily married to a French doctor.'

'I'm pretty sure that didn't work out.'

'I'm pretty sure you're wrong.'

He reached for his phone and made a quick search.

'Yeah, it didn't work out.'

* * *

Later, soon after they'd both turned in for the night, Dylan wandered down the corridor and knocked on Carrie's door.

'Come in.'

She was propped up in bed with a book, wearing wireframed spectacles and a Minnie Mouse T-shirt.

'What are you reading?'

'Tim Winton. Australian writer. Know him?'

'Can't say I do.'

'Change that,' she said.

'*My* bedtime reading.'

He dropped the Prius's owner's manual on the bed.

'I'll think I'll stick with Tim.'

'I've marked the page. Turns out it's not such a great car to steal, after all.'

Five minutes later, his phone rang. He reached for it on the nightstand, hoping it was Evie, finally returning his calls.

It was Carrie.

'Interesting,' she said.

'Could be.'

'It'll mean seeing Mrs. Chiltern again.'

'A price I'm willing to pay in the pursuit of justice.'

Carrie gave a soft chuckle. 'Goodnight, Dylan.'

It was the first time she had called him by his Christian name.

TWENTY-EIGHT

'It's me. I know where she is and where she's going to be for a while.'

'That's good.'

'I can tell you how to get into the house, and even which room she's in.'

'This isn't what you asked for.'

'I'm asking you to deliver on the service I've already paid for.'

'You said it had to look like an accident.'

'She's had one. Can you make it look like a complication related to the crash . . . a cerebral hemorrhage . . . a stroke?'

'I know what a cerebral hemorrhage is. I've heard of it being done.'

'Then find out how to do it.'

'No problem. And I'll handle it myself this time.'

'What does that mean? I don't know what that means.'

'It means you don't have to worry, it's as good as done.'

'Only, it isn't. And time is tight.'

'Yeah, yeah, you said.'

'Yeah, yeah, this has to happen ASAP. I need you to understand that.'

'I get it, I'm on it, the second you hang up.'

'Then I'll say goodbye now.'

TWENTY-NINE

The Garden Atrium at the University of Vermont Medical Center was Carrie's kind of place: a bright, double-height space, a soaring cathedral to health and well-being, with its tasteful wooden cladding and its vegetarian-heavy menu of locally sourced produce.

'This is the future. I'd come here any day for a mammogram if I could have a feta and warm green bean salad after. I don't suppose you know what a mammogram is.'

'I have a mother.'

'Who talks to you about her mammograms?'

'There's not much off-limits with my folks. I know for a fact they're having sex again since moving to Florida.'

'The heat will do that to a person.'

Mrs. Chiltern arrived five minutes late and in a fluster. They were understaffed at the pharmacy, and she hoped it was important.

'Let's see,' said Carrie, sliding a chair out for her. Dylan laid the Prius's manual on the table and turned to the relevant page.

'Have you ever heard of this — Safety Connect? It's a GPS service Toyota offers on subscription. It allows them to track your car if it's stolen, as well as other things. Were you signed up to it?'

'Obviously not,' came the aggressive reply.

'Mrs. Chiltern . . . ?' said Carrie.

Mrs. Chiltern let out a little sigh. 'Bernard didn't want to say yesterday, and obviously we're feeling a bit stupid now. The thing is, we don't believe in it . . . all that data gathering by the government . . . tracking everything we do, everywhere we go. We never use location services on our iPhones.'

'I don't think it's the government tracking you,' said Dylan.

'They're all connected, all in it together — big data, the deep state . . .'

'Hmmmm,' said Carrie, laying the skepticism on thick.

Mrs. Chiltern bristled. 'We're not the only ones who think it. One of my colleagues was saying the same thing just the other day. In fact, we were talking about the Prius and the way they can even keep tabs on us through our cars now.'

Dylan felt something close to an electric charge spark across the table between him and Carrie.

'Who?' Carrie asked, casually. 'Which colleague?'

'One of the orderlies.'

'The other day, you say? Can you be more specific?'

'Well, more like a few weeks ago.'

'Do you mind telling us how that conversation went, Mrs. Chiltern? Take your time. How did the subject of your car come up?'

'I don't understand. He's a friend.'

'No rush. Cast your mind back. Who brought up the subject of the Prius? Who mentioned it first?'

It was a while before Mrs. Chiltern replied. 'Holden did.'

'Holden . . . ?'

'Holden Truss.'

'Is he working today?'

'I don't know. I haven't seen him in a bit. Do you think . . . ?'

'We don't think, Mrs. Chiltern. We're detectives, we just gather facts; the rest is done by AI. You say he's a friend. Has he ever been to your house?'

'Not exactly a friend, but he was at our drinks party in June. He's not the only person from work who was.' Which sounded suspiciously like Mrs. Chiltern had a soft spot for Holden Truss.

'That's very helpful,' said Carrie. 'But we do have to warn you that if you communicate any of this conversation to either Mr. Truss or your husband, we'll have to charge you with perverting the course of justice. Do you understand?'

It sounded like complete nonsense to Dylan, but Mrs. Chiltern nodded vigorously.

'We'll know if you do. It'll come out; it always does. You can go now.'

They watched Mrs. Chiltern scurry away.

'You really don't like her, do you?'

'It shows?' Carrie drained the rest of her fennel tea. 'Let's go and see what Human Resources has on Holden Truss.'

They got directions and a map from the Information Center near the café. Human Resources was on Prospect Street, a five-minute stroll across the leafy campus.

'Hey, slow down,' said Carrie.

'I can't help it.'

'Enjoy the peace. If this is it, our back door, things are going to move fast from here . . . real fast.'

* * *

Human Resources was housed on the third floor of a somber old building that squatted at the corner of an intersection. Carrie showed her badge to the receptionist and explained the purpose of their visit without revealing Truss's name. A call was made, and a minute later a young woman with a big smile and a sweep of auburn hair bounced into reception and introduced herself.

'Hi, I'm Tonya Cliffe, one of our talent acquisition partners. How can I help you guys?'

'Is there somewhere we can talk in private?' Carrie asked.

'We have a couple of interview rooms.'

'Then we should feel right at home.'

'Oh, right, yes,' said Tonya, finally getting the joke.

It was a gaily colored room with a whiteboard on the wall and a weeping fig near the window that was losing its leaves. As soon as they were settled, Carrie explained that they'd like to take a look at the file of Holden Truss, an orderly in the pharmacy.

'Is there anything I should know?' Tonya asked warily.

'Only that we're in a hurry.'

'Personnel files are highly confidential.'

'Listen, Tonya, I don't know how *you* feel about hindering a police investigation, but I can tell you exactly what view a judge would take.'

'What view would a judge take?' Dylan asked, the moment Tonya had left the room.

'That she'd be perfectly within her rights not to show it to us without a warrant, but seeing as she offered it freely . . .'

It wasn't much of a file — a cardboard slip with a few sheets of paper tucked inside. Carrie gave them a once-over then asked, 'Any way of knowing his working hours over the last week or so?'

'I can call his supervisor.'

'Play it down, say it's an administrative matter, nothing important.'

Tonya left once more, and Carrie swiftly set about photographing the documents in the file with her phone.

'It's him,' she said. 'John Doe's accomplice.'

'You think?'

'I can see it in his eyes.'

They were heavy-lidded and wide-spaced, set in a long face topped by lank hair parted at the side, but only for the purposes of a job application, one sensed.

'He used to be in the Army. Catering at Fort Drum. And we've got a home address.'

When Tonya returned, she came with welcome news.

'He's been on vacation since last Wednesday, back at work next Monday.'

128

'Thank you, Tonya,' said Carrie, rising to her feet. 'You just made our day.'

Tonya looked genuinely moved by the statement. 'Hey, you know, whatever we can do to help.'

'You can keep this between us for now,' said Carrie. 'And don't worry, we'll see ourselves out.'

She turned as they were leaving the room. 'Oh, the weeping fig, you're overwatering it. That's why it's dropping its leaves.'

THIRTY

Lyndon was seated in one of the leather club chairs near the window at the far end of the library, ostensibly reading, but in reality planning how he was going to play it when Victor arrived. A simple stratagem occurred to him. His body might be falling apart, but his mind for now was alert enough.

Victor appeared a short while later, impeccably dressed in a lightweight dove-gray summer suit. He had always been something of a dandy, even when they were boys.

'Good of you to come, Victor.'

'Good to see you out of bed.' Victor dropped into the other club chair.

'Help yourself to coffee.'

The coffee service was laid out on the low table between them. Victor poured himself a cup: black with a dash of sugar.

'What are you reading?' he asked.

'Shakespeare's *King Lear.*'

It was a seventeenth-century edition bound in brown Levant that had set him back close to $25,000 in auction. Lyndon removed his spectacles, closed the book, and laid it reverently on his lap. The skin on the back of his hands was so pale and diaphanous that it looked like it might tear at any moment.

'Do you know the story of Lear?' asked Lyndon.

'I know he went mad.'

'Eventually. He disinherited a child and his world fell apart because of it. He lost everything, including his sanity. Such a vain and foolish old man.'

'Come on, Lyndon, you're neither of those things.'

'No?' He stretched out the pause, enjoying a moment of curious calm before casting his line. 'I want your opinion, Victor, about the changes I made to my will.'

'As your attorney, I'm simply here to execute your wishes.'

'As my friend, I'm asking if you think I've made a mistake.'

Victor glanced out of the window. 'It's dramatic, what you've done, no doubt about it.'

Ah, a nibble, thought Lyndon.

'I'm not sure I was thinking straight at the time.'

'Understandably. You'd just received your diagnosis.'

'I was thinking of my own legacy, not the pain I would cause my children.'

'Don't blame yourself. It's natural under the circumstances.'

Time to reel the hook in, thought Lyndon.

'What do you suggest I do?'

Victor leaned forward in his chair and said with eager deliberation, 'Lyndon, listen, there's nothing you've done that can't be reversed in a moment. I can have the papers here by the end of the day.'

Lyndon nodded several times, weighing the words. 'I have one more question, Victor, and I want you to take your time before replying. Think hard before you do, because if you lie to me, I'll know it and I *shall* destroy you.'

Victor drew breath as though to speak; Lyndon silenced him with a crisply raised hand.

'No, let me finish. You know I can destroy you, even from here. And yes, I'll be incriminating myself in the process, but look at me . . . I won't be serving a jail term, whereas you will.'

'Lyndon—'

'I'm not done yet. If you're honest with me, I'll do everything in my power to protect you. It may not be enough — there are other forces at play now that I can't control — but you have my word I'll do what I can. We both know it's more than you deserve.' He paused. 'Nod when you're ready to hear the question.'

Lyndon could see from the creeping look of desolation in his old friend's eyes that he knew what was coming. Victor eventually gave a nod.

'Who did you tell about the changes to my will?'

THIRTY-ONE

It was a twenty-minute drive east from the University of
Vermont Medical Center to the village of Essex Junction,
although the city never fell away at any point. The suburban sprawl had consumed the small communities in its path,
filling in the gaps with strip malls, used-car dealerships, gas
stations, Tire Warehouses, Subways and KFCs. Route 15 east
out of Burlington could have been anywhere in the United
States.

'Have you got a baseball cap?' Carrie asked.

'Do I need one?'

'Best if we stick that pretty face of yours in the shade.'

They stopped at a Sports Central and bought a couple
of baseball caps, one blue, one red.

The Vermont Department of Motor Vehicles had been
less than cooperative when Carrie had called them and asked
for details of any vehicles registered to Holden Truss at the
address they had for him in Essex Junction. Stymied, Carrie
had been forced to turn to Detective Safran for help.

'It's probably a false trail, but I'd kick myself if I didn't
check it out, having come all this way.' She had signed off
with: 'Thanks a bunch, Ernesto, you're a mensch.'

Holden Truss's registered address was a stone's throw from the halo of traffic lights suspended above the five-way intersection that gave Essex Junction its name.

'Take a right here,' said Carrie, checking her phone. 'That's it.'

There was a large, open parking lot on their right, with a few cars and a big, black dumpster in the far corner. It was bordered by a railway line on one side, and on the other there were a few doors punched into the back of the huddle of buildings that occupied the corner of the intersection: humble apartments, like a run of motel rooms.

'One of those is his. Keep driving.'

They bumped over the railway tracks and bore right toward some warehouses.

'We're in luck. Open ground.'

She was right; even from here, on the far side of the railway tracks, there was no vegetation to obscure their view across the parking lot to the apartments.

'We're going to stake it out?'

'Not from here. We'll stick out like a sore thumb later.' There were a number of cars parked out front of the auto parts warehouse where they'd pulled up, but later the lot would be deserted.

They turned around and settled on a small road on the other side of Maple Street, south of the tracks still, with curbside parking across the street from some houses. It was farther away, but there was still an uninterrupted view of Truss's apartment. Carrie pulled some binoculars from her bag.

'Is this when you send me out for coffee and doughnuts?'

'You've been watching too many cop shows,' said Carrie. 'Mint tea for me, no doughnuts. And take the back route.' She nodded over her shoulder.

It was a minute's walk to the Nest Coffee & Bakery on Main Street, where Dylan loaded up. When he got back, Carrie told him the call from Detective Safran had come in.

'Looks like our friend is home, not on vacation. That's his car right there . . . the mid-blue Ford.' Carrie handed him the binoculars.

The car was parked with its nose facing the middle door of the three.

'What now?' he asked.

'I drink my tea, you drink whatever that is, and if he doesn't poke his snout out of his hole, we check into our cabin and wait till dark.'

'Er, what cabin?'

'The one I just booked on Airbnb.'

Dylan handed Carrie the small brown paper bag. 'Lemon and blueberry muffin, homemade.'

'What are you going to eat?' she asked.

'Already did. Prosciutto bagel. Toasted.'

'Good?'

'To die for.'

'As some poor pig did. Let me tell you about pigs.'

'Do you have to?'

'Genetically, we're so close to them you might just as well have been eating a slice of flesh off your own thigh.'

'I don't believe that.'

'Okay, genetically we're closer to mice, but there's a lot of emerging evidence suggesting common ancestry between pigs and primates.'

'What, twenty million years ago?' scoffed Dylan.

'More like eighty million, actually.'

'Where do you get this stuff?'

'From things called books. They're made out of dead trees. Just think how much you're going to learn, cooped up in a car with me for endless hours.'

'Dear God.'

'Damn, this is one good muffin.'

* * *

After an hour there was still no sign of Holden Truss; no sign, in fact, of anyone coming or going from any of the three units that fronted the parking lot, so they called it quits for now. It was a short drive to the tree-lined road on the north side of Main Street. The cabin that Carrie had booked on Airbnb turned out to be a small weatherboard building that stood in the garden of a much larger house.

The owners — an elderly couple, charming and unsure on their feet — showed them around the modest little property. There were two bedrooms, a bathroom, and a kitchen just large enough to take a table. It was impeccably clean and well-stocked, right down to a bowl of cherries from the garden and a stash of capsules for the coffee machine.

'You take the double bedroom,' said Dylan.

'Why, thank you, I will.'

Carrie went straight to work, logging on to the Wi-Fi and digging into the information she had photographed in Truss's file.

'I'm good here for a bit. Grab a power nap, if you want. Could turn into a long night.'

Dylan unpacked his bag then took a shower. He lay on his bed and drifted off to the calming sound of Carrie talking on her phone. He was woken twenty minutes later by a text pinging in from Evie. She was rushed off her feet but would try to call him later. She just wanted him to know she'd be coming home a day early — tomorrow night, not Friday.

He joined Carrie in the kitchen, where she was tapping away at her laptop.

'Did you sleep?'

'Yeah, briefly.'

'Here, have some cherries.' She slid the bowl toward him.

Carrie had called Greg in Torrington and asked him to fire off a photo of John Doe to Fort Drum Army base in upstate New York, where Holden Truss had worked as a caterer for a few years up until September 2017, according to his employment record. If Truss was the missing accomplice from last Friday night, then maybe he and John Doe had met while in the service. It was a long shot but worth chasing up. Truss's resumé also revealed that he had attended Troy High School in New York State, leaving in 2005. Seeing as he and John Doe appeared to be close in age, Carrie had also asked

Greg to get the high school yearbooks from 2002 to 2008 couriered over to him, in case a younger incarnation of John Doe appeared in one of them.

'He's happy with what we've achieved so far. Surprised, even. I took all the credit for the breakthrough, of course.'

'Naturally, boss. Give me something to do.'

'You can make a quick walk-by of his place, discreetly, see if you hear noise from inside. And as soon as it's dark, you can fix this to his car.'

Carrie produced a rectangular, black, plastic object from her bag.

'A tracker?'

'Let's see how *he* likes it.'

THIRTY-TWO

Florence was seated on the back terrace, picking off a bunch of work emails on her laptop and seriously regretting making the call earlier. She had misjudged her mother's reaction, which wasn't so surprising, given how little they'd seen of each other in the last five years.

Her father's disappearance hadn't just punched a bottomless hole in her life; it had driven a wedge between the two women he'd left behind. Her mother had begged him not to go to Mozambique, and her anger at his refusal to heed her warnings had become a feature of their lives in the aftermath of his vanishing. Florence, quite naturally, had leaped to her father's defense. Arguments had flared, some of them vicious. They had said things to each other, cruel words that should never have been spoken and couldn't now be taken back.

In the end, it was the damage they were doing to each other that had driven Florence away, carrying her to Greece, to Kara Tepe, the gateway camp for refugees on the island of Lesbos that she'd heard about from a friend. Valentine had been volunteering there for two months already as part of a search and rescue crew, and was only a few days off leaving. He had stayed on.

Her own story had seemed so trivial compared to those of the people arriving in weary droves every day in their flimsy inflatables, cold and confused and terrified. It had come out eventually, though, and when Valentine hadn't tried to save her, when he'd just swum along beside her, a reassuring presence with a wicked sense of humor, she knew she had found a special man, one she would fight to keep a hold of.

There was nothing to be done now. Her mother was getting on a plane to New York, despite Florence's efforts to dissuade her. It was a worrying prospect; her mother wasn't someone who knew how to rein herself in when the situation called for it. Being a teacher, if she had an opinion, she was inclined to voice it. Florence had said nothing to her about the suspicious circumstances of the car accident, but she had foolishly mentioned that the other driver had died.

A genuine lapse of judgment? She wondered. Maybe some part of her needed her mother at her side right now. It was easier before, when she'd had a focus for her fear, her anger, even a personal mission that she could dream of and work toward: the destruction of General Ngomo to ensure her own survival, and the satisfaction of avenging her father in the process.

Gone. Snatched from her. Carrie Fuller hadn't said it in so many words — in fact, she'd gone out of her way *not* to say it — but she clearly suspected the answer could lie closer to home, with the changes that Lyndon had made to his will.

It was a thought she didn't like to dwell on, but one she couldn't shut out, just as there would be no laying her father's spirit to rest again any time soon. She had thought of him more in the past few days than she had in the past few years, the happy memories coming at her unbidden . . . the way it had once been for the three of them. No, maybe it wasn't so surprising that she'd picked up the phone to her mother after all this time.

Her ringtone cut short her thoughts. Dylan. She felt her heart soar a little as she saw his name on her phone.

'Bad time?' he asked.

'Good time.'

'I just wanted to see how you're doing.'

'All fine, except my mother's flying in from England and I don't want her here.'

'We can head her off at the pass, if it helps.'

'Like in the Westerns?'

'That's us . . . the sheriff and her deputy.'

'Any news on the dirty varmint who tried to kill me?'

'Could be. We'll see.'

A lead, then. She didn't push him. 'Where are you now?'

'In a shop, buying some earbuds for my phone.'

'Nothing better to do?' she joked.

'All part of our devilish plan. Where are you?'

'Me, I'm sitting on the back terrace, looking at a big guy walking up and down the lawn.'

'The bodyguards arrived?'

'A couple of hours ago. Russ and Gil.'

Muscled, thickset men with short hair, just like Bevan. They were from an executive protection firm whose services the Winslows had used before. Both were licensed to carry concealed weapons, and one of them would be on duty throughout the night.

'That's good to hear,' said Dylan.

'Yeah, it helps. She might even get more than three hours' sleep tonight.'

'Look, the sheriff's waiting for me. I better beat a trail.'

She cast around for something smart to say, without success. 'I'm all out of cowboy talk.'

'Me too, dang it.'

She laughed. 'Okay, you win.'

'Speak soon,' he said.

'It's great to hear your voice. Call me whenever.' She winced at her words; they sounded so desperate, so needy.

'Same goes for you. Day or night.'

She placed her phone back on the table. A delicate little dance, a gentle trade of intimacies, each sending the other a message? Or just a considerate man doing his job, his duty?

140

She no longer trusted her judgment on such things, she'd been out of the game so long.

She returned to her emails but had barely gotten going when Heather and Alice came hurrying from the house.

'Lyndon's not in a great way,' said Heather, with something close to urgency. 'He wants to see us all.'

THIRTY-THREE

'Ah, the Three Graces,' Lyndon said weakly as they entered the library.

Heather pushed ahead of the others. 'How are you doing, Lyndon?'

'Dying, last time I looked.'

He grimaced, as if in pain, which he wasn't. He was loaded up with morphine, prepared for the conversation.

'It's close. I can feel it. I need my family with me.'

'Of course,' said Heather. 'Of course.'

'I don't think I'm going to make it to the weekend.'

Heather rested a bony hand on his bony arm. 'I'll make the calls.'

'Do you mind, my dear?'

Had he ever called her that in the past? Did he care? Heather hurried from the library. One down, one to go.

He turned to Alice.

'I'm going to say this now, because a man in my position is allowed to say anything he wants. It also happens to be true.' He paused. 'I'm sorry I didn't get a chance to spend more time with you, Alice. You seem like a right fine person, as my grandfather used to say.'

'*Una persona per bene.*'

'Oh?'

'As *my* grandfather used to say. He was Italian.'

'Tell me one thing about him that I can take with me.'

She thought on it. 'He could balance a broom on his foot while singing *La donna è mobile* from *Rigoletto*.'

Lyndon laughed, loud and hard. 'I can't believe I'm going to die without seeing that,' he said, recovering. 'Do you mind, Alice? I'd like a word alone with Florence.'

'Of course.'

Alice left the library, and Florence pulled up a chair next to his bed.

'I've seen you laugh before, but never like that.'

'Too many things too late,' he said. 'Have you had a chance to think more about my letter?'

'Yes.'

'I worry that I've forced your hand. It's a lot to take on, and you have a life to live. Maybe you don't want to spend it doing good deeds. I know I wouldn't.'

This drew a smile from her. 'Did Joe have a hand in it?' she asked.

'Joe?'

'He called and suggested we have lunch a few weeks ago.'

'Yes, he mentioned it.'

'I know you two are close. I just wondered if he'd . . .' She petered off.

'Joe has always been a big fan of yours, but this was entirely my decision.'

Florence reached out and took his hand. 'You're right, it's daunting. But it's also an amazing gift, Lyndon.'

'Is that a yes?'

'Valentine would be so proud of you. And I'll make him proud of me.'

The mention of his son's name still cut like a dagger strike.

'Tell me about the place where you scattered his ashes.'

He saw her stiffen at the question. 'I can show you a photo.'

'No, describe it to me.'

'All right,' she said. 'It's on the north coast of Colombia, the Caribbean coast, where the river meets the sea, a place so beautiful you can't imagine. A big, fat river, sluggish, almost like a lake, with mountains rising up behind, and thick jungle either side of it . . .'

He closed his eyes and pictured it as she continued: the thatched house on the big rock at the mouth of the river, where they had stayed for a week. The meeting of two worlds; the stillness of the river on one side, the relentless beat of the waves on the other; and around the headland to the south, a virgin beach that seemed to go on forever, backed by palm trees, where Florence would sit in the shade and read while Valentine surfed.

'He was a good surfer, wasn't he?'

'So he said. I couldn't really judge.' She fell silent for a moment. 'I'm sorry I didn't bring him home to you. I had to respect his wishes.'

'I understand. It's just a body, a vehicle. His failed him, as mine has betrayed me.' He hesitated, groping for the courage to continue. 'I'll always regret not attending his memorial service back here. I couldn't, though. I would have fallen apart, and there were too many people there who wanted to see that.'

'I was one of them,' said Florence with disarming honesty. 'I was still angry then, not only with you, but with all of it, the unfairness . . .'

'Why did he choose that spot for his ashes?'

'He said it was the happiest he'd ever been, caught between the river and the sea with me.'

'Tell me exactly where you put him.'

'Exactly where he asked.'

The mouth of the river narrowed dramatically into a slender channel of fast-flowing water that cut through the beach below the house on the rock.

'I tipped him in and he was carried out to sea. The waves are pretty strong, I'm sure he didn't get far. He's probably part of the beach now, gray specks in the sand.' She gave his hand a light squeeze. 'You must have a happiest place, too.'

'Nowhere like that, not even close.' He cast his mind back. 'No, mine would be my student digs in Oxford, the little basement off the Banbury Road, huddled in front of a coal fire on a winter's night with Deborah and a bottle of whiskey . . . talking nonsense, trying to save the world.'

She smiled at him.

'It's the same place, Lyndon.'

THIRTY-FOUR

They knew someone was home, because Dylan had heard music coming from inside the apartment when he'd strolled across the parking lot earlier: a dull beat, hard to define, no vocals. Whether it was Holden Truss playing DJ or someone else, he couldn't say. He hadn't lingered, walking straight on by in his baseball cap and going in search of a shop that sold AirPods for his iPhone, as Carrie had instructed.

Now, with darkness finally descending, he was on the move again, Carrie ahead of him by some fifty yards or so.

'You there?' she asked.

'Whiskey Tango Foxtrot.'

'Very funny. Wait till I'm in place and you've got the all-clear.'

'You said.'

'I'm saying it again for the dim-witted.'

'I feel like Jack Bauer.'

'If you were Jack Bauer this would have been done with days ago.'

'True.' Jack sure could shift. Never more than twenty-four hours to save the world. Again.

Up ahead, Carrie turned left at the intersection.

'Okay, his car's still there but the lot's lit up like a landing strip. The neighbor's porch light is on . . . the apartment just this side of his. You may want to approach from the other side, out of the shadows by the trees and the dumpster.'

'Your call,' he said.

'Yeah, I reckon.'

They had made a dummy run earlier, Carrie demonstrating where to attach the tracker on the rear suspension, a flat surface, but not a moving part, so it was less likely to be shaken loose. There was a whole lot of metal around, but the GPS signal would bounce off the road surface. Dylan had taken the Chevy for a spin, meandering through the residential streets, and Carrie had tracked him all the way on her phone with pinpoint accuracy. They were good to go. It only remained to fix the little black gizmo to Truss's car.

Dylan carried straight on over the intersection, past the corner gas station, closed now. The next establishment along was anything but closed. It was live music night at the On Tap Bar & Grill, and the high deck out front was mobbed with people. He pulled out the AirPods and strolled by, turning left into the bar's big parking lot. There was another entrance to the place directly off the lot, with more outside seating. He skirted the building, replacing the AirPods as he made for the run of trees that marked the border between the On Tap's parking lot and the one fronting Truss's apartment.

'I see you,' said Carrie. 'You're good to go.'

Dylan made for the dumpster and stopped briefly. From here it was twenty yards or so to Truss's Ford. He ambled casually over then dropped into the slab of shadow cast by the porch light on the far side. He was on his knees using a rag to wipe clean the spot where he planned to attach the tracker when Carrie's voice came to him through the AirPods.

'Someone just killed the lights inside. Move to the back of the car.'

The blood was beating a tattoo in his ears as he did so. What if Truss planned to drive somewhere? He wouldn't be crushed, but there was no way he could make it back to the cover of the dumpster without being spotted.

'Just wait,' said Carrie in his ear, calm as anything.

Dylan heard a door opening and closing, and then footsteps.

'He's heading off the way you came. Move to the right-hand side of the car now, silent as you can.'

He was blind, totally reliant on her, and caught now in the glare of the neighbor's porch light. He didn't like it one bit.

'He's still going. I see him. He's in the other parking lot.' He could tell from her breathing that she was on the move. 'Did you attach it yet?'

'No.'

'Do it now.'

He crawled back to the other side of the car, pulled the tracker from his pocket and heard the reassuring click as the magnet locked on to the steel strut.

'Done.'

'Great,' she said. 'No, wait!' The air stilled in his lungs. 'You're okay, he's still going. Make for the railway tracks, toward me.'

The shadows beyond the pool of light thrown by the porch light soon swallowed him up. He kept going, stepping through the long grass that fringed the tracks.

'I'm over here to your right, the trees where the tracks divide.'

She stepped out of the darkness when he was almost on top of her.

'Christ, that was close,' he said.

'Just unlucky timing.'

'Was it him?'

'For sure. Jeans, sneakers, gray T-shirt.'

'Did you see where he went?'

'Across the lot but not all the way to the street. He turned right before.'

'There's a back entrance to the bar off the lot. The place is rammed. They've got a live music night.' It sounded like

Holden Truss had wandered round the corner to his local watering-hole.

'He could be meeting someone,' said Carrie. 'We need to get eyes on him.'

'Let's do it.'

'Just you. Old women stand out in places like that.'

'Could be a tribute band.'

Carrie laughed. 'Go check and see. How else are you going to learn?'

'Learn what?'

'How not to look at him even though you are. How to build a cover story in the minute it takes you to walk over there.'

'For real?'

'Best to have something up your sleeve for all the single ladies who're going to hit on you . . . probably the married ones too. Cop tailing a suspect is unadvisable banter. Or maybe Holden is gay and decides you're his type. Seriously, you never know. Hope for the best, plan for the worst.'

'Team Fuller motto?'

'It is now.'

Dylan glanced over at the parking lot. 'You going to wish me luck?'

'I don't believe in luck.'

'And the "unlucky timing" you just mentioned?'

'I definitely believe in unluck.'

THIRTY-FIVE

Dylan had a good feeling about the On Tap the moment he stepped inside. There was a down-home warmth to the place, a buzz in the air. Smiling waitresses hummed like bees through the many tables where people were eating, and a gang of appreciative fans with drinks in their hands was ranged in front of the five-piece band, who were the real deal. They knew their instruments and how to play them.

It was a judgment Dylan felt entitled to make, having played lead guitar for a similar outfit throughout much of his twenties. Nothing big, only small venues like this, sometimes weddings and bar mitzvahs, but they had touched people, made them dance, brought momentary joy with their R&B sound and second-rate musicianship. He had hoped for more — they all had — but they had also recognized their limitations, even joked about them. If you couldn't write a killer tune, which they couldn't, the prospect of a record deal would always remain a remote prospect. They had called themselves the Unforgiven. This lot had gone for the Mannequins, according to the front of the big bass drum.

There were a couple of empty stools at the bar. He grabbed one and ordered a beer. He was now free to turn and survey the room, which he did casually but thoroughly.

He only had one photo to go on, probably not a representative one, and the description from Carrie — jeans, sneakers, gray T-shirt — didn't yield results. Only when the barman dumped his beer on the counter and he turned back to pay did he see that Holden Truss was standing no more than eight feet away from him along the bar, getting some drinks in — three beers and a glass of white wine — which he then carried precariously in both hands to a table close to where the band was playing.

There was a lean, handsome man with long, dark hair swept back off his face and two identikit blonde women wearing pale satin blouses cut low at the front, the sleeves lopped off above the elbow. Their skin-tight jeans were tucked into short cowboy boots. More like a gathering of friends than a meeting of co-conspirators, thought Dylan. A voice — Carrie's voice — warned him not to leap to any conclusions.

That's when one of the women turned and caught his eye. He looked away, cursing himself for allowing his gaze to linger too long. He had been staring, curious and over-confident, and she had sensed it. Not even five minutes in and he had already failed to heed a key piece of advice from Carrie. Fortunately for him, their table was almost directly in his eyeline when looking at the band, and he was able to keep tabs on them easily enough.

There was a lot of talk. The guy with the long hair seemed to be holding the table in thrall, with Truss chipping in from time to time, often getting a laugh. The court jester. The woman with the straight blonde hair contributed more than her girlfriend, who seemed happy to drink and watch the conversation unfold around her.

Dylan ordered another beer. The band finished their set and promised to be back for more in a bit. Truss and the other guy grabbed their beers and headed for the front entrance, probably to have a smoke on the deck. There was no point in following them; he would never get close enough to hear what they were discussing, certainly if they were looking to have a private pow-wow.

His back was to the room, and he didn't see the woman with the straight blonde hair until she appeared right beside him. She signaled to the barman.

'When you have a mo, Joe.'

Dylan smiled. She glanced at him.

'Hi,' she said.

'Old joke?'

'Mojo? One of my best. I haven't seen you here before.'

'You a regular?' he asked.

'Hey, Joe, am I a regular?'

'A regular pain in the ass,' said the barman. 'What do you want, Lizzie?'

'Same again . . . three beers and a Chardonnay. Oh, and stick 'em on Holden's tab.' She dropped a couple of bucks on the bar then turned to Dylan. 'Passing through?'

'You don't want to know.'

'Try me, I'm very understanding.'

'Driving holiday with my mother.'

'Wow, weird. No wonder you need a drink.'

'You never go on holiday with yours?'

'Our mother fucked off to Oregon with the local pastor when me and Holden were kids.'

So, brother and sister.

'Lizzie,' she said, offering her hand. He took it.

'Danny.'

'Where you from, Danny?'

'Long Island, originally. Patchogue.' He had a whole storehouse of information he could draw on, stuff relating to his mother's cousin and her family, and the many trips he had made there over the years. 'I now live in Westport, Connecticut.'

'First time in Vermont?'

'Uh-huh.'

'Impressions?'

'The natives seem friendly enough.'

Lizzie laughed. The barman arrived with her drinks.

'Hey, you want to join us?' she asked.

He had the feeling she'd said it on impulse, but another scenario came briefly to mind: Holden Truss, as suspicious as a cat, instructing his sister to check out the loner at the bar. If he declined the offer, he would have to say it was because he was about to leave, which he wasn't ready to do right now.

'Sure,' he said. 'Here, let me help you with those.'

Her friend was called Ellen, and they both worked for an outfit that leased farm machinery. He told them he worked for his cousin who ran an art gallery in Westport, and he sang the praises of the Connecticut coastline, which they'd never visited. It was small talk, easy, light-hearted, humorous, and after ten minutes there was still no sign of Truss and the other guy.

The band were tuning up for their next set when the skinny, handsome guy returned. Alone. No sign of Truss. His name was Jack and he was politely wary, until he heard that Dylan was on holiday with his mother, at which point he felt entitled to sneer at the stranger in their midst.

'What a good boy you are.'

'Not really. She's great, fun, young.'

'So why isn't Mommy here?'

'She's fifty-four. She prefers books to bars.'

'Fifty-four's not so young.'

'Leave him alone, Jack,' said Lizzie.

'Yeah, Jack,' said Ellen.

Jack held up his hands in a gesture of surrender. 'Woah, just making small talk.'

Lizzie glanced at the entrance. 'Where the fuck is Holden?'

'He got a call,' said Jack.

Dylan was beginning to wish he'd turned down Lizzie's offer, made his excuses and headed back to the cabin. Instead, he was trapped in a fiction, in lies, any one of which could catch him out. Fortunately, the band struck up some lively numbers, and the talk gave way to dancing.

It was the first real indication that Jack and Ellen were an item. They danced well together, a sort of low-key lindy hop. Lizzie drew Dylan into some of the same moves, and he tried his best to keep up. Then suddenly he was alone with both women. Truss had finally reappeared and Jack had gone to join him at the table. It didn't take much to know that Dylan was the topic of conversation between the two men.

When they took a break from the dancing, Truss was friendly enough at first — 'Good to meet you, man' — but then the gentle interrogation began. 'So where d'you work? Your cousin's art gallery, huh? What's it called?'

Truss pulled up the Fish Factory's website on his phone but seemed to relax when Dylan beat him to the punch and named Evie Horn as the artist exhibiting right now.

'Hey, man, looking good,' said Truss. He had linked through to the gallery's Facebook page and found a photo of Dylan standing in front of one of the paintings with Evie and a few others.

'People pay money for that crap?' he asked.

'Big money. Eight thousand a pop.'

'Jesus, I'm in the wrong game,' said Jack. He was an eBay trader specializing in catering equipment from restaurants that had gone bust.

'My man's the king of deep-fat fryers, ain't you, baby?' said Ellen, planting a kiss on his cheek.

Soon after, they all returned to the dance floor. Dylan was itching to be gone but left it for three more numbers before he announced he was leaving.

'I'll walk you back, man,' said Truss.

'You don't have to.'

'My place is tiny. I'm always looking for overflow for when friends visit.'

Lizzie pulled a sad face when Dylan kissed her good-night. 'I thought I'd struck lucky.'

'Maybe you did; maybe I'm a psycho killer.'

She laughed. 'Fun, though.'

'Sure was.'

* * *

154

Dylan was on his guard during the short walk back with Truss, especially once they'd turned off the main drag into the unlit residential roads. Nothing happened, though, and they soon found themselves at the darkened cabin.

The front door was unlocked, and Dylan flicked on the light as he stepped inside, Truss at his shoulder.

'Hello,' Carrie called from her room.

'Ma, it's Danny.'

Carrie appeared in her Minnie Mouse T-shirt.

'Daniel . . . ?' she said, which was inspired.

'This is Holden. We met in a bar.'

'I hope you boys aren't looking to make a night of it. Anyhow, we're clear out of booze.'

'Holden's from around here, just wanted to look the place over for friends.'

'Shouldn't take too long,' said Carrie. 'It's what they call bijou.'

'Nice, though,' said Truss.

'Two bedrooms. This is mine.' Truss poked his head inside her room.

That's when Dylan remembered he'd left his holstered handgun on his bed.

'Bathroom's on the small side,' he said.

He showed it to Truss, and for a moment thought that he'd gotten away with it.

'This the other bedroom?' Truss asked, already reaching for the handle.

He opened the door and flicked on the light.

Dylan's gun was no longer on the bed.

'Daniel drew the short straw,' said Carrie.

'Daniel offered his mother the biggest bedroom,' Dylan replied.

And that was that. Truss thanked them both then left. They watched him turn right out of the driveway, back toward Main Street.

'Could be he'll come right back,' said Carrie, 'so why don't you give your old Ma a kiss goodnight, brush your teeth, and go to bed like a good boy. We'll talk in a bit.'

155

A bit turned out to be about twenty minutes later, when Carrie appeared in his room and perched on the end of his bed.

'Thanks for hiding the gun.'

'You never know,' she said. 'Interesting tactic, befriending the prime suspect. Not in the manual.'

'I'm sorry.'

'At least we know now he's guilty as hell. Wouldn't have walked you back otherwise.'

He told her exactly how his time in the On Tap had unfolded, the choices he'd had to make on the hoof, operating on instinct, out of his depth. On her side, Carrie had seen Truss pacing around the bar's parking lot on a long phone call.

'Any idea who he spoke to?'

'It didn't come up, and I wasn't going to ask.'

'Lesson learned,' said Carrie. 'You got too close.'

'Close enough for this.'

Dylan pulled up the selfie he'd taken on the dance floor: the four of them peering up at the camera, with Jack making rabbit ears behind Ellen's head.

'That's Jack. He sells used catering equipment on eBay.'

Carrie grunted. 'Okay, you're forgiven. Ping it over to me.'

THIRTY-SIX

'It's me.'

'What time do you call this?'

'I thought you'd want to hear the good news. It's all sorted. We're good to go.'

'When?'

'Tomorrow night. You going to be there?'

'I'll be there.'

'With thirty thousand dollars.'

'Out of the question.'

'That's what he's asking for . . . the guy helping me out. Take it or leave it. His words, not mine.'

'I'll leave it.'

'No problem. *Adios*. Have a good life.'

'Wait.'

'I'm waiting.'

'Thirty thousand?'

'Cash.'

'Okay. But I've got some bad news, too. A couple of bodyguards showed up at the house today.'

'Shit. That means the cops are on to us.'

'Maybe not. They have their suspect . . . an African general.'

'What the fuck . . . ?'

'Old history. It means you can deal with her any way you like now. I can get you past the bodyguards.'

'And the money? He's wants it up front.'

'I'll think of somewhere to leave it . . . somewhere outside.'

'If it's not there, we're gone.'

'How do I know you won't just take it and disappear?'

'Now there's an idea.'

'I hope you're joking.'

'Relax, for fuck's sake. I'm a man of my word. This time tomorrow she won't be breathing.'

THIRTY-SEVEN

As soon as they'd checked out of the cabin, they headed east from Essex Junction, in case they were being observed. Dylan had told Truss and his pals he was going hiking with his mother in Mount Mansfield State Forest.

Fifteen minutes later, when they stopped for coffee at a gas station near Richmond, Dylan called Annie at the gallery in Westport and explained the tangle he'd gotten himself into last night, posing as her cousin Danny, who also happened to work for her. Annie wasn't happy about it, but she agreed to cover for him and say that 'Danny' was on holiday in Vermont if anyone called the gallery asking after him.

'Great news about the commission,' said Annie.

'It came through?'

'Evie didn't say?'

'We haven't had a chance to talk. Last I heard, she was running all over with Angus Lovelock.'

Annie drew breath before speaking. 'Are you fishing?'

He knew her well enough by now to ask, 'Do I need to be?'

'I don't know, Dylan, I really don't.'

* * *

Truss's car was still parked in front of his apartment, and there wasn't much more they could do until the tracker alerted them to his making a move. Carrie suggested they swing by South Burlington PD and see if Detective Safran could dig up anything for them on Truss and his friends. It would mean taking him into their confidence, but given the speed at which things were moving, they couldn't continue to fudge it forever.

They jumped on the highway back toward Burlington. Satnav said fifteen minutes to South Burlington PD. After five, Carrie's phone trilled. It was Greg calling from Torrington, and there was a clear lift in his voice.

'We got an ID on John Doe. Personnel at Fort Drum just called. He's a former soldier, same time as Truss was there.'

'Are they sure?'

'As eggs is eggs.'

'Name?'

'They're not saying.'

'What?'

'And they won't send over his file. They say the information it contains is too sensitive to be fired off electronically. They're okay with us taking a look at it, though . . . hard copy, on site, in person.'

'Did you lean on them?'

'Hit them with everything I had, the whole enchilada. They're not budging.'

Carrie turned to Dylan. 'Looks like we're going to Fort Drum.'

'I'll see your clearance is sorted,' said Greg.

Carrie filled Greg in on the events of yesterday evening: the successful planting of the tracker on Truss's car, and Dylan's unexpected brush with Truss and his pals in the bar. She made no mention of his foolhardiness in accepting Truss's sister's invitation to join them or indeed the close call with Truss when he'd accompanied Dylan back to the cabin, clearly with a view to checking out his story.

'I just looked,' said Greg. 'It's a good four hours to Fort Drum from Burlington. Maybe Dyl should stay on Truss's tail.'

'I need him with me,' said Carrie. 'We're only where we're at because of him.'

'Whoa, has the world gone mad? Did I just hear you pay a compliment to a colleague?'

'Must be the menopause,' Carrie replied.

THIRTY-EIGHT

Florence and Alice strolled along the edge of the lawn, beside the ha-ha, enjoying a final moment of peace before the house filled once more with family. Sensing that the end was imminent, Lyndon had summoned them all back from the city for the final farewells. They were due to arrive any moment now, in time for lunch, which Mary the cook was working away in the kitchen to prepare.

Just beyond the hidden ditch, a handful of cows in the overgrown pasture tracked them as they walked, curious, lashing their flanks with their tails to fend off the flies. Florence knew nothing about cows — she was a city girl, born and bred — and up close they seemed improbably huge and alien to her, creatures from another time and place, with their large liquid eyes which seemed to be asking: *What are you doing here?*

Trying to stay alive. That's enough for now.

Carrie Fuller had called from the road a short while ago to say that she and Dylan were chasing down a strong lead up north. This news was for their ears only, though; the Winslows were not to know. This seemed to confirm what Florence had sensed already: that their true suspicions lay not with General Ngomo, but one of the family. Which meant she would soon be sharing a roof with the person behind the plot.

The thought of it sat like curdled milk in her stomach. She had said as much to Alice, who had tried to persuade her there was nothing good to be gained from wild speculation. Frustrating though it was, all they could do for now was wait and see what Carrie and Dylan turned up.

Florence drew to a halt. So did Alice, and so did the cows.

'Would they eat us?'

'Huh?' said Alice.

'The cows. If we were over there . . . dead meat lying in the grass. Pigs would, I know.'

'I don't know if cows eat carrion. Maybe. My guess is they'd have a good chow-down on me, but they'd take one look at your bony ass and say it wasn't worth the effort. No, they'd leave you to the birds and the bugs.'

'That's got to be about the sweetest thing anyone has ever said to me.'

They collapsed in laughter.

'Oh God, am I going mad?' said Florence.

'You'd be well within your rights.'

'I don't know what I'd do if you weren't here.'

'Don't worry, nothing's going to happen to you. I mean, look at the size of that guy . . .'

Alice nodded back the way they had come.

Gil the bodyguard had been tailing them at a discreet distance. He now stood patiently, still as a statue, waiting for them to carry on their way.

* * *

William was the first to appear, pulling up out front in his hulking black Audi SUV. Joe was with him, and also Amber, Ralph and Connie's daughter. She had grabbed a ride up with her uncle and cousin because Ralph had been held back in the city by work and wouldn't be appearing with Connie until after lunch. The last time Florence had seen Amber, she had been a teenager wound tight with adolescent rage and with bangs that covered her eyes like a curtain. Now she was a confident, young woman who sported a shimmering ponytail and walked with her chin up and her shoulders back, like a dancer, like her mother used to be. She had recently graduated with top honors from Yale Law School, and it showed in the way she carried herself. She pecked Florence on both cheeks.

'It's great to see you again.'

Even her voice had changed; it had a soft, mellifluous edge to it.

Florence received a warm hug from Joe, who then caught sight of Gil lurking nearby, a bulky sentinel.

'I couldn't believe it when I heard. None of us could. It's crazy.'

'If it's true,' said William. There was something almost accusatory in the look he fired at Florence.

'Jesus, Dad, she's not on trial,' said Joe.

But she was. When it came to Valentine's family, she had always been on trial. Always would be.

'Enough, Joe,' snapped Heather. 'Your father has every right to hear why the police are talking about foul play. We all do.'

'She can tell us over lunch,' said William. 'I need to freshen up.' He hauled a couple of suitcases from the trunk and headed up the steps. Heather and Amber followed.

'Ignore him,' said Joe, 'he's been in a foul mood all the way up.' He grabbed his suitcase and closed the trunk. 'Foul mood most of my life.'

Florence laid a hand on his shoulder. 'His father's dying.'

Joe looked at her in a curious fashion.

'How can you make excuses for him after the way he just treated you?'

'Years of practice.'

Joe glanced toward the house. 'It's so fucking embarrassing, just being associated with that kind of behavior.'

'But you aren't, Joe. You never were . . . never with me.'

'Never?'

'Only once . . . the first time we met, first time I came here. You were surprised what a good swimmer I was.'

Joe winced. 'I said that?'

'Racial stereotyping of the worst kind,' joked Florence. 'You were just a kid, I forgave you . . . then I whupped your ass over ten laps.'

Joe laughed. '*That* I remember.'

THIRTY-NINE

The route from Burlington to Fort Drum took them right through the middle of the Adirondack Mountains, east to west, the lakes and pine-clad slopes and soaring peaks sliding by on both sides. It was a first for Dylan, and a couple of times he caught himself thinking that Evie would fall hard for the elemental majesty of the landscape.

Carrie was on her phone for much of the time, working her magic on Detective Safran, brightening his day with sweet nothings, then deftly drawing him on board to see what he could turn up on Holden Truss and his associates. ('I wasn't holding out on you, Ernesto. Now I'm hurt; I thought this was the beginning of a beautiful friendship.')

In between the back-and-forth calls to Greg in Torrington, she made one to her partner (involving some light-hearted bickering about a vet's appointment for their dog), and another to the law firm run by Lyndon Winslow's attorney, Victor Penfold, who had made the adjustments to the will.

Penfold wasn't just out of the office; he was away on holiday.

'What do you make of that?' Carrie asked.

'Lyndon described him as his dearest friend. Not sure how *I'd* feel if my best buddy took off on holiday just as I was about to turn up my toes.'

'Damn right.' Carrie fell into a pensive silence. 'Alice Arnold. What do we know about her?'

'She's smart and funny.'

'No denying it. What else? I'll tell you . . . it was Penfold who found her, brought her in.'

That was the difference between them, it occurred to Dylan. He had known it — he was in possession of the information — and yet it hadn't struck him as significant. Maybe it wasn't, maybe it had no bearing on the case, but the thought should still have crossed his mind.

'Let's see if she knows where Penfold is.' Carrie put the call through the hands-free so Dylan could listen in.

Alice said she hadn't spoken to Penfold since yesterday, when he'd shown up at the house to visit Lyndon. He hadn't hung around afterwards, just took off in his car.

'How well do you know him?' Carrie asked.

'The first time I met him was yesterday.'

'So why did he hire *you*?'

'I doubt we were his first choice.' The 'we' in question was the law firm headed by her father. 'My dad had some dealings with him a while back.'

'Anything you can tell us about?'

'No . . . even if I knew, which I don't.'

'You have Penfold's cell number?'

'Yes.'

'Text it to me, please.'

Carrie revealed that they were chasing down a promising lead, but nothing worth spelling out for now, and nothing Alice or Florence should mention to anyone else. The moment she killed the call, Carrie phoned Greg back in Torrington and brought him up to speed. Greg was intrigued.

'Penfold drops off the radar right after his meeting with the old man?'

'Looks that way,' said Carrie. 'I'm guessing Penfold's the source of the leak about the will, and Lyndon Winslow knows it now.'

'Could also be Penfold didn't share the information with anyone but used it himself.'

'Why? What's in it for him if Florence dies?' Carrie asked.

'Hey, you want me to do your job for you? Just putting it out there.'

* * *

They broke the journey in Lake Placid, staying just long enough to find a restroom, stretch their legs and top up with tea and coffee. Not long after they'd hit the road again, Carrie got a call from her man in New York, the one she had asked to do some discreet sniffing around Cherwell, the Winslows' hedge fund. He had turned up something potentially interesting. It seemed that William, Olivia and Ralph had been looking to shift the bulk of the fund's holdings into the biotech and armaments sectors. This was a year ago, and they had tried to force Lyndon to fall in with their wishes, not knowing that the old man had structured the business in such a way that he still retained ultimate control over any significant reallocation of assets.

All this was explained to Dylan once Carrie had finished the call.

'Word is he was spitting mad they'd tried to railroad him.'

'So, what? The whole thing with Florence and the will is revenge for their treachery?'

'Fits, no? Could have been the trigger.'

There was more. Rumor had it that Olivia was the brains behind the palace coup and had only signed up her two brothers after much persuasion.

'Olivia hatched the plan, the one that's now gone to total shit. Just how pissed must she be . . . ethical investments instead of armaments?'

* * *

There were two lines of cars tailing back from the twin toll-booths at Fort Drum's Main Gate. The long roof above the booths bore a big, red banner sign with white lettering: WELCOME TO FORT DRUM . . . HOME OF THE 10TH MOUNTAIN DIVISION.

Greg had instructed them to go to the visitor control center, a low brick building on the right. It took a while for them to be processed. They were expected, their names were on the list, but as neither of them was in possession of a Department of Defense ID card, there were forms to be filled out, driving licenses and other ID to be checked. And although they had a sponsor on post, they still had to hand over their weapons and voluntarily submit to a National Crime Information Center background check, which could take a while.

'Sorry, but rules is rules,' said Sergeant Blake from behind the counter, wearing fatigues and a standard-issue buzz cut.

'No problem, Sergeant,' said Carrie. 'We're all part of the same family, all set to see out our days on government pensions. I have nothing but respect for what you guys do. It puts the rest of us to shame.'

'Thank you, ma'am,' said Sergeant Blake. He glanced down at the paperwork, fiddled with it aimlessly for a couple of seconds and then looked up. 'I tell you what, let's not bother with the NCIC check. I'll call your sponsor and tell her you guys are good to go.'

It was a couple of minutes before they received their passes, and another five before Captain Chelsea Parrish appeared in the waiting room, also dressed in fatigues. She was trim and tall, and somewhat wary, Dylan sensed, as she shook their hands in turn.

'Thanks for this,' said Carrie.

'Let's see.'

It was a short drive from the main gate to their destination: a massive brick-built structure with two protruding wings that could have been a state-of-the-art high school. Two parking lots, big as football pitches, flanked the building, and there was a wide expanse of wooded parkland across the way, where a troop of soldiers was running in a tight pack beneath the trees.

* * *

The personnel office was an open-plan arrangement, and they received a few furtive glances as Captain Parrish led them straight through to a small meeting room at the back. There was a jug of water on the desk, and she filled three glasses before settling down behind it.

'Detective Captain Dyson explained to my colleague the reason for your being here, but I thought I should hear it from you, too.'

If she was hoping to catch them out, she was behind the curve. Greg had played his cards close, anticipating a degree of obstructiveness on the Army's part if they knew the full and sordid truth of the case. He and Carrie had talked at some length during the drive about what he had revealed to them and how she should play it. The story Captain Parrish got from Carrie was this: that they were simply trying to identify a John Doe killed in a car accident in a remote corner of Connecticut, and that they'd turned up evidence suggesting that the dead man might once have been posted at Fort Drum.

'What kind of evidence?' asked Captain Parrish.

'We found a 10th Mountain Division baseball cap in the car.'

Carrie was making it up now. Did such a thing even exist? She must have checked while they were en route, because Captain Parrish let it go unchallenged, although she did say, 'Detective Dyson didn't mention a baseball cap.'

'He may be the boss, but he's no good on detail.' Carrie threw in a confidential look. 'I bet you have them here, too.'

Captain Parrish smiled. 'In spades. No other ID on him, the John Doe?'

'Wouldn't be here wasting your time if there had been.'

'Strange, no?'

Carrie shrugged. 'Not unheard of.'

'And the car?'

'Registered to a woman across the border in Vermont who we haven't been able to trace yet or—'

'—you wouldn't be here wasting my time.'

Carrie spread her hands. 'Hey, I'm sure we've all got better things to be doing right now.'

Captain Parrish's eyes flicked between them. Then she pulled a bound folder from her attaché case and slid it across the desk.

'His name is Kyle Hackett.'

She also produced a pad of lined paper and a ballpoint pen.

'I'm going to need your phones. You can't make copies, only notes.'

'House rules?' Carrie asked.

'It's . . . sensitive. He left us under something of a cloud.'

They handed over their phones, and Captain Parrish rose from her chair.

'I'll be outside when you're done.'

The moment she left the room, Carrie flipped through the file.

'Sensitive? Half the fucking file's been redacted!'

It was true; large chunks of the text were obscured beneath strips of black ink. They went to work with what they had, Carrie scribbling away in her own notebook.

The stuff of interest came toward the end of the file. Hackett had seen action in Afghanistan, having been deployed there in 2015 as a sergeant first class with the 2nd Brigade Combat Team of the 10th Mountain Division. It had not ended well for him. There was a brief mention of 'an incident' in June 2016 while he was out on patrol from the combat outpost where his unit was based. There had clearly been a firefight of some sort, with a number of fatalities, although no indication that Hackett's unit had taken any casualties. The phrase 'court-martial' appeared briefly in the unredacted text, but nothing had come of it. Rather, Hackett had been shipped out, back to Fort Drum, where in August 2016 he had been issued with a less-than-honorable discharge for serious misconduct.

'What do you make of it?' Carrie asked.

'No wonder they're nervous.'

'Yeah, and no wonder they were so quick to identify him from the photo. Black sheep of the family.'

'I'm no expert, but it smells like a cover-up,' said Dylan.

'Could be.'

'Like they wanted rid of him, the whole matter buried, forgotten.'

'Who knows? They're certainly not going to tell *us*. Let's get her back in here.'

Captain Parrish breezily announced that she was happy the Army could be of assistance.

'Except all his personal details have been redacted,' said Carrie.

'That's not information I'm at liberty to disclose.'

'We need to inform his next of kin of his death.'

'I can tell you he had none: no siblings, mother long dead, father took off when he was a kid.'

'Last known address?'

'I'm not able to give that out, I'm afraid.'

Carrie nodded a couple of times. 'Can I ask you something, Captain?'

'Sure.'

'Do you really work in the personnel office?'

'Something like that.'

'Sounds more like the damage limitation office to me.'

Captain Parrish gave a thin smile. 'Something like that.'

Carrie leaned forward. 'I'm going to take a crack at something; I'm going to be honest with you, because we've all been feeling each other out, nice and polite, dancing around the truth. Hackett was a shit-bag and an embarrassment to you guys, and I don't suppose anyone's going to mourn him. But it's not Hackett we need; it's a friend of his we're after. This man is at large and extremely dangerous, and our only way of getting to him is through Hackett, who — as we all know — is no longer in a position to help with our inquiries.'

'That all sounds very interesting,' said Captain Parrish, 'but there's nothing I can do.'

'Let me show you something.' Carrie tapped at her phone and then handed it to Captain Parrish.

'Her name is Florence Winslow. She runs a charity in New York. That photo's off their website. A good person. Beautiful, too, don't you think?'

'Yes.'

'Well, she's going to be beautiful and very dead if we don't find the man I'm talking about. Hackett's all we've got to go on. We need to find where he was living, and soon . . . like, yesterday soon.'

Captain Parrish slid the phone back across the desk, her eyes locked on Carrie's. 'Why does he want her dead?'

'Money. A lot of money. An inheritance that others will get if she's out of the picture.'

'Are you bullshitting me?'

'No, begging you . . . woman to woman.' Carrie glanced at Dylan. 'Don't worry about him, he's in touch with his feminine side.'

Another faint smile from Captain Parrish, but she said, 'I'm sorry, but you're going to have to leave.' She replaced the file in her attaché case.

Carrie didn't budge.

'I get it, I used to be FBI. I've been where you're at, sat on that side of the desk . . . so let me put it another way. This is going to happen with or without you. With you, you get a good shot at spinning it in the Army's favor. Without you . . . ? I don't know, you tell me. Who do *you* think the top brass are going to throw to the wolves when the shit hits the fan? Which it will if anything, anything at all, happens to Florence Winslow.' She leaned a little closer. 'I'll come gunning for you, Captain, and I won't stop till you're stretched out, dead and done for.'

The two women glared at each other across the table like two animals poised to pounce and tear each other's throats out. Dylan was thankful to be a spectator, more than thankful.

'Two minutes,' said Captain Parrish eventually.

She left the room.

'What?' asked Carrie, catching Dylan's look.

'Told you you were a big softie at heart.'

Carrie laughed.

'Don't ever talk to me like that.'

'Don't ever give me cause to,' she replied.

'Nice touch . . . ex-FBI.'

'Going back a ways.'

Dylan shook his head. 'No, I'm not going to believe anything you say ever again. You're just too damn convincing.'

'Pass me the file.'

Captain Parrish had foolishly left her attaché case on the table, and Carrie used the torch on her phone to backlight the first page of the file, on which Hackett's redacted personal details were listed.

'Photocopies. No text showing through.'

The file was back in the attaché case and they were waiting patiently, a picture of innocence, when Captain Parrish returned to the room. She didn't take a seat; she just handed Carrie a folded slip of paper.

'You didn't get this from me.'

Carrie opened the slip. 'Where's Sangerfield?'

'About two hours south of here.'

'Thank you, Captain Parrish, you're a star.'

'I'll see you back to the main gate,' came the curt reply.

FORTY

Lyndon hit the button and felt the sweet flood of morphine spread through his limbs, dulling the jangling. It was getting worse, as if all the cells in his body were lighting up and vibrating. He was dosing up more as a result. Sleeping more, too, given the soporific effect of the drug.

Things weren't as bad as he'd made out yesterday — that was done to force a gathering of the whole family, to summon all the suspects — but it was becoming increasingly difficult to navigate the fine line between pain control and mental alertness.

He needed to have his wits about him right now, though, and he resisted the temptation to thumb the button another time. Meanwhile, Nina Simone was singing 'Baltimore' in the background, her sublime voice sliding over the notes as though she alone owned them. His favorite songs, put together by Bevan and piped into the library. His death playlist.

He heard footsteps and turned his eyes from the intricately stuccoed ceiling toward the door.

'Daddy.'

'Olivia.'

'How are you feeling?'

'Better for seeing you.'

He reached out a hand. Olivia squeezed it briefly before taking a seat beside the bed. Lyndon stared at his daughter and wondered what forces had combined in her to turn the serious little girl into a cold-hearted monster. It brought to mind the disturbing installation he had seen at Palazzo Grassi in Venice.

Olivia must have read something in his eyes. 'What are you thinking?'

'My trip to Italy, a few years ago. Venice in January.'

'I remember.'

'Antonella took me to an art exhibition at Palazzo Grassi.'

'Antonella?'

'A friend from Rome.'

Olivia grinned. 'You old dog. You never said.'

'Who wants to hear about the private lives of old people? It conjures up disturbing images.'

'True.'

'It was quite a show, a great space crammed with lots of stuff I don't naturally go for . . . Koons and Hirst. No offense, I know you have pieces by both.'

'Investments. Good investments.'

'No doubt. But there was one work there that stood out for me, an installation . . . a room, and kneeling in the far corner of it was a small schoolboy in a tweed jacket and shorts and little leather boots, his face to the wall. You had to go closer, of course, you didn't have a choice, it was such a sad sight. And when you got there and you looked at the little fellow, you saw that he had the face of an adult Adolf Hitler.'

'That's shocking,' said Olivia quietly. 'Why were you thinking about that?'

'I suppose it was the artist's way of saying that even the very worst people — the tyrants, the genocidal maniacs, the psychopaths — they were all innocent children once, before something evil rotted their souls. Who knows what? Society? Upbringing? Or maybe not nurture, but something in their nature, something essential to them. What do *you* think, Olivia?'

Olivia had fallen very still. 'It wouldn't be art if there was an answer.'

'An excellent response. Have you heard from Victor in the last twenty-four hours?'

'Victor? No. Why?'

'Because it would mean the end for him if he'd tried to contact you. I gave him a way out, and I'm offering you one, too. Call them off, Olivia.'

'Who?'

'Your attack dogs, the ones who tried to kill Florence, because it sure as hell wasn't General Ngomo.'

'Daddy—'

'Don't!' snapped Lyndon. 'I know Victor told you about the new will. He's confessed.'

'He came to me . . .' said Olivia eventually, feebly.

'Yes, but why you? That's what I've been asking myself. Why not William? Isn't William the king of the castle? Apparently not. Apparently you're the true power behind the throne, the Iago scheming in the shadows.'

'Don't say that about me!' She looked to be on the brink of tears.

'It's strange, just the other day Connie told me I under-estimated Ralph. It seems I've underestimated you, too. Who else knows about the will, Olivia? Does Chester?'

'He's my husband. I needed to speak to somebody.'

'Oh, I bet you did.'

'I was upset! I couldn't believe you would do something like that to us.'

'You mean, after you'd tried and failed to wrest control of my business from me?'

'We've given our lives to it, too.'

'You think that justifies murder? Murder, Olivia. What possessed you?'

'Daddy, I swear I had nothing to do with Florence's accident. I swear it on Mom's life.'

'She's dead.'

177

'Her memory . . . you know what I mean. My own life, Chester's, the boys' lives . . .'

'Words.'

'You can't really think that of me?'

'But I do.'

There was a slow shift in Olivia's expression, a hardening around the mouth and eyes.

'Well, you're wrong. I know it, even if you don't. And sure, that's got to be hard for you to accept, because Lyndon Winslow is never wrong about anything, never at fault. Even now you can't believe it, can you? You can't see the damage you've done to this family. You cast out one son, you've demeaned Ralph for most of his life, and you've just said things to me I'll never forget or forgive you for. That's quite a record, quite a life. Despised by three of your children, tolerated by the fourth, because William is such a . . . brainless dick.'

'Valentine never despised me.'

'Don't be so sure of that.'

'Wow, it's good to meet you finally,' said Lyndon quietly. 'But you should know, that sharp tongue of yours isn't going to save you. The police are on your trail. Two detectives. They're smart, smart enough not to let on what they're really thinking.'

'You haven't been listening. I've got nothing to fear from them because I've done nothing.'

'Who, then? Because I can't see Chester plotting a murder while hatching another of his hare-brained business schemes.'

Olivia was about to speak but held herself in check.

'What?' Lyndon demanded.

'No, because you'll take it the wrong way, see it as something it isn't.'

'I think we're way beyond that, don't you?'

Olivia briefly dropped her eyes. 'I told William about the will. We went to see him . . . him and Heather.'

'Oh Christ . . .' That made four of them in the know. How many more? 'Ralph and Connie?' he asked.

Olivia shook her head.

'Why not?'

'Connie's right: you underestimate Ralph. He's tougher than you think.' She hesitated. 'We weren't sure how he would react.'

But what if Ralph had somehow gotten wind of it without them knowing? What if his youngest son *had* reacted? Ralph, the watcher, the quiet one, stubbornly close-tongued, except for one night when the liquor had loosened it, the night he'd learned that Valentine and Florence were married. An ugly rant with racist undertones, for which he had apologized the following day, ascribing his outburst to a sense of insult that he hadn't been invited to the wedding. Hollow words. None of them had been invited to the tiny ceremony in Italy.

And what of Heather? Lyndon had been surprised, moved even, by her decision to stay on at the house over the past week, given her evident disgust at his unsightly decline. Had he misread her mastery over her own revulsion? Had she remained simply to monitor and control developments at close quarters?

Questions. Too many questions. And the morphine was dulling his ability to reason.

'Do you believe me, Daddy?'

'Yes, Olivia, I believe you.'

She didn't reply immediately. 'I'm not sure you do, but it's okay.'

'No, it's far from okay. This is going to end badly, and the Winslow name will be stained forever by the scandal.'

FORTY-ONE

Sangerfield was a crossroads town, just like any number of such places they'd traveled through over the past couple of days: a straggle of houses giving way to an intersection with traffic lights, where the usual businesses were clustered. There was a gas station, a post office, a convenience store and a coffee shop, and not much evidence of anyone using them. The heat outside the air-conditioned cocoon of the Chevy was pitiless, coming off the road in shimmering waves.

'Left at the lights,' said Carrie, eyes on her phone.

The address they had for Kyle Hackett led them to a rutted dirt track that ran south off the highway about half a mile east out of town. The track served just the one property, a rundown single-story clapboard number, its pale green paint job flaking away as though the building beneath were diseased. It was backed up against a copse of tall trees, and there was no vehicle out front, just a rusting child's swing choked by ivy.

Dylan pulled up close to the front steps and killed the engine. The heat hit them with the force of a slap as they got out of the car. Not a breath of wind stirred. Carrie led the way, mounting the steps to the front porch. There was a fern in a plastic pot beside the front door. She crouched and poked at the soil, then showed her fingers to Dylan: moist earth, recently watered. Hackett had been dead almost a week.

Carrie pulled open the screen door and knocked. A voice from inside, but it was impossible to make out the words. She tried the handle.

'Gun, just in case.'

Dylan unholstered his Sig and let it hang at his side. Carrie eased open the front door. 'Hello,' she called.

'Through here,' came back the cracked voice of an elderly man. 'In the kitchen.'

He was extremely old, gnarled like a piece of weathered wood, a few desultory strands of silver hair sprouting from his sun-spotted pate. He was seated in a rocker, dressed in filthy denim dungarees and little else. There was an electric fan in his face and a piebald mongrel curled at his feet, as good as dead.

'Some heat.'

'Sure is,' said Carrie.

'You the carers?'

'Not us.'

'Didn't think so. Don't come till later.'

'We're friends of Kyle's.'

'Don't know no Kyle.'

'Kyle Hackett.'

'Hackett,' said the old man, dredging what was left of his memory. 'Hackett was the one done sold this place to my son.' He fixed them with his rheumy eyes. 'Some friends . . . that was two years back.'

'We lost touch,' said Carrie. 'Happened to be passing, thought we'd look in on him for old times' sake.'

'What can I say? Ditched this shithole on my boy then got hisself another place. Not so far, is what I heard. Ain't seen him since, but then I don't get to stir much, not since these old pegs gave out on me.' He slapped his thighs.

'Do you think your son might know where he moved to?'

'Couldn't say. Been gone more'n a year, not a squeak outta him. Good boy, though. Set me up in this place, sorted the carers n'all. I paid my taxes; now the government gets to wipe my ass. It's called the social contract. Does that one speak?'

He pointed a crooked finger at Dylan.

'He's the quiet type,' said Carrie.

'Looks kinda faggoty to me. You a faggot, son?'

'Promise not to lynch him if he says yes?'

The old man chuckled, coughed, then rocked forward and put his face in the fan, baring his toothless gums like he was trying to dry them off.

'Sorry I can't help you folks.'

* * *

'What now?' asked Dylan as they dumped themselves back in the welcome cool of the Chevy.

'You see that bar back down the road, the one with the pickups out front?'

'The Black Cat?'

'Looks like the sort of place Hackett might hang out.' Carrie looked at him askance. 'He's right, you do look kind of faggoty . . . not ex-Army at all.'

She mussed up his hair.

'Really?' he moaned.

'Just don't bring any friends home this time.'

* * *

The Black Cat was the kind of place Dylan had only ever entered as a patrolman, in the early days of his career, usually when trying to locate an offender of some kind. On those occasions, the reception he'd encountered had been less than welcoming. This time, it wasn't far off that.

Heads turned, eyes narrowed, unheard words were mumbled. It was the five o'clock crowd, the ones who liked to start early, laying claim to the bar stools and the pool tables. Blondie was blasting out 'Heart of Glass' from the jukebox against the back wall, a pop tune just retro enough to be acceptable to the hardcore home crowd.

He skirted a table of three construction workers — leather utility belts and steel-capped boots — and made for an empty stool at the bar. The barman sported a shaved head, a handlebar moustache, and a spider's web tattoo on his neck.

'What can I do you for?'

'Beer. Damn heat . . . got a throat like sandpaper.'

The barman pulled the beer and slid it over. Dylan downed most of it in one and replaced the glass on the counter.

'Passing through?'

'Kind of. Looking for an old buddy of mine . . . Kyle . . . Kyle Hackett.'

'You know Kyle?'

'From back a ways.'

'Yeah?'

'We holidayed together.'

'Sweet. Where'd you go?'

'Afghanistan. Don't bother. The food's crap and the locals ain't exactly welcoming.'

The barman smiled, but his eyes were clouded with caution. 'What's your name, buddy?'

'Dylan.'

'Kyle never mentioned no Dylan.'

'Maybe 'cause everyone called me Dildo?'

He was beginning to enjoy himself, maybe a little too much.

'Nope, no Dildo neither.'

'Well, fuck him. Guess I won't look him up after all.'

The barman wandered off to serve a couple of guys hunched down the end of the bar. Words were exchanged, and when the barman returned, one of the men came with him, short but solid as a stump.

'What unit were you with, brother?'

'2nd BCT with the 10th.'

'Out of . . . ?'

'Fort Drum.'

'How'd you like it in Afghanistan?'

'Better'n Kyle.'

'Oh?'

Dylan eyed the guy. 'If he ain't told you what went down, he don't want you to know.'

'Oh, I know. Question is, do you?'

'Fuckers stitched him up, didn't they? Needed a fall guy so they hung him out to dry.'

The short guy glanced at the barman.

'Listen, Kyle said to look him up if I was ever near Sangerfield. But I also got other places to be, so if you ain't going to call him and tell him I'm in town, I'll be on my way. You got a pen?'

The barman handed him a pen and Dylan grabbed a paper napkin off a pile. 'Do me a favor and give him this.' His instinct was to leave a fake cell number, but in the end he scribbled his own. It wasn't like Kyle Hackett was ever going to rumble him.

It turned out to be right thing to do, because after he'd settled up for the beer and was heading for the door, his phone rang. An unknown number. He answered.

'How's tricks, Dildo?' said a voice.

Dylan turned to see the barman on his phone. He gestured for Dylan to return.

'Kyle's kinda private. Needed to be sure.'

He started drawing a map on a napkin.

'He went backwoods a couple of years ago. You'll never find him without this.'

* * *

At the coffee shop where she'd been waiting for him, Dylan slid into the booth beside Carrie and laid the napkin on the table.

'Got us a map.'

'They bought the hard-ass commando act?'

'Unless those are directions to an ambush.'

'Getting better at the lying game,' said Carrie, pocketing the napkin. 'Evie's back tonight, right?'

'Yeah.'

'Odds are we're not going to be now. You should let her know. I just called my partner.'

'What does he do?' Dylan asked.

'Runs a fishing charter boat out of New Haven, old forty-eight-footer with a flybridge. She's called Abby.'

'Strange name for a boat.'

'Boat's called *Falcon*.'

Dylan let out a slow sigh, taking a moment.

'Just how fucking stupid am I feeling right now?'

Carrie smiled. 'Don't . . . all the evidence was against it, the two husbands and the daughter.'

She pulled a photo from the back of her wallet and handed it over: a woman standing on a sunny dock, long dark hair tied back in a ponytail, big-billed cap, mirrored Aviators, and a face-cleaving grin.

'Cradle-snatcher,' said Dylan.

'She's older than she looks. She has a son who lives with us, the cutest little boy, Arlo. He's nine.'

Dylan handed the photo back.

'I wasn't going to tell you, but I'd like you to meet them,' said Carrie.

FORTY-TWO

The map led them east out of town, up into the wooded hills, the blacktop giving way to wide gravel trails that wound through the thick forest, then dirt tracks with hedgerows pressing in on both sides, then a makeshift gate held together with orange plastic string that blocked their path.

A sign read: KEEP OUT. DOGS.

'Dogs are bad,' said Carrie.

'Not all dogs.'

'Dogs that haven't been fed for a week are definitely bad.'

He could feel something coming off her, an edginess he hadn't sensed before.

'What's your radar reading?' he asked.

'That Kyle Hackett's definitely not at home, but someone else might be. Let's ditch the car and go on foot from here.'

* * *

The lack of wind made for an unearthly silence, punctuated by the eerie cries of unseen birds. The lowering sun clipped the treetops, the odd stray shaft of sunlight slanting through the thick canopy overhead. There were tire marks in the deep dust of the track.

They didn't speak. They hadn't spoken since the gate, when Carrie had suggested they put some distance between themselves: two targets rather than one. She had insisted on leading the way, Dylan some twenty feet behind her. She moved with an easy grace, relaxed but alert, her gun drawn, and it struck him that her talk of the FBI might not have been a lie to win over Captain Parrish.

Soon after the track begun to dip away, Carrie dropped into a crouch. Dylan followed suit. Carrie pulled some small binoculars from her pocket and scanned the forest before waving him forward to join her.

He could make out a shingle roof below them, some fifty yards down the slope, just visible through the under-brush and the trunks of the trees.

'Cover's too thick,' whispered Carrie. 'We'll make less noise sticking to the track.'

It dropped away sharply then dog-legged to the right, at which point they got a better view of the house. It was a single-story shack, low but large, with a front porch that ran the length of the building, and a pan of dirt out front. There was no sign of a vehicle. Drawing closer, Carrie scooped up a rock.

'How's your arm?' She didn't wait for a reply, just handed him the rock. 'Land it on the porch.'

The rock hit the wall to the right of the front door with a loud thud and clattered across the boards. Nothing. No barking dogs. And when no one appeared from the shack after thirty seconds or so, Carrie edged forward.

'I'll check round the back. You cover the front.'

She seemed to be gone for an eternity but finally appeared around the far corner of the shack.

'No one here,' she called. 'Stay off the tracks out front. Forensics are going to have a field day with that lot.' There had been no rain in an age, and all manner of tire tracks and footprints were preserved in the dust.

Dylan joined her at the front door. He was sweating, more from nerves than the heat, and he dragged his forearm across his brow.

'There's a generator round the back in a small lean-to, and also a workshop. The windows aren't shuttered from the inside like they are round here. It looks neat as anything in there . . . magazines arranged in a fan on the table in front of the couch, cushions plumped, draining board clear. Full OCD. There are some dead flowers in a vase on the kitchen table, which suggests he expected to be back, and soon.'

'You want me to break in?'

'I don't know.'

'It's not like he can sue us.'

'I don't know.'

'Come on, Carrie, we could be standing a few feet from everything we need.'

'The guy's ex-military, trained in all kinds of shit, and now it looks like he's taken that knowledge and gone freelance. Three years out of the Army, odds are Florence wasn't his first job, which means he's wary, and he's sure as hell tidy, which means thorough.'

'What are you saying, that he might have rigged the place?'

'It's possible.'

'We're up against the clock here.'

'It's not a risk I'm willing to take.'

The look was back in her eyes, a quiver of genuine disquiet. He'd seen enough of her at work to respect her instincts, even if his own were telling him the opposite.

'Okay, you're the boss.'

'We've done what we can. Time to call in the big guns. Time to call Greg.' She checked her phone. 'We lost cell signal way back up the track. Same formation, you behind.'

FORTY-THREE

Olivia lay stretched out on a lounger beside the pool, deep in dark thoughts, a faint prickle teasing her skin as the sun dried off the water from her recent dip. To her right, Heather was flipping through a copy of *The New Yorker*; on the other side, Chester was tapping away at his laptop, dealing with emails.

William appeared from the house.

The grim set of his face said it all, but Olivia still asked, 'How did it go?'

'How do you think? He went at me . . . hard.'

'I warned you he would.'

'And I warned you it would end like this.'

'Did you, Will?' she said. 'Because I don't remember it that way.'

'Keep it down,' hissed Heather, nodding toward the pool, where Joe and Amber were drifting around on air mattresses.

'She's right,' said Chester. 'And Ralph and Connie will be along any second.'

William caught her eye. 'Let's take a walk.'

Olivia pulled on her sarong wrap, and the two of them made off, skirting the pool as they went.

'You're next, Amber,' said William.

Amber squinted up at them. 'What's that, Uncle Will?'

'Grandpa wants to see you.'

* * *

'Fucking Victor,' said William as they entered the rose garden. 'Couldn't keep his mouth shut. Pa must have bluffed it out of him.'

'Threatened him, more like,' said Olivia.

'Have you been able to get a hold of him yet?'

'His PA is stonewalling me, and he's still not answering his cell. Maybe he's cut and run for good. Maybe he's the one behind this.'

'Victor's an opportunist, not a murderer. He was looking to the future, his own future, with us.'

'Only, he was wrong,' she said. 'It turns out that challenging the will after Daddy is gone isn't a slam-dunk, even with Victor testifying he wasn't of sound mind when he altered it. I ran the scenario past someone else.'

'Who?'

'Discreetly, don't worry,' she said.

'You only tell me this now?'

'I only just found out. A long and dirty fight, he said . . . public, too. It all depends on whether Florence is up for it or not. What do you think?'

'I don't know. She's tougher than I thought . . . even gave Heather a piece of her mind the other day.'

'Good for her,' said Olivia. 'Someone has to.'

'Look to your own marriage, Liv, and your loser of a husband.'

William had always enjoyed belittling her — it was a big brother/younger sister thing — and she had long ago learned to remain icy calm, never to rise.

'We can maybe get her to back off the family trust if we don't fight her over Valentine's share of the inheritance.'

'Thirty million bucks!'

'Pre-tax,' said Olivia. 'It hurts less when you think of it that way.'

'It's the principle. What the hell has she done to deserve it? Fuck our brother for a year?'

'A bit longer than that.'

'Whatever . . . Saint Valentine's little black trophy.'

He was parroting the phrase that Ralph had once blurted out when drunk, on hearing they were married.

'You want to fight her all the way?' Olivia asked.

William stopped in his tracks, obliging her to do the same. 'What I want to do, Liv, is turn the clock back a year.'

'Oh please, not this again,' she groaned.

'It all goes back to that. You tried to blindside Pa and you screwed up.'

'You and Ralph both signed up to it.'

'Based on your assurances it was a done deal.' William gave a snort of disbelief. 'A done deal? Christ, all you did was resurrect the ghost of Valentine for Pa . . . oh, and cost us a *fucking* fortune in the process.'

Olivia glared at him. 'You know your problem, Will? You're weak, you always were. You hit a wall, you sit down, hang your head. Sometimes you have to go looking for a ladder.'

'Did you get that from a book you bought in an airport?' he shot back at her with a sneer.

'I'm just saying . . . it's not over till it's over, not for me.'

FORTY-FOUR

Florence was making for the sanctuary of her bedroom when she heard the voices, distant, muffled, raised in anger. They were coming from a room at the far end of the corridor. Curiosity drew her closer, just close enough to establish that the room in question belonged to William and Heather.

It wasn't husband and wife arguing, though; it was mother and son. Heather and Joe were going at each other, but not quite loud enough for Florence to make out the heated exchange of words. The fear of being caught snooping when one of them stormed from the room dampened the urge to creep forward and press her ear to the door.

She turned and headed back down the corridor, ignoring her own room. Just four more walls. She needed air, she needed to be outside, where she could breathe.

If Joe had also been drawn into the ugly atmosphere infecting the house, then what hope was there for her?

* * *

It had started at lunch, when William had pressed her hard on the anomalies that had led the police to interpret the accident as an attempt on her life. Olivia and her husband,

Chester, had arrived from New York as Mary was serving the salmon en croute, and they had folded themselves seamlessly into the interrogation. Olivia had been particularly keen to know how the police investigation was progressing, and Alice had trotted out the party line laid down by Carrie Fuller about General Ngomo's likely involvement.

At least Joe and Amber had been there to temper the charged mood with some levity. Joe had always been her ally in the family. He had adored Valentine from an early age, in the way that boys so often prefer their uncles to their own fathers. It was a role that Valentine had embraced, teaching his young nephew to play tennis and how to swim when not romping with him and generally making him feel loved and wanted, making up for William's glaring failings as a father.

Joe had been devastated by Valentine's death and had often phoned Florence in the aftermath to see how she was doing, to console her. She was usually the one who had ended up comforting him, which had been fine by her. Being strong for Joe had made her feel more in control of her own crushing grief. It was probably no coincidence that Joe had followed in Valentine's footsteps, finding the courage to turn his back on the family business and strike out on his own. She knew it hadn't always been easy for him, but he saw the world in its proper perspective. As he had said during their lunch a month ago: 'In the grand scheme of things, a privileged little shit crashing at his folks' downtown brownstone while chasing his dream using investment funding from his wealthy grandfather hardly registers on the Richter scale of human miseries.'

They had laughed about that.

Amber's story was different. It had never been in doubt that she would fall in with her father's wishes and join the family firm, which she was set to do in the fall, after traveling in Europe for a few months — a concession she'd fought hard to extract from Ralph, who thought the idea frivolous. It was strange to think of Ralph looking to exercise that sort of control over his daughter. He had always been the meekest of Lyndon's children, passive and a little browbeaten by Connie.

Olivia was the first to have been summoned by Lyndon after lunch. Since then, the others had trooped through the library one by one, saying their farewells when not hanging out by the pool or gathering in rooms, where the conversations would awkwardly shift tack the moment Florence appeared.

Feeling put-upon, shunned and really quite paranoid now, she had headed for the safe harbor of her bedroom before dinner, only to be driven back downstairs by the sound of Heather and Joe's argument.

* * *

Alice was nowhere to be found, so she made off across the back terrace and along the lawn to a bench backed up against a stand of tall rhododendron bushes. She called Dylan. She didn't know what she planned to say to him; she just needed to hear his voice.

He answered almost immediately. 'Hey, you okay?' he asked, almost in a whisper.

'You sound like you're in the middle of something.'

'We're up to our necks here.'

'Where's here?'

'Waterville.'

'Anything you can tell me?'

'Give me a second.' She heard him walking and a couple of doors closing behind him, then he was back: 'We know who he is, where he lives — the guy who smashed into you.'

'Really?'

'That's for you, no one else, not even Alice.'

'Why not Alice?'

'Because I'm asking. Promise me.'

'I promise.'

'I shouldn't have told you. Forget I did. How are you?'

She had never heard him like this; he was usually so unflustered.

'Not great. It's all too weird, knowing that one of them—'

'We don't know that, not for sure.'

'*Might have* is enough,' she said. 'I don't feel right here.'

'Nothing's going to happen to you, you've got personal protection. Two guys, right? Just hang in there, we'll be back before you know it.'

'When?'

'Tomorrow . . . lunch at the latest. Trust me, it's the best place for you to be. And where else are you going to go?'

'My mum's hotel at JFK. She lands any minute now. I persuaded her not to drive out here tonight.'

'Don't do it,' said Dylan firmly. 'Seriously, Florence, you shouldn't be out there on your own; you're much safer where you are.'

'You think?'

'For sure. Trust me.'

She let his words wash through her. 'Maybe that's all I needed to hear.'

'Hey, happy to oblige. Like I said, day or night.'

'Thanks.'

'Look, I better get back,' he said. 'I'll see you tomorrow.'

'Yeah, see you tomorrow.'

She laid the phone aside on the bench. He was right, she needed to get a grip of herself. The prospect of dinner, of playing happy families around a table, was getting to her.

'There you are.'

Alice materialized from the gloom. She glanced at Gil, who was patrolling the far side of the lawn, a dark mass in the dying light.

'I knew he'd have you in sight, but you shouldn't wander off like that.'

'I had to make a call and I needed some space.'

Alice settled down on the bench beside her. 'Dylan, by any chance?'

'Purely business.'

'Naturally.'

195

She had made the mistake of confessing to Alice last night just how attractive she found him.

'Where are they?' Alice asked.

'Waterville.' She probably shouldn't have said, but it was out now.

'Any more news?'

'He didn't say.'

'You didn't ask?'

'He wouldn't say.' Why was she lying to Alice, of all people? It didn't seem right. 'I tried to find you.'

'I was with Lyndon,' said Alice. 'He wants to see you.'

'How is he?'

'Weaker . . . much weaker. Are you okay?'

'Honestly? Not really.'

She spelled out the turmoil of the past hours, the claustrophobia of living at close quarters with her in-laws, the creeping conviction that one of them was definitely behind it. And even if she was wrong, the future offered little consolation.

'I want to do the right thing by Lyndon . . . there's so much I can do to make a difference. But you've seen how they are with me; they don't want me in their world. The thought of working with them, having to deal with them . . . I'm not sure I can.'

'Then don't,' said Alice. 'Take your share of the inheritance and split. I'm guessing it's more than enough to make a difference still.'

'Walk away from the family trust?'

'If what you want is a clean break from them.'

It would be a betrayal of the faith Lyndon had placed in her — a betrayal of Valentine's vision, too — but in that moment it was a seriously tempting prospect.

'Is that what you think I should do?'

'I think it's entirely your decision, and not one you should take until you're thinking straight, which you can't be right now. When you are, I'll be here to talk it through with you.' Alice laid a hand on her thigh. 'Now go and say goodbye to Lyndon. He's waiting for you.'

FORTY-FIVE

After the dose of fresh air, the smell of pizzas and body odor hit Dylan hard in the nostrils when he returned inside from his call with Florence. Now that the four black-clad members of the special operations response team had finally arrived from Albany, there were twelve people jammed into the small police field office, which itself was jammed into a corner of the Waterville Fire Department building.

Carrie was in the thick of it, in her element, rounding up the briefing. Kyle Hackett's military background was of genuine concern, and no one was making light of the challenge. The other people seated in chairs or perched on desk corners consisted of a couple of detectives from the Criminal Investigation Unit of the Oneida County Sheriff's Office in Oriskany, three investigators from the Forensic Investigation Section, and a local patrolman. They had Greg to thank for mobilizing such an impressive team at such short notice; he was the one who had made the calls to his counterparts across the state line, stressing the urgency of the situation, arguing that a search of Hackett's property couldn't wait until morning. A night lost now could easily equate to a life lost down the line.

Dylan felt a stab of sadness as he observed the proceedings from the back of the room. The investigation no longer

197

belonged to Carrie and him. The machine had taken over. No doubt that was always the way of it, but he hadn't seen it coming.

Carrie fielded a couple more questions and then announced: 'Okay, let's get this caravan on the road.'

* * *

They led the way in the Chevy, the response team's sinister matte black truck behind them, followed by the forensics officers in their van, then the two detectives from the sheriff's office, with the patrol car bringing up the rear. A few people stopped and stared at the odd cortège as it snaked along Main Street through the gathering gloom.

It was a fifteen-minute drive from Waterville to Hackett's place, and a chance for Dylan to fill Carrie in on his conversation with Florence.

'She's right: it's not ideal,' said Carrie. 'But we're on a roll here, we'll deal with it as soon as we're back.'

Dylan also raised another matter with Carrie, one that had been puzzling him.

'Where's Hackett's car? Because it's not at his place.'

'Could be anywhere,' she said.

'I don't think so. I think it's back in Burlington, and it can tie him to Truss.'

'I'm all ears.'

The most obvious explanation seemed to be that Truss had stolen the Prius and driven it south to Connecticut, with Hackett heading over from his place in his own car. They had then switched vehicles for the purposes of the crash. But then what? They only had one car once the deed was done — Hackett's. It made sense for Hackett to drive Truss back to Burlington, drop him off and carry on home. Yes, it was a nine-hour round trip, but it meant both men would be back in their beds before sun-up.

'Only, it didn't work out. Hackett is dead, Truss is panicked. What does he do? He drives himself back to Burlington in Hackett's car and dumps it, stuffed with his own DNA.'

'Unless he torches it.'

'I don't see it. The cops would identify the vehicle from the engine number, and the last thing he wants is to draw attention to Hackett. No, I reckon it's sitting in a backstreet somewhere. Might be worth getting your pal Ernesto to put out an APB on it.'

'First thing tomorrow.' Carrie peered at him. 'Has your brain always worked this way?'

'I was an odd kid.'

'I can just see you playing with your Rubik's Cube in your bedroom.'

He smiled. 'You don't know how right you are.'

The talk of Truss prompted Carrie to pull up the tracker app on her phone.

His car still hadn't moved from out front of his apartment in Essex Junction.

* * *

Only the forensics van and the response team's truck drove right down to Hackett's shack; they both had kits on board that couldn't be lugged. The others left their vehicles at the gate and walked the rest of the way, flashlight beams needling the darkness.

A couple of arc lights had already been set up by the time they arrived, and the shack stood out starkly in the night. The rest of them held back while Carrie took the four special operations officers on a tour of the building. She then retreated and left them to do their thing, which involved hauling several big boxes of equipment from the back of their truck and dumping them on the front porch. A heavy-duty laptop came to life and was put to work. They then ran some kind of handheld device around the front door and the window frames before vanishing round the back. When they reappeared, they stooped to examine the laptop again.

It was their unit leader, Lieutenant Kerber, who wandered over and spelled it out for them.

'Okay, here it is,' she said. 'Looks like he's got five motion detectors in the house and two in the workshop out back. They're wireless PRIs, all tuned to the same frequency, so connected to the same hub, which has got to be powered by a battery because he's not connected to mains electricity and the generator isn't active right now. The bad news is we can't say for sure where the battery is, so we can't kill the power. The good news is we can jam the wireless signals with radio noise, neutralizing the system.'

'Let's do it,' said one of the detectives.

Lieutenant Kerber glanced at him. 'I'm not done with the bad news. Jamming the system could trigger it. There's no way of knowing, not without getting a good look at one of the sensors, which we can't. It depends on their age, their sophistication. Plus we can't say what the system's rigged to. Could be an alarm to scare off intruders, could be something much worse.' She turned to Carrie. 'You tell me . . . is he the sort of guy who's happy to blow up his own house because, I don't know, some drifter breaks in while he's away?'

'Hard to say. Probably not.'

'Okay, let me put it this way,' said Lieutenant Kerber. 'How much do you need this?'

Carrie hesitated, all eyes on her. 'It's got to happen sometime. Might just as well be now.'

Lieutenant Kerber nodded. 'Okay, you should all move back behind our truck.'

They did as she said. The response team removed their gear from the front porch and joined them behind the truck. Kerber set up the laptop and tapped away for a while.

'Good to go.'

Her finger hovered over a button. Everyone braced themselves.

Click.

'That's it?' Carrie asked.

'Uh-huh. Sensors are knocked out and there's no trigger. Best to leave it a bit, in case he rigged a delay.'

Five minutes later, the response team came to life again. The plan was to go through one of the windows at the back and disable the battery, on the off-chance it was rigged to other trips inside. It was going to take them a while to check the rooms over, and one of the forensics investigators requested that they wear crime scene suits to avoid contaminating the space.

'You may have to force the front door,' said Kerber. 'Depends what we find on the other side.'

Ten minutes later, that was exactly what happened. The tall detective from the sheriff's office took a single step toward the front door and expertly kicked out, popping the lock and earning himself ten bucks from his colleague, who had bet him he couldn't do it in one. The three forensics investigators were ready by now, kitted up, their equipment laid out on a trestle table on the porch, a smorgasbord of the hi-tech and the basic: digital cameras, Ziploc bags, fingerprint kits, sterile swabs, forensic lasers, portable vacuum cleaners for sucking up trace evidence, and the like. It was going to take them a good while to complete their sweep of the place, and there was also the workshop round the back to be dealt with. The fun bit was over, and the patrolman made his excuses and left.

Carrie went with him, in search of a cell signal so she could fill Greg in on developments.

A few minutes later she was back, appearing out of the darkness at a run.

'Truss is on the move,' she said, catching her breath.

'Where?'

'South of Burlington . . . heading south. We need to hit the road.'

FORTY-SIX

'You're a good man, Bevan.'

'Bits of me, sir.'

'Everyone has a right to leave their past behind them.'

Bevan cast an eye around the gloomy recesses of the library. 'Well, you helped with that.'

'Do you mind moving the light?' said Lyndon. 'It's hurting my eyes.'

Bevan rose from his chair and shifted the standard lamp beside the bed a little to the left. 'Better?'

'Thank you, yes.'

He waited for Bevan to sit back down before breaking the news.

'I've made a provision for you in my will. It's enough to get you a place of your own, and a bit more besides.'

Bevan looked stunned. 'I . . .' He couldn't find the words, and he dropped his gaze toward the floor.

'Are you tearing up, big man?'

'Damn dust allergy,' muttered Bevan.

'It might be the time to make an honest woman of Helen.'

Bevan looked up. 'You know about Helen?'

'You think you're my only spy?'

Bevan shook his head. 'I don't get you, sir. Not sure I ever have.'

'Me neither,' said Lyndon. 'Here I am at the end of my life, and I don't recognize myself. I don't mean this dried-up husk lying in a bed.' He tapped a finger against his temple. 'Up here. In my head. We spend a lifetime forming a view of who we are, and yet I'm going to die a mystery to myself.'

He was about to apologize for the rantings of his diseased brain when Bevan said with unexpected force, 'We all do, sir, even the saints.'

Lyndon grunted, an old quotation coming to mind, pushing itself upon him. '"When we remember we are all mad, the mysteries disappear and life stands explained."'

'Sir . . . ?'

'Mark Twain.'

It was more than a consolation. It excused what he was about to do to his own flesh and blood, for in the final analysis all people were deranged. He looked around him. Of all the words in all the books that surrounded him, maybe he had at last found the ones that went to the true heart of the human condition.

'I have one last favor to ask of you,' he said. 'I need you to deliver a letter to Detective Fuller . . . the woman.'

'I remember.'

'Striking, no? Very attractive.'

'Short hair isn't my thing. I'll still deliver the letter, though.'

'I need you to write it, too. This hand is no longer up to it. And as for my eyesight . . .'

It seemed to be fading by the hour, blurring around the fringes, narrowing down to a fine point. Like everything, shrinking back until it was finally extinguished.

'No worries, sir. You dictate it, I'll write it.'

'Before I die would be good.'

Bevan slid his chair back. 'I'll get some paper from the study.'

'And put on some music while you're at it.' He thought on it. 'David Bowie. You choose the album.'

'There's only one that's worth it.'

'I'll tell him you said that when I see him.'

'Trouble is, Bowie went to heaven, sir.'

Lyndon laughed.

'What on earth was I thinking when I hired you?'

FORTY-SEVEN

Dylan drove, foot to the floor whenever possible, which was often. Highway 20 east toward Albany was a straight, fast road through sparsely populated countryside, and a four-laner for long stretches. Carrie, meanwhile, worked away at her phone, flipping between the tracker app and Google Maps.

'How's it looking?'

'He's still headed south. Just passed through Granville on Route 7.'

As *they* had two days ago, although in the opposite direction, driving north to Burlington. Was it really only two days? It felt like an age away.

'Jesus,' said Carrie as they ripped past an eighteen-wheeler. The trucker hit his horn and flashed his lights in protest.

'Don't worry, I'm an advanced driver,' said Dylan. 'Got the certificate and everything.'

'Tell that to the buck deer when it steps out in front of us.'

'Not much we can do if that happens.'

They flew over some railway tracks, the Chevy bellying out on the far side.

'Maybe we should put in a call to Ray Hoskin,' said Dylan.

He hadn't seen Ray since they'd questioned Florence together at the hospital, but as the local chief of police, Ray was right there in Canaan, where they were headed.

'First thing I did was call him when I saw Truss was driving south,' said Carrie. 'We worked a domestic abuse case together a year back. Ray's the real deal. He's on call, ready to help if Truss is headed for the Winslow place.'

'He is. He's going back to finish the job.'

'If so, he's about two hours out, which means we're on target to beat him by twenty minutes . . . probably more at the breakneck fucking speed we're going.'

'You want me to slow down, just say.'

A farm flashed by on their right, a couple of giant barns briefly glimpsed then lost to the night.

'No, it's kind of exciting. Reminds me of the old days.'

'The FBI days?'

'Not those days,' she said. 'I was strictly back office, an analyst.'

'For real?'

'Is it so hard to believe?'

Dylan hesitated. 'What happened? I know something happened. I think maybe I saw a bit of it back at Hackett's place.'

Carrie took a while to reply. 'I like you, Dylan, but that's my stuff. No offense.'

'None taken.'

* * *

They had skirted Albany and were headed south on the New York State Thruway when Satnav rerouted them. It sometimes did this to knock a minute here or there off their journey, and they generally ignored whatever sinister algorithm lay behind it. This time, however, it added a full twenty minutes to their journey time, suggesting that they keep heading south on the Thruway, ignoring the exit to the bridge over the Hudson River.

They prayed it was an error, but when Carrie went on Twitter, she picked up some early reports of a vehicle pile-up on the Castleton-on-Hudson Bridge, closing off all eastbound traffic. They had no choice but to carry on south for another twenty-five miles in order to cross the Hudson. Doubling back to Albany would take them even longer, Carrie swiftly worked out.

She recalculated their respective ETAs. They had lost almost all of their advantage over Truss, who was now driving south through Massachusetts toward the Connecticut border.

'We're talking a matter of minutes,' said Carrie. 'Four, maybe five.'

As long as they arrived before him, they were okay. They had the benefit of knowing exactly where he was, which played hugely in their favor, and it wasn't like they had planned to intercept him before he could incriminate himself. They needed to catch him in the act of breaking into the grounds if they were to build a case against him. Anything less than that and he would beat the charge.

They crossed the river at the Rip Van Winkle Bridge and were barreling east when Carrie asked, 'What do you make of Truss? He strike you as the brains behind something like this?'

'No, he strikes me as a weaselly little shit.'

'What if he isn't alone?'

'Then we get to make two arrests.'

'I mean, what if someone else is making their way there separately? It was a two-man job before. Why not this time? Could be there's someone else already on site.'

'If they are, they'll be waiting for Truss to show up.'

'It's a variable we can't control. I think we need to get Florence out of there now.'

'She's safe,' said Dylan. 'Bevan sorted out a couple of bodyguards.'

'Yeah, but who is Bevan? What do we really know about him?'

'You said the same thing about Alice.'

'And I stand by it.' Carrie hesitated. 'I got my man in the city to check her out. He couldn't turn up much on her, only that she works with her father and a couple of other lawyers. All very hush-hush, total discretion guaranteed.'

That's when they heard the siren and saw the flashing lights behind.

Carrie twisted in her seat. 'Seriously? You got to be fucking kidding.'

The two state troopers didn't put up a fight, but by the time they had parked up behind, then swaggered over like in the movies, and heard what Carrie had to say, and then checked her badge, and then sent them on their way with an apology, a good few minutes had ticked by.

Precious minutes. Vital minutes. It was too tight now. They didn't have a choice; they had to get Florence out of the house.

'Who do I call?' Carrie demanded as the Chevy's engine screamed, lurching up through the gears. 'Alice or Florence?'

'Alice.'

'What if you're wrong?'

'I think she's kosher. I think we need her. I think Florence needs her.'

'Okay,' Carrie finally conceded.

It made no difference; Alice didn't answer her phone.

When it went straight to voice message a second time, Carrie tried Florence's number.

FORTY-EIGHT

Florence knew she wasn't asleep, not properly asleep, because she identified the sound almost immediately. She had turned off the ringer, but her phone was vibrating on the nightstand, drumming against the wood.

She reached for it in the darkness. It was Carrie Fuller calling.

'Hello . . . ?'

'Florence, it's me. You're on speaker. I've got Dylan here with me. We're in a car about twenty minutes away. Listen very carefully. You need to get dressed, then you need to go and find Alice. Is her bedroom near yours?'

'Just along the corridor.'

'Don't turn on any lights and make as little noise as possible.'

Her heart was racing now. Something was wrong, badly wrong.

'What's happening?'

'Nothing to worry about. It's only a precaution; try to stay calm. We just need you and Alice to relocate.'

Relocate? It sounded like polite speak for flee. She wasn't wrong.

'Can you put your hands on some car keys?'

'I don't know.'

She pictured the small cupboard mounted on the wall in the entrance porch; she saw Bevan hanging the Ranger Rover keys on a hook when he drove her back from the hospital.

'Yes. Maybe.'

'Good. Now get dressed as quickly as you can, then go and find Alice. No lights, no noise. We'll stay on the line.'

Florence hauled on her jeans. The T-shirt she was wearing in bed would have to do, and she pulled a light cotton hoodie over it. She had been wearing heeled ankle boots at dinner. They were on the floor by the chair, but she imagined the noise they would make on the stone staircase, she imagined trying to run in them, and she hurried to the cupboard and dug out some sneakers. Tying the laces seemed to take an age; her fingers were so clumsy.

She snatched up the phone from the bed as she made for the door. 'Are you there?'

'We're here.'

'Okay, I'm going to find Alice.'

'Check the corridor first. If you see anything, anyone, close the door and lock it. Can you lock it?'

'Yes, there's a latch.'

But she was thinking about what Carrie Fuller had just said: someone in the corridor. Only a precaution? That was nonsense. They thought there could already be an intruder in the house. Fear rooted her to the spot for a moment. She breathed deeply, from the diaphragm, the way she'd been taught to when the panic attacks began to hit her after Valentine's death. It always amazed her how calming it could be, how rapidly it worked.

She edged the door open. There was a lamp on a console table at the far end of the darkened corridor. It threw enough light for her to see that the coast was clear.

She stuck to the narrow runner, to avoid the soles of her sneakers squeaking against the polished floorboards.

Alice's bedroom door was open, so were the curtains, and a pale of wash of moonlight guided her across the room to the bed.

Alice sat up with a start before she got there.

'What? Who is it?'

'Florence.'

'Florence . . . ?'

'It's Carrie Fuller.' She handed over her phone.

Alice was out of bed almost immediately, unabashed by her nakedness, already pulling on clothes as she listened to Carrie: 'Sure . . . okay . . . I don't know . . . I don't think the first floor is alarmed since the bodyguards arrived. One of them's on duty down there throughout the night . . . Trust them? I don't see why not . . . No, I've never carried a gun . . .'

Breathe, Florence told herself.

FORTY-NINE

'Alice, listen, I need to check on something,' said Carrie. 'I'll call you right back. Make sure your phones are on silent.'

She killed the call and went straight to Google Maps to confirm their location before switching to the tracker app.

'Okay, you need to slow down, or we're going to crash into him,' she said to Dylan.

Truss had been on Route 7 all the way from Burlington, and they were set to intersect with it any moment now, just north of Sheffield. From there it was ten minutes to the house, if that.

'We can just sneak ahead of him,' said Carrie, 'but I reckon we slow down and fall in behind.'

'Sure.'

Dylan eased off the gas. It was an odd sensation: the first time since leaving Hackett's place that he hadn't been pushing the Chevy to the max.

'Hell of a trip,' said Carrie. 'One to remember.'

It felt good. They'd made it. After a wild thrash across two states for close on three hours, they were about to drop onto the tail of their chief suspect, whose guilt now appeared to be beyond question.

There was a wide track winding off into the trees just shy of the junction where the road from Egremont hit Route 7.

'Pull in and kill the headlights,' said Carrie.

She called Ray and told him that they'd made it with a minute to spare. Sure enough, across the triangle of low scrub that separated the two roads, they soon saw the headlights of a car heading south on the 7 toward them.

Carrie checked her phone. 'That's him, that's Truss.' The car passed by. 'Technology . . . what a thing. Might just have saved a life.'

Dylan waited for the taillights to disappear from view before firing the engine.

'Hang well back,' said Carrie. 'We can afford to.'

Her phone rang.

It was Alice. They hadn't been able to find any car keys.

FIFTY

'I'm telling you, they're not here,' Alice whispered into her phone.

The box on the wall in the gloomy entrance porch was empty; no sign of any car keys hanging on the hooks. Her phone still pressed to her ear, Alice hurried to a side table and checked the drawers. 'Nothing. They must put them away at night.'

Or someone else has moved them, taken them, thought Florence.

Under instruction, Alice made for the front door. It was bolted top and bottom, but the key was in the big brass lock.

'It's open,' said Alice.

She slid back the bolts and was about to unlock the door when the security light outside came on. There was a fanlight above the front door, and the small porch area where they were standing was suddenly illuminated. Florence dropped to the floor, searching for the shadows. Alice had the presence of mind to put her eye to the peephole in the door.

She was down on the floor beside Florence in a moment. 'There's someone outside,' she hissed into her phone: 'The security light came on. I saw someone running . . . a man.'

Alice listened, firing back brief responses: 'I don't know . . . I'm sure we can . . . Okay.'

The light outside went off, and they were plunged into welcome darkness once more.

'We need to find somewhere to hide,' Alice whispered to Florence. 'Can you think of anywhere?'

FIFTY-ONE

'Why get them to hide?' said Dylan. 'Why not just get them to wake the house? They'll be safe that way.'

'And when the place lights up like a Christmas tree? What then?' Carrie didn't wait for a reply. 'It's over, is what. Whoever's outside hightails it and puts in a call to Truss to pull out.'

'You're using them as bait?'

'No, Dylan, I'm thinking on my feet here, balancing the risks. We need a result and we need them safe. What if the bodyguard on duty has already been taken out of action? What if the guy Alice saw outside is entering the house right now? How hard is it for someone to leave a back door on the latch?'

Convincing enough questions, but they still sounded like excuses to Dylan, excuses that played to his earlier suspicions that Carrie hadn't exactly gone out of her way to ensure Florence's safety.

'Only you know what you're really up to, but I trust you.'

'Don't. I'm winging it here. Forget the last couple of days, that's the easy bit, following a trail. This is a live situation, and the next hour of your life is going to be unlike any other you've known.'

Her phone pinged with an incoming text.

'Okay, they're holed up in the boot room. No lock, but they've jammed a chair under the door handle.'

Carrie texted back.

They were well south of Sheffield by now, approaching the outskirts of Canaan, and when Carrie flipped back to the tracker app, she saw that Truss had just taken a left. She called Ray immediately, putting him on speaker.

'Looks like he's skirting Canaan to the east. Why would he do that, Ray?'

'Must be planning to come at the house across the fields at the back. There's a track runs close to the river on the south side.'

'Can we box him in?'

'Both of us, yeah. He's got another exit to the west.'

'Shit.'

'What's the problem?'

'He's not alone, and the guy he's joining is already there. We need to get the women out, which means you with your car. I don't want them running around the grounds in the dark.'

They tailed Truss at a good distance, tracking him on the phone. Sure enough, he took the dirt road that skirted round the back of the Winslow property, which left them free to meet up with Ray near the front gates. Ray hadn't come in his police cruiser, but he was wearing his uniform.

The wrought iron gates weren't just closed; they were secured with a chain and a chunky padlock.

'Never seen that before,' said Ray.

'Probably a precaution,' said Carrie. But they were all thinking the same thing. Had it been done to keep intruders out, or those on the inside from leaving?

'You know Bevan?' Carrie asked.

'By sight,' said Ray. 'He's got a thing going with a local woman. You still carry bolt-cutters with you?'

'Always,' she said. 'I'll get them. You check out Bevan's place.'

Dylan scaled the stone wall and helped Ray up after him. They dropped into the darkness that was the back garden, stepping cautiously across the small square of lawn and rounding the building. Ray rang the doorbell several times, forcefully enough to wake the dead on the last occasion, but nothing stirred inside the gatehouse.

Carrie appeared at the front gates, and they hurried over to join her.

'He's not there,' said Ray.

Carrie slipped him the bolt-cutters through the ironwork. 'Then he's involved.'

'I don't know,' said Dylan. 'Look . . . the padlock's on your side.'

He hadn't registered it before; none of them had. It suggested the gates had been chained from the outside.

'Good point,' said Ray.

'Could be that someone paid Bevan a visit then chained the gates as they left,' said Dylan. 'Just because he didn't answer doesn't mean he's not in there.'

Carrie glanced at the gatehouse. 'We need to know.'

Ray cut through the chain, and together they went round to the back of the gatehouse. Ray used the bolt-cutters to break in through a French window, smashing the small panes of glass and the latticework of wooden frames.

'I'll stand guard,' said Carrie.

Ray insisted on leading the way, wielding the flashlight, Dylan at his shoulder, handgun drawn. It took them no more than a minute to search the warren of tiny and modestly furnished rooms. There was no sign of Bevan.

'We have to assume he's in the mix,' said Carrie when they re-joined her outside. 'Which means we have to get them out of there right now.'

'Me and Dyl will do it.'

'We'll all do it, Ray,' said Carrie.

'You want Truss? Someone needs to jump him when he runs, which he will . . . back to his car.'

FIFTY-TWO

Florence had never felt fear like it. Her body was screaming at her to move, begging her, and yet she and Alice had to sit there, huddled at the base of the wall, perfectly still and silent, cowering in the darkness.

She had started to shake before, an uncontrollable shiver, and Alice had put an arm around her. It was still there, the arm, and Florence was leaned into her, ears straining for the slightest sound that might warn them of an approaching threat. The one they were both dreading most was the sound of the door handle turning, for what good would that chair really do if someone tried to force their way inside the small boot room that had become their sanctuary?

Alice's phone lit up beneath the coat she'd placed over it so that the glow of an incoming text didn't alert someone on the outside to their presence. There were no curtains on the window above our heads.

Alice put her lips close to Florence's ear and whispered, 'Dylan's coming to get us. We need to be ready to move in two minutes.'

Dylan. Two minutes.

She felt the sharp terror ebbing away.

FIFTY-THREE

The car crept down the darkened driveway, no headlights, Ray steering by the light of the moon.

'Pull up,' said Dylan. 'I'll track you on foot, off to the right there, through the trees.' Two targets were better than one. 'There's a turning circle out front. Stop short or you'll trigger the security light.'

'Got it.'

Dylan slipped out of the car and eased the passenger door shut behind him. He then hurried off across the grass toward a cluster of big trees and the deep shadows beneath their spreading boughs.

A brisk walk was enough to keep pace with Ray's car, and he trod lightly over the hard ground, acutely aware of every tiny twig that cracked beneath his feet. It was a warm night — a southern night, unnaturally humid — and a stiff breeze played through the treetops, reducing the sound of the motor to a low purr off to his left.

The driveway took a long, lazy turn to the right as it approached the house, and Dylan was able to cut the corner, which drew him toward a stand of tall shrubs.

A shadow shifted up ahead.

A trick of the light?

No.

He froze, instinctually dropping to a crouch and leveling his gun.

Something was moving at speed, flitting through the moon-dappled darkness from right to left, toward the car, toward Ray.

Dylan came out of the crouch, no time to think, his brain already plotting a course to intercept the danger. He took off, running stealthily through the trees, bearing down on the darkened figure from behind. When the car slowed and pulled onto the grass beside the driveway, he realized with a spasm of alarm that he wasn't going to make it in time. Fortunately, the man also slowed, changing direction so that he could sneak up on the car from the rear.

He heard Dylan's footfalls at the last second and was turning when Dylan dropped his shoulder and slammed into him, sending him sprawling. A natural-born street fighter would have stepped in immediately and finished him off. It was only a momentary hesitation, but it was time enough for the man to roll away as Dylan kicked out hard, landing only a glancing blow, not a crippling one.

Then the man was back on his feet, rushing him, bundling him to the ground in a bear hug. The impact as they hit the deck winded them both, and although Dylan was the first to recover, he couldn't slip the grip of the other man, who was soon astride him, going to work with his fists. Dylan blocked what he could, but they landed like hammer blows. Just when he realized it was a battle he was destined to lose, the man fell suddenly still then collapsed onto him.

Someone was standing over them.

'Ray?'

'Shhh . . .'

Ray sank to his haunches and swept the surroundings with his gun, expecting consequences. When there weren't any, he whispered, 'You okay?'

'Yeah.'

The low glow of Dylan's phone was enough to reveal the unconscious, pistol-whipped man to be Bevan, the back of his head sticky with blood. Dylan searched the pockets of his pants, hoping to find a phone, a link to the others, but all he turned up was a set of car keys.

Ray felt for a neck pulse.

'Let's cuff him and put him in the trunk.'

Easier said than done. Bevan was a big man, thickset and absurdly heavy, difficult to maneuver. They managed it eventually. Ray ensured he was lying in the recovery position so that he didn't asphyxiate before gently closing the lid on him. Bevan could scream and holler all he liked, but he would play no further part in what was about to happen.

Dylan crouched at the back of the car and texted Alice.

Ready out here. Kill the security light if you can and turn left out of the door.

FIFTY-FOUR

'Time to go,' whispered Alice.

She helped Florence to her feet and removed the chair that was jammed under the door handle. They had about forty yards to travel to the front door, down the narrow corridor and across the cavernous entrance hall. The temptation would be to run, but they had to move as silently as possible through the darkness.

Alice eased open the door and led her by the hand down the black tunnel toward the vague light of the entrance hall. Halfway along, she stopped to listen. All Florence could hear was the blood beating in her ears.

Alice stopped again at the end of the passageway to survey the entrance hall. She gives Florence's hand a brief squeeze by way of an all-clear and they bore right, hugging the wall that led to the foot of the main staircase.

Alice froze. She pointed up the darkened stairwell then put her finger to her lips. They waited. And then Florence heard it, too: the creak of a floorboard.

Someone was moving around on the floor above.

There was nowhere for them to hide, and the small porch was right there, across the flagged floor. Alice drew her toward it — out in the open now, as exposed as they'd been

— and then they were there, and Alice was forcing her down into a corner, out of sight of anyone descending the staircase.

Alice examined the panel of light switches on the wall but gave up in frustration and turned her attention to the door. She slid back the door bolts, top and bottom. The brass lock offered considerably more resistance. The key groaned in protest as she turned it, and then there was a loud CLICK that landed like a thunderclap in the deafening silence.

That's when they heard the footsteps, light yet urgent, descending the stone staircase.

'Quick,' said Alice, grabbing Florence's hand and yanking open the door.

FIFTY-FIVE

The moment the security light came on, Dylan broke from the bushes at the side of the house where he was crouched with Ray, running unsighted at first as his eyes adjusted to the blinding white glare flooding the facade.

He saw them now — like actors on a brightly lit stage — hurrying down the front steps, hand in hand. They raced toward him along the slender strip of lawn between the house and the parked cars. Alice cast an urgent glance over her shoulder, and as she did so, a tall man dressed all in black burst from the house.

He was raising his gun when a shot rang out, and he darted back inside.

Dylan spun round. It was Ray who had fired from the bushes, and he urgently swept his arm, indicating for them to take cover behind the cars. As Dylan bundled Alice and Florence between the two vehicles, a bullet slapped into the bodywork just behind them. Another kicked up some gravel nearby. The shots could only have come from the man at the entrance, and he was clearly using a silenced weapon.

He had the angle on them. They would be sitting ducks if they broke for the safety of the bushes, and he could fire freely at them without exposing himself to Ray's covering shots, another of which now rang out.

That's when Dylan remembered the car keys he'd taken off Bevan.

He fumbled them from his pocket and hit the unlock button. The indicator lights of the Range Rover parked in front of the Audi SUV flashed three times. Dylan hauled open the rear door and forced Florence inside.

'Stay on the floor.'

He thrust the keys into Alice's hand.

'Turn right out of the gates. Head for Torrington. I'll let you know where.'

'What about you?'

'I'll use you as cover. Go.'

He hurried round to the front of the vehicle, staying low, and when the man in black tried to draw a quick bead on the vehicle, Dylan let loose three shots in quick succession, forcing him to retreat once more.

Alice fired the engine and pulled away, not too fast as she made off around the carriage circle, allowing Dylan to use the Range Rover as a shield. When he darted for the safety of the bushes, she floored the accelerator and the car roared off down the driveway.

Dylan lay panting in the darkness, belly to the ground among the bushes. He heard a rustling off to his right.

'It's me.' Ray appeared beside him. 'You okay?'

'Yeah.'

'He took off round the other side of the house.'

Dylan scrabbled to his feet, but Ray gripped his arm. 'Don't risk it. They'll be looking to clear the hell out.'

'Yeah, and Carrie's on her own out there.'

'She knows what she's doing. They won't get past her, which means there's only one way out for them. Best we can do is block off the other end of the track.'

* * *

Dylan put in the call as they were tearing back down the driveway.

Carrie answered immediately. 'I heard shots.'

'We're okay. Florence and Alice got out and we've got Bevan in the trunk. No sign of Truss but he's probably headed your way right now with the other guy.'

'I've got two cars here.'

'He has a gun, Carrie, and he's not afraid to use it.'

'Gotcha.'

'I mean it, they're not worth it.'

'Message received. STOP. Touched by your concern. STOP.'

'We're going to try to close off the other end of the track.'

As the car swung left out of the front gates, Dylan dialed again. Florence answered on the third ring.

'You okay?' he asked.

'Yes. You?'

'I'm going to text you an address. Go straight there. Don't tell anyone. I mean no one, got it?'

'Sure,' said Florence.

'Got to go.'

'Alice says thank you. So do I.'

'Hey, our pleasure.' He hung up.

'Speak for yourself,' said Ray, 'I'm too old for this shit.'

'Didn't look that way to me. Saved my ass twice, you did.'

Ray took a racing line through a bend. 'It's going to be tight. We got a ways to go still.'

Dylan dialed again, Evie's cell this time. She finally picked up.

'Hey . . .' she said groggily.

He kept it simple. The woman involved in the accident and the lawyer representing her needed a place to be, a place to sleep. He wouldn't be with them, but he'd show up later. He tried to strip the urgency from his voice, but of course she picked up on it.

'You're not in danger. Tell me you're not in danger.'

'No, nothing like that,' he soothed, the lie tripping easily off his tongue.

His phone lit up with an incoming call. It was Carrie.

'I've got to go. I'll call again when I can.'

He accepted the incoming call and knew immediately that Carrie was in a car, driving hard, her phone on speaker.

'They're on the move, two cars, Truss behind.'

He wanted to ask what had happened, but she was alive, and that was enough.

'How are we doing?' he asked Ray.

'Couple of minutes.'

'We're two minutes out,' Dylan said into his phone.

'That means nothing to me, I'm driving blind in a cloud of dust here. Stay on the line.'

Ray gave it everything he could, but it wasn't quite enough. As they flew round a bend, they saw a car fishtail into the road up ahead, near the top of a long rise.

It was Truss's Ford, which meant the other guy was already gone.

'We've got Truss in our sights,' Dylan told Carrie. 'He hung a left when he hit the road.'

'Coming now,' she said.

Dylan saw her headlight beams dancing in the trees to their left. 'That's her.'

Ray eased off the throttle to avoid a collision, and Carrie slewed into the road just in front of them. Some ten seconds separated them from Truss, but when they cleared the rise, there was no sign of his taillights up ahead.

'I'm pulling over,' said Carrie.

'You sure?'

'No choice. I can't drive *and* track him. Tell Ray to head back to the house and deal with things there.'

The switchover was a swift business, Carrie sliding across to the passenger seat, Dylan dropping in behind the wheel. A brief screech of tires and they were back in pursuit. Carrie tapped away at her phone.

'Bastard took a couple of pot-shots at me.'

'Truss?'

'Hard to say.'

'You get the other car's plate?'

'Yeah.'

It could make all the difference if Truss managed to give them the slip. For now, though, he was ripping south on Route 7, and according to Carrie, they looked to be gaining on him.

A few miles of forest-bordered road flew by.

'Okay, he's taken a sharp left . . . up ahead, after the bend.' Then almost immediately: 'He's stopped. Yes. Could be he's killed his lights, hoping we'll overshoot.'

'Let's give him what he wants.'

They tore past the mouth of the narrow lane, then Dylan slowed, extinguishing the headlights as he hung a slow U-turn and pulled in.

'He's on the move again,' said Carrie. 'No, wait. He's stopped. He's turned around . . . he's coming back.'

There was just enough moonlight for them to make out the entrance to the lane, and Truss switched his lights back on as he crept from it, heading north, back toward Canaan. Dylan took off after him along the moonlit road, slowly gaining, only switching on the headlights once he'd built up a head of steam and closed the gap.

Truss accelerated away, but they had the advantage in terms of momentum and fell in right behind him.

'You want me to give him a nudge?' Dylan asked.

'I thought they didn't teach the PIT maneuver in Connecticut.'

'They don't. Thank God for YouTube.'

'Christ,' said Carrie.

'He's not going to pull over.'

'Okay. Try not to kill him.'

Maybe Truss knew what was coming, because he fought hard to keep the Chevy from drawing alongside, swerving left and right to block it off. Dylan finally got him with a feint to the left that lured him into the middle of the road, followed by a nearside nudge when Truss moved back to close off the gap.

The Ford was knocked off its axis. It slewed side-on through ninety degrees, almost gracefully, before spinning hopelessly out of control. There was a spray of gravel from the side of the road, then the car disappeared off the edge into a ditch.

Dylan hit the brakes. They both drew their weapons as they ran back up the road. The Ford lay on its roof, upside down in the ditch. Truss wasn't just conscious; he was grunting, struggling in vain to get out. He was folded over on top of himself, caught up in his seat belt.

Carrie fired the flashlight beam into his face.

'Good to see you again, Holden.'

'What the fuck . . . ?'

Carrie turned the beam on herself and then Dylan.

'I knew it!' spat Truss.

'No you didn't, you little fuck, or you wouldn't be lying upside down in a ditch.'

'Get me out of here.'

'Is it me or is that arm bent all out of shape?' said Carrie. 'Oh Christ, it is. That's disgusting.'

The shock had obviously dulled the pain. 'Fuck,' said Truss. 'Fuck, fuck.'

'I'm no doctor, but I reckon you could lose that.'

'Get me out of here,' Truss pleaded pathetically.

'How about you tell us who the other guy is first.'

'What other guy?'

'Wrong answer, Holden.'

'Fuck you, Grandma.'

'That's more like it,' said Carrie. 'Makes what I'm about to do to you a whole lot easier.' She turned to Dylan. 'Go call it in.'

'Carrie—'

'We don't need this piece of shit. We've tied him to Hackett. It's enough.'

'Hey, I know my rights,' hollered Truss. 'Read me my rights. I want an attorney.'

'See? He's just going to drag it out, turn it into a circus. This is my last case. I need a clean win, not a court battle.'

'Crazy fucking bitch.'

Carrie jammed the muzzle of her handgun into Truss's cheek. 'Say that again, Holden.'

'You're not going to shoot me.'

'You think I'm that stupid? A fatal car accident?' She glanced at Dylan. 'Go call it in.'

'Carrie—'

'I said call it in!'

Truss gave a plaintive cry as Dylan headed off up the bank. 'Don't do it, man, don't leave me with her. . .'

After that he heard nothing more from Truss, and he hoped to hell he hadn't misread the situation, playing along with Carrie's charade when in fact she'd meant every word of it.

He got his answer a few minutes later, when she appeared at the car as he was finishing up his call to the dispatch officer.

'He's clammed right up, won't give me anything.'

'I'm not going to lie, you had me worried there.'

'I'm not going to lie, I was tempted.'

FIFTY-SIX

Lyndon was woken by the sound of a siren bleeding into his dream, becoming one with the cry of gulls. It plucked him off the pebble beach where he was walking through a thick sea mist while unseen waves sucked and sighed nearby.

Something had happened. Something bad. A siren in the dead of night meant nothing good. The only light in the library came from the machines ranged at the side of his bed, and they winked at him as if to say: *Not long now.*

Footsteps. He was barely able to move his head, but there was no need. William appeared from the darkness and stared down at him.

'What were you thinking? You bring her back into our lives, our home, and this is what happens? Men with guns! Well, now she's gone, disappeared . . . for good, I hope.'

Gone? Where? Not dead . . . please not dead.

The words wouldn't come, though. All he could do was lie there in impotent anguish, skewered by his son's hate-filled gaze.

'It's all your fault. It's always been your fault.'

'Dad, don't.' Joe appeared at his father's shoulder. 'The police want to speak to us. They know where Florence is. She's safe.'

Safe . . .

William turned and left, but Joe lingered a moment.

'I'm sorry, Grandpa, but he's right.'

Yes, but so am I, Joe . . . so am I.

Alone once more, he searched for the pebble beach shrouded in sea mist. He had been strolling along it aimlessly, yet somehow with purpose, and he was curious to discover what lay at the far end.

He hoped it was Deborah, waiting for him.

FIFTY-SEVEN

There was a low glow in the east when Dylan let himself silently into the house.

'Hello,' came a voice from the darkness, Florence's voice.

'It's only me.'

He switched on the lamp beside the front door. Florence was on the couch, buried in a duvet. She swung herself into a sitting position. She was wearing Evie's T-shirt, the one with THIS WAY UP printed upside down.

'Alice get the guest bedroom?'

'I knew I wouldn't sleep. And I wanted to be sure.'

He had called a couple of hours ago to say that he was back at the Winslow place but headed home soon.

He dumped himself in the armchair opposite. 'How you doing?'

'Evie's been amazing. She *is* amazing.'

'Yeah.' He felt like a slug of whiskey, but 4:20 a.m. wasn't exactly cocktail hour. 'How much did you tell her?'

'Probably more than we should have. We were pretty shaken up when we got here, even Alice.'

'Of course you were. It's okay.'

It puzzled him just how calm he had remained throughout, even when being shot at. Maybe the shock would kick in later, but right now he was feeling fine, just bone-tired.

'We got two of them. One is Bevan, the other's not talking.'

'Bevan? No . . .'

'That's what he's saying. We'll see tomorrow.'

'What happens now?' she asked.

'Well, you can't go back to the house. Carrie's got an idea. She needs to run it past our boss first. In the end, it'll be your call. Let's see how you feel in the morning.'

'It *is* the morning.'

'I still need to lie flat for a bit.'

'Sure. Of course.'

'Don't worry, you're safe here.'

'I've heard that before,' she replied.

'I don't know what to say.'

'I don't know, maybe something like, "I was wrong last time."'

He could forgive her the sarcasm, given what she'd just been through.

'I was wrong. I'm sorry. I'm new to this. I fucked up.'

She held his gaze a while. 'No plans to fuck up again any time soon?'

'None I can think of right now. Ask me again in the morning.'

Her smile suggested he was forgiven, at least in the short term, and he levered himself to his feet.

'Try to get some sleep; it's going to be a long day.'

Florence also stood, then without warning stepped forward and hugged him.

'Thank you.'

He felt the tight, lean heat of her in his arms, her breath against his neck. And as he headed for the stairs, he wondered if they hadn't held each other just a little longer than was absolutely necessary for her to convey her gratitude.

* * *

He stripped off in the bathroom and gave his teeth a cursory brush. Evie stirred as he slipped into bed beside her.

'Badger . . . ?'

'Hey.'

She twisted round and draped an arm across his chest. 'The hero returns.'

'Hardly.'

'That's not what they said.'

They lay in silence, and he thought for a moment she'd dropped off again.

'It's weird, when they told me what you did, I couldn't see it . . . couldn't picture you. I still can't.'

'Me neither. It was pretty surreal. It's all been pretty surreal.'

'You think you're cut out for it?' she asked.

'I've done okay. I've got a great teacher.'

'Yeah, they said that, too.'

He stroked her arm. 'Thanks for helping out.'

'I think what I'm trying to say—'

'Evie, I know what you're trying to say. If you can't picture me, how can you picture you?'

She said nothing at first. 'I can picture you with Florence. I think she can, too . . . but I guess you know that already.'

Dylan took a moment; he was still buzzing from before and liable to let fly with something he'd regret.

'It's a bit rich, you playing the jealous partner under the circumstances.'

'Meaning?' she asked.

'Meaning we both know what I mean. Meaning let's not argue about it now . . . not ever.'

Evie twisted onto her side to face him. 'You're not going to fight for me?'

'Is that what you want?'

'I don't know what I want, Badger.'

'I think you do. I think you've known for a while. And it's okay.'

Hearing himself utter the words made him realize he was finally coming to terms with it.

FIFTY-EIGHT

Florence had slept, but only briefly, snatched moments of semi-conscious limbo. With her jittery with exhaustion, a shower was exactly what she needed. The hard hammering of the water against her body not only revived her, it felt like a symbolic purging, a washing away of last night's terrors.

Evie had sweetly laid out some clothes for her on their bed. She opted for a pair of denim shorts and a short-sleeved navy cotton shirt. Other people's bedrooms had always fascinated her; they were such intimate spaces. A dressing table could reveal more about a person than the books on their shelves. Evie's spoke of a woman who cared little for make-up but was happy to drop a small fortune on French exfoliators and face creams.

She should have known he'd have a girlfriend, and a special one, too. Men like him didn't go home to empty houses at the end of the day. She was so out of touch with life, with the ways of normal people, it was almost embarrassing.

She helped herself to a guilty dab of *crème nutritive hydratante* and then headed downstairs, drawn by the smell of freshly brewed coffee.

Evie was at the range, making scrambled eggs.

'Thanks for the clothes.'

'Wish they looked that good on me.' Evie nodded toward the back door. 'They're all outside.'

She was surprised to find Carrie Fuller seated at the table in the backyard with Dylan and Alice. There was also another man present: short, balding and with a slight squint that wasn't completely masked by his thick spectacles. This turned out to be Carrie and Dylan's boss, Detective Captain Dyson, although he insisted that she call him Greg. She liked him immediately, his gentle manner and the birdlike blink of his eyes. He looked more like an academic than a detective, like one of her mother's coterie of eccentric friends.

He explained that Lyndon's house had been locked down, turned over to the forensics team, and that Carrie had a plan for keeping her safe until the case was solved. He then asked that Alice drive him to the Winslow house in the Range Rover.

'I want her with me,' said Florence.

'Sure you do,' said Greg, 'but I need her to walk me through exactly what happened with the two of you last night.'

'Afterwards, then.'

'Let's see,' said Carrie.

Florence had the uneasy feeling that they viewed Alice as a suspect, and she wondered if Alice sensed it too.

'They're right,' said Alice. 'The fewer people who know where you are, the better.'

They left before the eggs arrived, Alice giving her a parting hug at the front door.

'Stay strong,' she said. 'Just think, next time we see each other this will all be over.'

Carrie was also keen to get going, and Evie helped Florence throw together a bag of clothes to tide her over. She didn't see them to the car, fielding their thanks at the front door.

'Will I see you later?' she asked Dylan.

'Hard to say,' Carrie replied on his behalf.

Dylan received a parting peck on the cheek from Evie, which seemed surprisingly formal after all that had happened. Even he seemed a bit put out.

* * *

Carrie spelled out the plan as soon as they were on the move. Friends of hers had a holiday home on the north shore of Long Island, a place called Mattituck Inlet. The house was empty right now, theirs if they wanted it. They were going to drive to the coast to New Haven, where her partner would take them by boat across Long Island Sound.

'There's a local man, Abel. He'll be there to show you the ropes and look after you. I'd trust him with my life. You can, too. That said, if you don't feel comfortable, Dylan will stay on with you. I'll be honest, he's a lot more use to us back here, but it's your call.'

'I'm sure I'll be okay.'

'Let's see how you feel when we get there. One thing's for sure: you'll love the place. It's an old saltbox right on the water.'

They drove on in silence for a bit.

'Is that all I'm getting?' said Florence. 'You were gone two days.'

'Things are still pretty sketchy.'

'Sketchy is better than nothing.'

Carrie glanced at Dylan before responding. 'Okay, here it is. We tracked down the driver, the guy who died in the accident. His name is Hackett, Kyle Hackett. He's ex-military, probably a professional hitman. They're tearing his place apart right now. No leads yet, nothing that ties him to Truss . . . that's the guy we arrested last night. We're pretty sure Truss was also there the night of your accident, but he's still not talking. Maybe he will, maybe he won't. Even if he does, we're not sure how much he really knows about who's behind this. Hackett and Truss are looking like foot-soldiers.

We're guessing the man who got away last night knows a lot more.'

'What man?'

'I didn't tell her about him,' said Dylan.

'We're hoping he's the one who set it all up, brought Hackett and Truss in on the job. We find him, we find who hired him.'

Florence sat with the information for a few seconds. 'It sounds like a lot of guessing and hoping.'

Carrie twisted in her seat. 'Nothing wrong with that. They got us this far in just a few days.'

'And General Ngomo?'

'Not in the picture for us right now.'

'Was he ever?'

'For a while,' said Carrie.

'So, it's one of the Winslows.'

'We've got nothing concrete, but it's looking that way . . . one or more.'

Strangely, it hadn't occurred to her before. More than one. Or maybe they were all in on it together, like in *Murder on the Orient Express*.

'Is that what this is really about, just money?' she asked.

'A whole heap of the stuff,' Carrie replied.

'They're rich as Croesus already.'

'Exactly the kind of people who don't know the meaning of the word "enough."'

Florence found herself thinking of her father. He had taught her from an early age to embrace with pride the color of her skin ('You're not just black, you're both. How cool is that?'), and to never assume that it alone was the reason for her poor treatment at the hands of others ('It could be that they just don't like you, Flopsy, which doesn't make them racist, just stark raving mad.'). But she distinctly remembered the welcome she had received when Valentine first introduced her to his family, their polite bewilderment when he'd shown up at the house with a black woman on his arm. They had talked about it at the time, and Valentine hadn't tried to persuade her she was imagining it. He knew it wasn't his place to adjudicate on such matters. You had to be black to interpret the dumbshow of awkward body language and stolen looks that betrayed white people like the Winslows when you stood before them as an equal.

'It's not only about the money.'

She wasn't looking to start a conversation on the subject, but Dylan wasn't afraid to go there anyway.

'Race?' he asked tentatively.

'Maybe. I don't know for sure.'

'Let's run with it anyway,' said Carrie, turning again to look at her. 'Did you ever sense it was more of an issue for one of the Winslows than the others?'

'Olivia,' she replied unthinkingly.

'Anything specific?'

'Heather, too.'

FIFTY-NINE

The City Point dock in New Haven lay near the mouth of the West River, and as Dylan pulled the Chevy to a halt in the parking lot, he had a vague memory of being here before. Probably when he was a kid. One of their weekend trips, driving all over, exploring for the sake of it. They had done a lot of that sort of thing as a family, him happily sandwiched between his two bickering sisters in the back.

A small boy with an untidy mop of dark hair came running up as they were getting out of the car. He launched himself at Carrie, throwing his arms around her waist.

'I missed you.'

'Me too, Arly,' said Carrie. 'Hey, wasn't Mommy going to dump you on the Calders?'

'She tried.'

'Weren't having it, huh?'

'Is this them?'

'Manners, munchkin.'

Arlo thrust his hand out at Florence. 'Hello, I'm Arlo.'

'Hello, I'm Florence.'

Dylan took Arlo's tiny hand in his. 'Dylan. Good to meet you, young man.'

'Do you like boats?'

'Not really,' said Dylan.

'Nah, me neither.'

'Hey, what happened to being a skipper when you grow up?' asked Carrie.

Arlo shot her a sharp look. 'I changed my mind.'

'Fair enough. Are we good to go?'

'Mommy's just doing some checks.'

Mommy had her head buried in the engine well at the back of the boat. Dylan had always had a mild fear of the ocean, and he was happy to see that *Falcon* was a substantial craft, with large decks fore and aft, and a big cabin in between, topped by a flying bridge. It certainly didn't look like it was going to sink any time soon.

'Permission to board,' said Carrie.

The two women kissed each other on the lips, and Dylan saw the pieces falling into place for Florence. Carrie had said that Abby looked younger than she was, and she appeared to be about forty years old, with faint laugh lines bracketing her mouth. In the flesh she was even more beautiful, limber and with a glow of vitality about her. Her long, dark hair was tied back in a ponytail, as in the photo Carrie had shown him, but she wasn't wearing the mirrored shades. Her eyes were preternaturally blue and carried a clear hint of humor in them.

Her hands were covered in oil, so she offered her elbow for Dylan to shake. 'It's good to meet you. Thanks for looking after her.'

Dylan glanced at Carrie. 'She's a handful; it hasn't been easy.'

Abby turned to Florence. 'You must be Florence. Welcome aboard. Conditions are great. It shouldn't take us more than an hour to cross the Sound.'

* * *

As soon as they were clear of the headland, Abby opened the throttle and *Falcon* came up on the plane, leveling out the light chop. There was hardly a cloud overhead, and

243

from high on the flying bridge they seemed to be suspended between the sea and the sky. It was exhilarating: the speed and the bracing, briny tang of the wind in their faces.

Arlo tugged at Dylan's hand. 'Do you want to see my fishing rod?'

'Sure.'

'Can I come too?' Florence asked.

'I guess,' said Arlo, not exactly bursting with enthusiasm.

Florence smiled. 'No problem, I get it, it's a guy thing.'

Dylan didn't just get to see the rod; he received a long lesson in trolling for bluefish and striped bass off the back of the boat. He sat and cooed as Arlo delved into boxes and pulled out a colorful array of jigs and plugs, tubes and spoons, each of which served its own particular purpose. Arlo's favorite fish in the world was weakfish, which Mommy cut into cubes and fried in batter.

After that, there was a tour of the boat and the offer of a chilled beer from the fridge in the galley, which Dylan turned down in a favor of a soda water. They were still below decks, bent over a bunch of nautical charts, when Carrie found them and dispatched Arlo up top. 'Mommy needs her look-out. We're about to enter the inlet.'

'Come with me, Dylan,' said Arlo eagerly.

'He's right behind you, munchkin.' Carrie waited for Arlo to scamper off up the steps. 'Sorry about the limpet. It's not always easy for him, living with a couple of lesbians.'

'Come on, he adores you.'

'Doesn't have a whole load of men in his life, though.'

'His father?'

Carrie's expression darkened. 'Not what you call a role model, that one.'

They stopped en route to the bridge to pack away the various lures and other fishing paraphernalia that now littered the aft deck.

'Evie seems like a great girl,' said Carrie. 'You two get a chance to talk?'

'Enough to know our thing has run its course.'

'I wondered. That's too bad.'

'It's okay, I've got a lot else to be excited about. I'm just sorry . . .'

'What?'

'That you're retiring. That this is it . . . you and me.'

'I know the feeling.'

'You sure I can't persuade you to stay on?'

Carrie gave a rueful smile. 'It's complicated.'

'Abby?'

'She'd never tell me what to do. No, it's my call.'

They tucked the rods and the boxes of fishing gear away in the big locker at the back of the deck.

'Is Abby the reason you left Philadelphia?'

'Good reason, no?'

They had met on a river cruise, the fortieth birthday bash of one of Carrie's colleagues in Philadelphia PD, who happened to be Abby's cousin.

'It was the weirdest thing, a first for both of us. I mean, I once kissed a girl in high school for a bet . . . ten bucks for two seconds of French.'

'A small fortune back then.'

'Fuck you,' grinned Carrie.

Dylan wondered if the relationship had triggered the breakdown in Carrie's relationship with her daughter, but that wasn't the question he asked.

'Does Greg know?'

'Greg is a dark horse. Greg knows everything about everything. Spotted you for a natural, and he was right.' She hesitated. 'He's a good man. Great boss, too. He'll pair you off with the right person.'

Yeah, but it won't be the same, thought Dylan.

SIXTY

The entrance to Mattituck Inlet was bordered by a narrow breakwater, hundreds of feet long, which pointed straight and true like an accusatory finger toward the distant Connecticut shoreline. It slipped ceaselessly by on their port side before they finally entered the channel proper, which soon took a turn to the left behind the dune-backed beach. Low, marshy ground lay ahead of them at the next bend, a dog-leg right with a couple of waterside properties set among the trees on the far bank. Just beyond, Abby guided *Falcon* into a looping side channel, where a man stood waiting for them on a jetty at the foot of a sweep of lawn.

'Abel!' called Arlo from down below on the foredeck, waving wildly.

'You've got competition,' Carrie said to Dylan.

'I hate him already.'

Abby laughed and brought *Falcon* alongside the jetty, where Abel set about securing the mooring lines that Arlo tossed to him. Though not particularly tall, Abel was lean, muscular, with a face and arms that were tanned to a light mahogany and a five-day beard flecked with silver. Everything about him said outdoorsman. He ruffled Arlo's hair then greeted the rest of them warmly with an iron handshake and a shy smile that showed a chipped front tooth.

'You've not got long if you're to get off,' he said. 'Tide's on the ebb.'

The weatherboard saltbox that stood at the head of the gently rising lawn was much as a child would draw a house: two stories, a pitched roof, and windows arranged symmetrically around a central doorway. The inside was sparsely but elegantly furnished, a tasteful blend of rustic and mid-century modern. Arlo launched himself onto a giant leather couch.

'This is my favorite place in the *whole* world,' he declared.

Carrie, Abby and Arlo were regular visitors and knew their way around the house. Abel kept an eye on the place when the owners were absent, as they were now, on holiday in Newfoundland.

'It's yours for ten days if you need it,' Carrie told Florence. 'We're hoping you'll be out of here long before then.'

As the tour moved on from the kitchen to the front yard, Dylan held Florence back.

'Abel is ex-Coast Guard, so he's allowed to carry a weapon, not that he'll need it. No one will ever know you're here. I'll still stay if you want, though.'

'I do want, but don't worry,' she said. 'Carrie needs you. So does Evie.'

'Evie's moving to New York.'

She had broken the news to him earlier, just before Carrie and Greg showed up at the house. She had been offered a shared studio space in the East Village, as well as a place to stay until she found her feet.

'For good?' Florence asked.

'Looks that way.'

The moment was broken by the scampering of tiny feet, as Arlo came hurrying back into the house.

'Come and see the pond, it's got giant fish in it.'

* * *

Their brief interlude on Long Island ended with them sliding down the shrinking channel, past banks of oily mud. As soon as they were clear of the breakwater, Abby gave *Falcon* full throttle, picking a path through the sailboats that speckled the Sound.

Dylan and Arlo stood in the prow, the wind whipping their hair.

Carrie joined them.

'Hey, little man, mind if I have a word with the big man?'

'Work stuff?'

'You got it.'

Arlo went off to join his mother on the bridge.

'Try to put her from your thoughts,' said Carrie.

'Since when did you get so good at reading them?'

'The saucer eyes are a giveaway. So's the dribbling. You realize you're screwed now, don't you?'

'How's that?' he asked.

'Saving the damsel in distress from the bad guys with guns. That's not something she's ever going to forget.'

'Me neither. First time I've fired my Sig not on a range.'

'How did it feel?'

'Weirdly natural. There was a threat . . . it had to be neutralized.'

Carrie glanced off briefly. 'Look, Ray's telling anyone who'll listen how you handled yourself last night. I know you won't, but don't let it go to your head. We need to stay focused. We're a way off cracking the case.'

They might have Truss in custody, but there was still only a loose tie between him and the stolen Prius, and no hard evidence so far that he'd been present the night of the accident. As for the connection between Truss and Hackett, that could be described as flimsy at best: the possibility that their paths had crossed at Fort Drum years ago.

'I just got off the phone to Greg. Truss is still playing dumb, and they've got nothing from Hackett's place. Also, Lyndon's lawyer is looking like a dead end for now.'

Greg had tracked Victor Penfold down to the Bahamas, where he had a holiday home. Penfold's wife was saying that he'd picked up a bad bug on the plane and was bedridden with respiratory complications, too ill to talk. Probably bullshit, but bullshit they had to accept, seeing as it came with a doctor's certificate attesting to the severity of his illness.

It was a sobering analysis of their situation.

'Stay positive,' said Carrie. 'It's normal for an investigation to take a dip after a high like last night. The dust settles, you take a look at what you've got . . . it can be demoralizing. This is our dip. It's for us to find a way out of it.'

She tapped his skull with the tip of her finger.

'Forget about Florence for now and get those cogs of yours turning.'

SIXTY-ONE

There was a discernible buzz in the detective bureau when they showed up a couple of hours later.

'Going out with a bang, Fuller,' called Doug Thwaites, raising his takeout coffee in a toast.

Carrie ignored him. No one liked Thwaites. Dylan had brushed with him last year on a joy-riding case which had left two young men, high as kites on a cocktail of weed and amphetamines, badly messed up after they'd lost control of a stolen Lincoln and smashed into a wall. Thwaites had shown little sympathy for the victims and even less for their distraught families.

'Word is the rookie's got half a brain,' called Thwaites.

'Half a brain but still twice the man you are,' Carrie fired back as they pushed into Greg's office.

Greg was at his desk, looking exhausted and strung out. He blamed it on Florence's mother, who had shown up at the Winslows' place in a cab from her hotel near JFK Airport.

'That woman is a force of nature.'

Denied access to her daughter, she had turned her attentions on the family she had never known, never met, including Lyndon Winslow.

'The old man's pretty much gone, just lying there, and she's got this crystal on his chest, and she's chanting all kinds of weird shit and holding her hands over him.' He swept his hands around above his desk.

'She's still out at the house?' Carrie asked.

'Couldn't budge her.'

'Are you sure that's wise?'

'Feel free to try. She's staying on till the old man "crosses over."' He made speech marks in the air.

'They're all suspects, Greg.'

'Yeah? Show me the evidence. We've questioned them thoroughly. They're all pleading ignorance about last night. A bunch of them are heading back to the city later.'

'That doesn't seem right.'

'We've no grounds to hold them. What have we got? One brother who suggested Florence head out to the house via Torrington the night of the crash . . . a sister who masterminded a failed takeover of the family hedge fund . . . and a sister-in-law who may or may not have an issue with the pigmentation of Florence's skin. What do you think the DA's going to say when we hit her with that lot?'

'Fuck off?' Carrie suggested.

'If she's in a good mood.'

'Jesus, Greg, look how far we've come in just one week.'

'You're preaching to the converted. I'm blown away by what you've achieved . . . but it's not enough.'

'What about Bevan?' Dylan asked.

'Bevan's saying you didn't identify yourself as a police officer before tackling him.'

'Shit, I don't think I did.'

'Bad mistake if it turns out he's involved. But he's sticking to his story and I'm beginning to believe him.'

Bevan was under guard in hospital, nursing a stitched scalp and concussion. He was claiming that he'd been in bed in the gatehouse when he'd heard a car cruise slowly past the front of the estate a couple of times. Suspicious, he had gone outside to discover that someone had secured the front gates with a chain and padlock. Grabbing the spare keys to the Range Rover, he had then hurried to the house to investigate. There he had found the on-duty bodyguard unconscious, gagged and bound near the pool house. It was soon after that he'd heard the car approaching down the driveway, the one with Ray at the wheel, not that he'd known it at the time. All he knew was that any car approaching from that direction had gotten through the chained gates and clearly presented a threat.

'Could be,' said Carrie.

'Could also be he was the one who took out the body-guard,' countered Dylan. 'Did the guy see anything?'

'*Nada*,' said Greg. 'He was tasered from behind and chloroformed while making a routine tour of the outside.'

His assailant — presumably the man in black — hadn't taken his keys to the house, choosing instead to get a ladder from the gardeners' cabin and enter the property via Florence's balcony. All of which screamed inside job. He knew which room was hers and also that she kept her door locked at night.

'Stuff Bevan would have known,' Dylan pointed out.

'My guess is he's clean,' said Greg. 'It's Ray's gut, too. He was with me at the hospital when I questioned him.'

As for Truss, he was only speaking through his attorney, who was offering them nothing at all.

'There was shit on his shoe. Forensics are looking to tie it to a cow pie in the pasture out back. Even if they do, all it proves is he was there or thereabouts, and he can come up with any number of reasons for that: got lost, stopped for a leak, heard gunfire, went to investigate, freaked out, fled. As for the gunfire, they found no residue on his hands or clothes, so he's clear on that count. The guy who got away was the only shooter.'

Carrie had taken down his license plate, but the trace had turned up a stolen car, so another dead end for now.

Carrie's assessment of their situation on *Falcon* had been depressing enough; as spelled out by Greg, their prospects appeared even bleaker. All they could do was sit back and hope that the search of Truss's apartment turned up a lead or that Detective Safran located Hackett's car. Greg had dispatched a couple of detectives to Burlington to assist in both matters.

He held up his hand to silence Carrie before she could speak: 'I know, I know, it's your case. Still is.'

'Doesn't sound like it.'

'We need all hands on deck right now or Truss is looking good to walk. We've got nothing else. If he had a phone on him, he must have tossed it while you were chasing him.'

The words lodged themselves in Dylan's brain, and it took him a few moments to figure out why. Meanwhile, an argument was building between Carrie and Greg about control of the case. Voices were being raised. Dylan soon silenced them.

'How fucking stupid are we?' They both looked at him. 'He tossed it. Hackett tossed his phone.'

'What are you talking about?' said Greg. 'Hackett didn't have a phone.'

'We figured he must have had one when we turned up the tracker in Florence's car. We assumed Truss had grabbed it from the wreck before leaving.'

'Which never sat well with us,' put in Carrie, 'because if Truss had enough sense to do that, why didn't he finish off Florence?'

'Think about it,' said Dylan. 'In order to kill her, Hackett has to slam into her hard. There are risks. Does he really want his phone on him? It's a burner, for sure, so does he even need it anymore? It's served its purpose. The moment has arrived.'

'He tosses it,' said Greg quietly, as though picturing it in his mind's eye.

Carrie leaned forward in her chair. 'He can see her headlights coming, knows for sure it's her.'

Greg's eyes flicked between them.

'I like it. I'll like it a whole lot better if you're right.'

SIXTY-TWO

They hardly spoke on the drive north from Torrington, almost as though to discuss it further would somehow jinx the theory. They both knew how much was riding on it, and Dylan was in an agony of anticipation when they arrived at the intersection.

They took the side road on the left that Hackett had shot out of in the Prius. They had been here before, on foot, and at the point where the lane widened, Dylan turned the Chevy around so that its nose was pointing back down the slope toward the intersection. They got out of the car and began searching the hedgerows on both sides, and also the pastures beyond. They made slow progress; the hedges were threaded with angry brambles.

They continued to work their way down the lane, but dejectedly now, the dream slipping away from them with every extra yard they covered.

Then out of the blue Carrie said with surprising composure, 'Well, hello. Exhibit A . . . one cell phone.'

Dylan hurried over to join her.

It was lying jammed in the fork of two branches at the foot of a blackthorn bush. Carrie pulled a pair of surgical gloves from the back pocket of her jeans, snapped them on and delved one-handed into the hedge.

'Bastard thorns,' she said, her forearms already beaded with blood from the bramble scratches.

She held up the phone in a pincer grip between thumb and forefinger. It was an old Samsung with a scratched screen. The weather was with them; thanks to the heat wave over the past week, there would be no water damage. Better yet, there was still some juice in it.

The screen lit up with standard-issue wallpaper, which then switched to a passcode protection screen when Carrie pressed the home button.

'Shit,' she said.

It would have been too good to be true for it not to be locked.

'I know this phone,' said Dylan.

'Why am I not surprised by that?'

'It's a Galaxy S8. Evie had one. She loved it . . . mainly because it was one of the first to have face ID.'

Carrie turned to him. 'That's sick.'

'Sick as in cool, or sick as in disgusting?'

'Both.'

* * *

Satnav said it was just over an hour to the state morgue in Farmington. Carrie put in a call to Dr. Vaughan, the associate medical examiner they'd dealt with before. She was in the middle of an autopsy but would be finished by the time they got there. Carrie also called Greg and asked him to clarify the legal position regarding any information they managed to extract from Hackett's phone, assuming it *was* his phone. Greg was back in touch five minutes later. Legally, they were good to go ahead: the dead had no right of privacy.

Dr. Vaughan was waiting for them in the lobby when they arrived. Hackett's corpse had already been removed from the body storage refrigerator and was waiting for them on a gurney in a small room off the autopsy suite. It was a first for Dr. Vaughan. She had heard of a dead person's face being used to unlock a phone before but never witnessed it.

For a while, it looked as though she wasn't going to any time soon.

Hackett's features had, understandably, lost some of their defining character in the past week. His cheeks were gaunt, drawn, so they used cotton balls to plump them up. His hair was arranged to conceal the stitches across his forehead, and they forced his lips into a faint smile in a bid to animate the pale, staring death mask, which was then touched up with make-up to lend it some warmth.

'Open sesame,' said Carrie.

It had finally worked. They were in.

A lab assistant was dispatched to find a suitable charger to keep the phone juiced up, and Carrie went straight to the call log. There wasn't much, but there was enough to be excited by. All the calls had been made the Friday of the accident, or the day before it.

Carrie pulled out her own phone and shot a short video as she scrolled through the phone's log again, then another of her digging deeper into the log whenever a number of calls had been made to the same number, in order to get the exact timing of them. There were no texts, but Google Maps history offered up some stuff, which Carrie also recorded on her phone. The other apps yielded nothing, but among them was one that corresponded to the tracker planted in Florence's car. Only the tech guys knew what they could get from that.

'There could be other stuff on here, stuff he's deleted that can be recovered.'

Carrie recorded a final video on her phone: of Dr. Vaughan attesting to what she had just witnessed and reading off the phone's serial number.

All of the videos had been fired off to Greg by the time they said their farewells to Dr. Vaughan in the lobby.

'That was great work, Dyl,' said Carrie as they headed for the Chevy.

'Let's see if it leads anywhere first.'

'It will. Hackett fucked up. There was a landline number in the call log.'

'Could be a bar, any kind of public phone.'

'Big picture says different.'

'Big picture never lies?'

'Only once.'

Carrie didn't elaborate, and Dylan didn't push her. She would have offered more if she had wanted to.

* * *

Carrie's confidence turned out not to be misplaced. Greg had been hard at it in the time it took them to drive from Farmington back to Torrington PD. The landline number was registered to a residential address just outside of Ravena, New York. The account holder's name was Vincent Greer.

'He's a known felon with ties to the Albanian mob in Westchester County. Short rap sheet, but fruity, including a murder charge that was dropped when a key state witness disappeared in suspicious circumstances. He looks to be some kind of enforcer.'

Albany PD had already been drawn into the frame and were making an application to a judge for an arrest warrant. There was no reason to think it wouldn't be forthcoming within a couple of hours.

Of the three cell phone numbers in Hackett's phone log, there was one that had been called many times in the lead-up to the accident, which suggested it was a burner phone being used by Truss. Long gone, no doubt. And there was little chance of proving the connection, not without convincing CCTV footage from the store where the SIM card had been purchased, which they all knew wasn't going to happen.

'Albany want you there when they move in. *I* want you there, especially you, Dyl. There's a good chance Greer is the guy in black, the one who fired on you at the Winslow place. You got a better look at him than anyone.'

'Not much of one. It all happened so fast.'

'No one's asking you to pick him out in a line-up, but an impression would help. If you're sure it's not him, we need

257

to reassign our key assets elsewhere.' Greg caught Carrie's grimace. 'That's how we talk now. I've been on courses and shit.'

'So glad I got through it without having to.'

'Another thing,' said Greg. 'Ray just called. Florence's mother is kicking up a fuss, demanding to see her daughter.'

'I don't see why not,' said Carrie. 'If Florence agrees to it.'

'Seems she has. They've been in touch.'

'I don't know,' Dylan offered hesitantly. 'It's a potential security risk.'

'Not if it's handled right.'

'You want us to stop by the house en route to Albany?' Carrie asked.

'Yeah, see if you can't sort it out.'

SIXTY-THREE

Florence was walking on the beach with Abel when her phone trilled into life. She was dreading another angry exchange with her mother, but she saw that it was Dylan.

'I'm sorry, I have to take this.'

'Go ahead,' said Abel, drifting off toward the water's edge to give her some privacy.

'Settling in?' Dylan asked.

'Yeah, Abel's showing me the beach.'

The strip of pale sand, a few minutes stroll from the house, stretched off into the distance, straight as a hoe handle and studded with pods of people soaking up the sunshine. Carefree.

'I don't want to get your hopes up, but it looks like we've got a lead on the guy who gave us the slip last night.'

'How?'

'It's complicated. We'll know more later. Listen, we just wanted to hear it from your side. Are you really okay with seeing your mother?'

'I don't have a choice. She's come all this way.'

'You *do* have a choice.'

'Then I'll go for Alice over my mother.' Alice's sudden absence was more than an ache; it was a void she couldn't fill. 'I know you don't trust her, but I do.'

'We're just trying to do what's best for you.'

'Then give me my old life back. Can you do that? No, you can't.' When he didn't reply, she let out an apologetic sigh. 'I'm sorry.'

'Are you sure you're okay?'

'I am. Really. I like Abel. I feel safe with him.'

He was a kind man of few words, gentle and slightly awkward. He had mentioned a wife and a young daughter, and she knew already that he was a good husband and a good father.

'You can have your old life back, Florence. You can have anything you want when this is over. Take the money from the inheritance and walk away from all the other stuff. It'll be just like before, only better.'

'Alice said the same thing.'

'Obviously a woman of high intelligence,' he joked. 'What exactly did she say?' he added, trying to sound casual.

'The same as you. It's good advice. It helps.'

He knew it was a brush-off, but he didn't push for more.

'Just so we're clear, you're okay with your mother joining you there?'

'I am.'

'We'll arrange it.'

'Good luck.'

'With what?' he asked.

'You'll see.'

SIXTY-FOUR

The carriage circle in front of the house was sealed off by yellow incident tape that declared in repeating bold capitals: POLICE LINE — DO NOT CROSS. A couple of forensic trucks lay within the perimeter, together with the Audi SUV, still standing near the front entrance, as it had been last night.

The whole Winslow family was fanned out across the front steps. A departure. Ray looked on as the bags were loaded into the back of the car. He was standing with a tall woman dressed in a white peasant blouse and a long, faded purple skirt, possibly Florence's mother.

Ray and Alice broke away from the group and made their way toward them. 'Need to let the car through,' said Ray, untying the incident tape.

'You're leaving too?' Carrie asked.

'My work here is done,' Alice replied with mock grandiosity.

'We'll be in touch.'

'I'd appreciate that, seeing as Florence has engaged me as her lawyer.'

'Yeah? She didn't say. A lucrative appointment . . . not going home empty-handed.'

'It came from her, I didn't push for it.'

'No need to be so defensive,' said Carrie.

'I'm feeling defensive,' said Alice. 'To be honest, I'm feeling like a suspect.'

'You're not . . . but the man who hired you is.'

Alice nodded a couple of times. 'Okay, I see where you're coming from now. You think I'm Victor Penfold's plant, his eyes and ears.'

'Are you?'

'No.'

'Then you'll be able to tell us why you advised Florence to take her cut of the inheritance and leave the hedge fund to the three Winslow children.' Carrie turned to Dylan. 'That's what Florence said, right?'

Dylan nodded.

'That's not how it was,' Alice said indignantly. 'It was getting to her, all of it, the family, the thought of having anything more to do with them. I was just trying to make her feel better. It wasn't advice, not as such. If you don't believe me, ask her.'

'You can be sure of it,' said Carrie. She nodded past Alice. 'Looks like they're ready to leave.'

Alice glanced at the front steps. 'You know, it's a shitty way to go, after everything we've been through together.'

'It's a shitty situation, period,' said Carrie. 'But we're all grown-ups, we'll get through it.'

Alice turned and left, skirting the steel sculpture on the circular lawn.

'Did she pass the test?' Dylan asked.

'What do *you* think?'

'I think you really upset her.'

'The guilty do upset better than anyone,' said Carrie.

Sensing the tension in the air, Ray had kept his distance until now. 'Want to tell me what that was about?'

'Bit of due diligence,' said Carrie.

Farewells were being exchanged on the front steps.

'Is that Florence's mother?' Dylan asked Ray.

'Uh-huh. Tamsin. Apparently it means "free spirit" in Scottish. In American it means fruitcake.'

Joe Winslow gave Tamsin a big hug before getting into the car with his cousin Amber and her mother, Connie.

'Kind of tight, aren't they, after just one day?' Carrie observed.

'He's a good kid . . . funny, considerate, keeps me in coffee.'

'Never trust an ingratiator, Ray.'

It was odd. Joe Winslow hadn't struck Dylan as an ingratiator last night, when they'd headed back to the house following the car chase with Truss. Joe had been the mouthpiece of the family, demanding to know what the hell was going on, not afraid to put noses out of joint in his quest for answers.

'How's the old man doing?' Carrie asked.

'Hanging in there,' said Ray. 'Just.'

They stepped aside to let the SUV pass, blank faces staring back at them from the interior. Dylan caught Alice's eye, and she nodded at him.

'We got a lead,' said Carrie. 'An address. Could be the shooter's from last night.'

Ray was genuinely shocked by the news. 'How in the hell . . . ?'

'Turns out Hackett had a phone on him the night of the crash.' She talked Ray through the discovery, crediting Dylan with the breakthrough that had led them to Vincent Greer.

'We've got Greg to thank,' said Dylan. 'If he hadn't talked about Truss tossing his phone . . .'

'Modest with it,' said Ray.

Carrie grimaced. 'Sickening, huh?'

They made for the house. The remaining members of the family were filing back inside, together with Florence's mother.

'Who have we got left?' Carrie asked. 'Just Lyndon's three kids?'

'Yeah, and Heather. I did like you said . . . no mention of Truss's arrest, and I kept all the talk to General Ngomo.'

'Greg says Florence's mother is being a pain in the ass.'

'Can't blame her,' said Ray. 'Flies all the way here from London to hear that the man who had her husband killed is now trying to kill her daughter. I feel like a heel lying to her.'

'You a fan?' Carrie asked.

'She's impressive, if a little nuts.'

'She'll find out the truth soon enough. Dyl spoke to Florence; she's okay with seeing her mother.'

'That's good news . . . as it should be,' said Ray.

'The bad news is Greg wants us in Albany when Greer's arrest warrant comes through, and I don't trust anyone else to deliver her safely and in secret.'

'Where are we talking about?'

'Long Island. It'll mean taking the ferry from Bridgeport, then an hour's drive the other side.'

'What's that, an eight-hour round trip?'

'Give or take. Could be you make the last ferry back, or you can crash the night at the house, head home in the morning.'

'I might just do that.'

'Thanks, Ray, I know it's the last thing you need right now.'

'You reckon? A good night's sleep while you and Poirot here are chasing all over New York State?'

SIXTY-FIVE

'Impressive, if a little nuts,' turned out to be spot-on.

Florence's mother had an air of easy authority about her, in spite of the hippy clothes and the leather sandals. Her handshake was firm, her gaze steady, unyielding. They asked for a word in private, and the moment they were alone with her on the back terrace, she demanded to know why the police appeared to be doing everything in their power to keep her from seeing her daughter.

Dylan explained that there were certain procedures they were obliged to follow, protocols to be observed.

'No offense, young man, but that sounds like complete and utter crap to me.' The accent was pure *Downton Abbey*, even if the words weren't.

Carrie's faintly amused expression told Dylan that he was on his own.

'Complete, not utter,' he said to Tamsin.

That gave her pause for a second. 'Intriguing. Go on.'

'Not yet. Soon, though. We need you to trust us, need you to play along for now, do as we say.'

She eyed him warily. 'If it means I can see Florence.'

'Before nightfall,' said Carrie. 'But you can't tell anyone where you're going. If they ask, say we're taking you to police headquarters in Torrington.'

'Why? What's wrong?' demanded Tamsin, the concerned mother beginning to show through the cracks in her steely composure.

'Later,' said Carrie. 'That's the deal.'

The two women eyed each other: similar ages, one with a mad ash-blonde mane that cascaded around her shoulders, the other a silver pixie crop.

'All right,' said Tamsin.

'Be ready to leave in fifteen minutes.'

As soon as Tamsin had made her way inside, they headed across the back lawn. Carrie wanted a word with the forensics team, whose last task was taking molds of footprints and tire tread patterns from the track on the far side of the pasture. They were pondering how to negotiate the deep ditch that separated the lawn from the field beyond when Carrie's phone rang.

It was Greg calling. The arrest warrant for Greer had come through sooner than expected; Albany PD was waiting for them. The chat with the forensics team would have to wait.

'What about the Winslows?' said Dylan.

Carrie turned and surveyed the house. 'Greg rattled their chains already, got nothing. No, let them sweat. Back door, like I said. Greer could be the key that unlocks it.'

They made a beeline across the lawn for the front of the house.

'If Greer's the shooter from last night he must have figured by now we're holding Truss,' said Dylan. 'Odds are he's bolted. I know I would have.'

'There are always traces. Look at Hackett . . . had it all worked out, made one small mistake.'

They were nearing the Chevy when Dylan said, 'I think we should take a good look at Joe Winslow.'

'Oh?'

'Just a hunch.'

'They're allowed.'

He explained his thinking to Carrie.

'Interesting,' was her guarded verdict.

'Last night he's the guy pushing for more information, today he's the guy cozying up to Ray.'

'More than interesting when you put it like that.'

'Sounds like his radar's working overtime.'

'Yeah, yeah, I get it. You drive, I'll see what I can turn up on him.'

SIXTY-SIX

'It's me.'

'No shit. Now fuck off. Don't ever call this number again.'

'Eighty thousand dollars and this is what I get?'

'Listen to me. You listening to me? Damn right this is what you get, 'cause I got shot at last night, which means they were waiting for us, which means someone fucked up at your end, which means *you* fucked up. Eighty thousand doesn't even come close to covering the shit I'm looking at here.'

'You got away, didn't you?'

'Just. No such luck for the guy I was with.'

'That's not what I heard.'

'Who from? The cops? Wake up. They're lying, playing dumb. It's what they do. They're all over this thing. The guy who died in the crash, fuck knows how, but they worked out who he is. I just heard they're crawling all over his place. That means two men down, one who can't talk, one who won't 'cause he knows what I'll do to him if he does. Same goes for you if the cops come calling. You still there?'

'Yes.'

'Get over it . . . the money's gone; me too, in about ten minutes. This number ceases to exist the second I hang up, so don't bother trying it. Just remember what I said — they come for me through you it'll be the dumbest thing you ever did, and one of the last. Understood? I want to hear you say it so I don't feel bad when I put a bullet in the back of your head.'

'On past record, you'd miss.'

There was a short snort of laughter. 'That's funny . . . really. Jesus, where do you people come from?'

'The top of the pile, and not by chance.'

'Yeah, well, enjoy the view from up there while you can.'

The line went dead.

SIXTY-SEVEN

Vincent Greer's house lay at the end of a residential cul-de-sac that threaded off through the trees a mile or so west of Ravena. They knew what to expect because they had sat together in the Coeymans police department and surveyed it from on high using Google Maps, and from out the front with Street View. It was a low-slung affair sheathed in vinyl cladding, with an overgrown front yard and a detached double garage at the head of a short driveway. They had also spotted a track running through the trees from behind the garage back toward the highway. It was overgrown but passable, affording Greer a second point of exit.

The first thing they did when their little convoy of vehicles showed up on site was to block off the track with a police cruiser where it hit the blacktop. As arranged, the other police cruiser and the forensics truck hung back, well out of sight, at the entrance to the cul-de-sac. This left two unmarked cars to approach the house: Carrie and Dylan's Chevy, and the anonymous brown sedan belonging to Detectives Wallace and Tanner, who had driven down from Clarksville, where the Criminal Investigation Unit of the Albany County Sheriff's Office was based.

It hadn't taken much persuading on Greg's part to get the CIU on board; Vincent Greer was known to them as a suspected trafficker of narcotics north out of New York City. This presented a possible conflict of interests; Wallace and Tanner were there for themselves, to piggy-back on a warrant issued for an unrelated, out-of-state offense. Carrie wasn't too troubled by this. They were after the same thing in the end — evidence — and with any luck they'd find more than enough to go around.

On Street View, there had been a white RV parked in the driveway. There was no sign of it now. In fact, there was no sign of any vehicles, and the house appeared to be empty. When no one answered the 'Ride of the Valkyries' doorbell, Detective Wallace — a balding, bluff, no-nonsense type — went and got a steel battering ram from the trunk of their car and breached the front door with a few practiced thrusts. They had discussed it before; time was a factor, and forensics would have to wait before doing their thing, even if it meant dealing with a degree of contamination.

It was immediately apparent that someone had left the place in a hurry. The drawers in the master bedroom were open, and clothes lay scattered about. They discovered more evidence of a hasty departure in the study at the back of the house, where papers were strewn all around.

'A mess like this, he's sure to have missed something,' said Carrie.

They could make a cursory first search, but everything would still have to be boxed up and carted away. Detective Wallace took charge of the situation, calling the forensics team and telling them they were good to approach the house. He then contacted the County Sheriff's Office and instructed them to put out on an APB on Greer. Two police officers were set to work questioning neighbors, and they soon learned that Greer had been spotted driving off in the RV a couple of hours earlier. Wallace couldn't get a license plate — there was no such vehicle registered to Greer on the

Department of Motor Vehicles database — but the image on Street View was enough for one of his colleagues back in Clarksville to identify the make and model of the RV.

Meanwhile, Carrie, Dylan and Detective Tanner, a lugubrious beanpole of a man, kept up their search. Carrie discovered that although Greer had remembered to delete the messages from the answering machine before leaving, there was a list of the last numbers called stored away in both the handsets. She recorded them in her notebook and dialed *69 to get the details of the last incoming call to the property. The boxes provided by forensics began to fill with credit card bills and bank statements, invoices and insurance documents, and anything else that might prove useful.

Dylan turned up three cell phones tucked down the back of the couch, all without SIM cards. Tanner went through the trash out back then began tapping walls and yanking up the carpets, searching for hiding places. The shallow loft space above the guest bedroom yielded a dusty cardboard box crammed with vintage porn magazines — *Playboys* and *Hustlers*. If Greer had a girlfriend, there was very little evidence of her other than an open packet of tampons in the cupboard beneath the bathroom sink, together with a pink razor.

A couple of hours flew by. Outside in the lowering sunlight, the forensics team was growing restless. Eventually, Detective Wallace let them loose on the house. There wasn't much more that Dylan and Carrie could do until, with luck, Greer was apprehended.

'Call Evie and tell her you'll be back in time for dinner,' said Carrie.

It was a pleasing thought: his own bed and a chance to catch up properly with Evie after the brief, blunt exchanges of last night and this morning. He got hold of her as she was finishing up for the day at her studio.

'I'm too tired to cook. Can we go out?' She sounded low, like she was entering one of her dips.

'Sure. You choose where.'

'Sasso's?'

'Fine by me.'

Ten minutes later, he and Carrie were on the road back to Connecticut. Carrie was in a good mood.

'Of the three men we know are involved, one's dead, one's in custody and the other's on the run. We've tracked all of them down in under a week and we're tearing their places apart. I'm not saying it's a done deal, but we're close to the tipping point . . . when the weight of evidence swings in our favor and nothing can stop it.'

'When did you get so optimistic?'

'About the time I found this.' Carrie held up an evidence bag. It contained an old envelope stained with reddish food waste. 'I double-checked the garbage out back once Tanner was done with it. The name Truss is written on it next to a cell number . . . the same number we found in Hackett's phone.'

It was the missing link that gave them their three-way connection, tying Truss to both Greer and Hackett.

'You kept quiet about that.'

'Didn't want to show up Tanner in front of his partner. We need them both on our side right now.'

She was about to call Greg and fill him in when Ray rang from Long Island. Carrie put him on speaker. He and Tamsin had made good time, so Ray had decided not to stay the night at the house but to hurry for the last ferry back to Bridgeport.

'Three hours in a car with her will do me for now,' he said.

What with them having to dash off to Albany, it had fallen to Ray to spell out to Tamsin the likely involvement of one or more members of the Winslow family in the attempt on Florence's life.

'How did she take it?' Carrie asked.

'How do you think? Disbelief. Anger. Relief that her daughter's safe at last.'

'Did you tell her about the will?'

'Not much. Thought I'd leave the details to Florence.'

SIXTY-EIGHT

Darkness had fallen outside, bringing unsettling memories of last night with it. Florence said nothing to her mother, who was at the sink, washing the dishes and still singing the praises of the meal that Abel had cooked for them: a seafood extravaganza, with tempura prawns to start, followed by mahi mahi in a ginger glaze. Several large glasses of white wine had loosened her mother's tongue.

'Honestly, darling, he should open a restaurant. You should tell him.'

'Mum, I hardly know him.'

'Then I'll tell him.'

'You already did.'

'Did I? Well, maybe we should back him.' She realized what she had just said, and she was quick to correct herself. 'You. It's your money.'

But it was out now: she saw Lyndon's legacy as hers, too. It wasn't a problem for Florence. Since her father's disappearance, her mother had led a simple life on an English teacher's salary, never once complaining, counting herself lucky compared to most in the world.

'I'm sorry.'

'No, it's okay, Mum. You'll never have to worry about money again.'

Florence took a dish from the draining board and began drying it. Her mother's eyes were shining with soon-to-be tears.

'I don't deserve it. I haven't been there for you.'

'I haven't needed you. I kept you away. It was my way of dealing with it. Alone.'

It was how she had always been — never one to reach for girlfriends when a relationship ended, far happier to mourn on her own and then move on. The truth was, though, she had leaned heavily on friends following Valentine's death, knowing that she wouldn't get through it without them. Only her mother had she pushed away. And if she didn't tell her the truth now, she never would.

'That's a lie. I just couldn't go through it all again with you . . . another death. Dad was enough. It was hell. I needed you to tell me he was gone, so I could let go. But you couldn't give me that, you kept insisting he was alive, making *me* feel bad for not believing it. You even told me if he turned up dead it'd be my fault for not believing it. Do you remember? You were hurting and what did you do? You attacked me, your daughter. It wasn't normal. It *isn't* normal.'

Her mother stared at her, stung by the words. She would normally have struck right back. Not this time.

'*I* wasn't normal,' she said. 'Am I now? Probably not. Will I ever be? I doubt it. Your father was the only man I ever loved.' The tears came now, coursing down her cheeks. 'But I've worked hard at it. I've tried. I've sought help. I can't do more than that.'

'Help?'

'You'd hate him,' she said with a manic laugh. 'Dr. Grogan. He specializes in grief . . . from his fancy Georgian townhouse in Dulwich. What can he possibly know about grief, right? Enough, is the answer. I wouldn't be here now without him. I wouldn't know what a shit I'd been to you.

Such a shit. Such a terrible mother. I'm so sorry, sweet pea, I'm so very sorry . . .'

Florence had never heard her mother speak like this. She had never *seen* her like this: broken, raw, revealed. She stepped forward and wrapped her arms around her.

'You came as soon as you heard about the crash.'

Her mother sobbed into her shoulder.

'It's nothing . . . one stupid flight.'

'It's everything.'

And now Florence was crying too. Mother and daughter bawling like babies over their dead menfolk. And in hopeless gratitude that they still had each other.

SIXTY-NINE

Lyndon's internal clock had somehow reversed itself over the past forty-eight hours, sending him off to sleep during daylight hours and leaving him hopelessly awake at night. In truth, there was very little to distinguish between the two states. Inert, on his back, no longer able to move much more than his eyelids, he might just as well have been asleep.

At least he was pain-free, and the morphine injection administered by Nurse Ratched earlier was enough to ensure he would remain so throughout the night. The drug had sent his thoughts spiraling off on some rather pleasing flights of fancy, an absurdist hodgepodge of memory and imagination, his own private Bunuel movie.

When he heard the footsteps, he didn't open his eyes immediately, conserving the strength for when it was required. Who on earth would be looking in on him at this hour? Not Ratched or Klebb; they never had. Only one person had, and he caught the scent of her a second or two after the footfalls ceased.

He forced open his eyelids.

Heather stood at his bedside, peering down at him dispassionately.

She said nothing. He was the one who spoke, or at least tried to.

'What was that?' she asked.

He tried, and failed, again.

Heather leaned down and put her ear to his lips.

'You're too late,' he said.

He wasn't sure if she had heard the words until she replied, 'Too late? Let's see.'

She stroked his forehead and then slowly ran her hand around to the back of his skull, cradling it for a moment, before raising it up so she could remove the pillow.

The last thing he saw before she pressed the pillow to his face was the curious mix of pity and pleasure in her eyes.

He didn't struggle — what was the point? — and his final thought before the deep darkness wrapped him in its shroud wasn't for himself, but for her. A day here or there meant nothing to a man in his condition, whereas she had just gambled away the remaining years of her life.

He would have laughed, had he been able to breathe.

SEVENTY

Dylan was woken by the muffled ring of his phone, buried beneath the pillow. He answered blind, too bleary-eyed to see who was calling.

'Morning, partner,' said Carrie brightly.

'What time is it?' he growled.

'Time to go to work. Wallace and Tanner came good. Vincent Greer was picked up a couple of hours ago at the Canadian border, trying to slip across in his RV . . . Rouses Point, one of the smaller crossings. He's being shipped back to Albany.'

Dylan was fully awake now. 'That's great news.'

'It gets better. They found Hackett's car, not half a mile from Truss's apartment. Seems you were right; Truss drove it back there after the accident. Forensics are sure to find something.'

'The tipping point . . .'

'It's looking that way. I just went past Naugatuck. You've got half an hour to wash behind your ears.'

'Where are we going?'

'Albany, of course, to have a little chat with Greer. Another thing . . . Lyndon Winslow died last night. Greg just heard.'

'That's too bad,' said Dylan, surprised that he was so saddened by the news.

'Or not. His will stands, which means Florence is safe. There's no longer any incentive to kill her.'

'I guess.'

'Half an hour,' said Carrie.

When Dylan wandered downstairs he found Evie cross-legged on the couch, flipping through a photo album.

'Who was that?' she asked.

'Carrie. They caught Greer . . . crossing into Canada.'

He had told her more than he should have over their pizzas at Sasso's last night. His indiscretion had seemed acceptable, given that she'd helped them out. And later, they had gone to bed and talked some more and held each other. Friends, no longer lovers.

'Congratulations, Badger.'

'Let's see.'

She nodded at the photo album. 'Good times.'

'They'll always be there. And I'll always be here for you.'

She tilted her head at him. 'Have you always been so fucking magnanimous?'

'No, does it suit me?'

'No, it's freaking me out.'

He smiled. 'Coffee?'

'Sure.'

'Remind me how you take it . . .'

'Asshole.'

* * *

He was ready and waiting out front when Carrie pulled up in the Chevy. She vacated the driver's seat for him.

'News just in . . . we need to make a pit stop.'

'Yeah? Where?'

'The Winslow place. Seems Lyndon wrote me a letter.'

Greg had learned of the letter when he'd dropped by the hospital to inform Bevan of his boss's death.

280

'Bevan says the old man dictated the letter to him then made him swear not to mention it until he'd passed. It's hidden in the house.'

'Where?'

Carrie dropped into the passenger seat. 'That's where you come in.'

* * *

They were approaching the house along the driveway when they saw an unmarked black panel van approaching in the opposite direction. Dylan guided the Chevy onto the grass to let it pass. The driver raised his hand by way of thanks. He was wearing a black jacket and black necktie, as was the man seated beside him in the passenger seat.

'Funeral director's van?'

'No hanging around,' said Carrie.

The state trooper on duty out front of the house was the same young guy with the wispy, wannabe mustache who had been turning back traffic at the crash site a week ago.

'Phipps, right?' said Dylan. 'Bodine, accident reconstruction.'

'I remember. Is this connected?'

'You'll have to ask Detective Fuller here.'

'Ma'am,' said Phipps, his curiosity swiftly curtailed.

He had recently fended off a local reporter who had somehow gotten wind of an incident at the house. She had left her card. Carrie took it from Phipps and tucked it into the back pocket of her jeans.

* * *

They found Lyndon's three children seated at the big table in the kitchen, along with Heather. Mary the cook was at the fancy Italian coffee machine, running steam through a jug of milk. Understandably, the mood was somber, subdued.

Olivia had clearly been crying and still had a handkerchief in her hands.

'We just dropped by to express our condolences,' said Carrie. 'He was a special man. He had a way about him.'

'You met him?' asked William.

This drew a flicker of a glance from his brother Ralph, Dylan noted.

'Briefly,' said Carrie. 'Do you mind?' She pulled up a chair. 'We also wanted to fill you in on Bevan. Seems we were wrong about him. His story stands up.'

'What story is that?' asked Ralph.

Dylan's phone rang. He didn't need to check to know it was Carrie calling him; she had surreptitiously thumbed her own cell, as they had planned.

'I'm sorry, I have to take this.' He made for the door, already launching into the phantom conversation: 'Hi, give me a second . . .'

In the corridor leading to the library, he passed a uniformed nurse with some sheets bundled up in her arms. She nodded at him grimly as they crossed.

Lyndon Winslow's bed had been stripped and pushed back against the wall, along with the machines, which now lay ominously silent. Maybe all deaths were sad and pathetic, but the grandeur of the surroundings made it seem even more so for Dylan. All that effort, all that money made, all that beauty accumulated — all these books bought! — only to find yourself dumped in the back of a Ford cargo van.

The letter was exactly where Bevan had said it would be: to the right of the fireplace, three shelves up, tucked into the first volume of Charles Darwin's *The Descent of Man*. Something told him the hiding place hadn't been chosen at random.

A silver-framed photo on the mantelpiece above the fireplace caught his eye. It was of a young man standing in the shallows of a swimming pool, arms raised, gripping the hands of a skinny boy standing on his shoulders. Valentine and Joe, uncle and nephew, years ago, both of them beaming wildly at the camera.

The staccato tap of heels on wood announced the arrival of someone in the library. Dylan quickly slipped the letter down the front of his pants, but there wasn't time to return the book to its place on the shelf.

He turned to see Heather Winslow approaching him.

'What are you doing here?' she asked, not unpleasantly.

'Having a last look. I've never seen a room like it . . . well, not in a private house.'

She held out her hand for the book. 'Are you a big reader?'

'Yes, I am.'

'Of Darwin?'

He dredged his memory for anything intelligent to say on the subject, or even something unintelligent. The History Channel came to his aid.

'Do you know the story about his nose?'

'Darwin's nose?'

'The captain of the *Beagle* almost didn't allow Darwin to sail with them because of his nose. He didn't think it was the nose of a man who was up to making such a long and tough sea journey.'

'Fascinating.'

Not exactly sarcastic, but not far off.

'It is when you think it could have changed the course of human history.'

'For the better, some would say.'

'I guess . . . if you think ignorance is a virtue.'

'It can be,' said Heather, reaching past him and pushing the book back into its slot. 'Are you done snooping?'

'I'm sorry, I didn't mean to—'

'It was a joke,' she said, almost convincingly.

Dylan nodded at the photo of Valentine and Joe. 'Great shot.'

'That was the first day of the new millennium.'

'Looks like they were close.'

'Not particularly,' said Heather. 'Shall we?'

She seemed eager to be gone — too eager — and as they returned to the kitchen, he held back, saying he had a call to make.

To be sure of some privacy, he cut through the drawing room and out onto the back terrace before pulling up Florence's number.

* * *

'She lied to me,' said Dylan. 'Florence says Valentine and Joe were tight as anything, peas in a pod. Why would Heather lie to me about something like that?'

Carrie pulled open the passenger door of the Chevy. 'Who knows? Maybe Lyndon's got something to say on it.'

Dylan dropped behind the wheel and pulled the letter from the front of his pants.

'Nice,' said Carrie.

She sat and read the letter in absorbed silence while he drove them north through Canaan; and as soon as she had finished, she read it through again.

'Well . . .' was all she could manage when she was done.

'What is it?'

'An apology, a farewell . . . a theory. You get a mention.'

'Can I read it?'

'Sure. Pull over.'

Dylan read the letter in the gravel lot of a fencing store just south of Sheffield. It was hard to believe Lyndon Winslow was dead; his voice came through so clearly in the words he had dictated to Bevan.

'He couldn't leave it alone . . . you were right.'

'So were you, it seems,' said Carrie.

'It's meaningless without proof, which he admits he doesn't have.'

'Yeah, only a theory,' she conceded, 'but one we can now test.'

'With Greer? You hit him with this, he'll just deny it.'

'There's more than one way to skin a cat.'

SEVENTY-ONE

The Detective Division of Albany PD was based out of the South Station, a nineteenth-century brick building tucked behind the blandly modern City Courthouse. Dylan found a space in the scrappy parking lot that ran the length of both buildings.

Detectives Wallace and Tanner were exhausted but in high spirits. They'd just had the lab results back on a package of powder they'd found hidden in Vincent Greer's garage. It was carfentanil, a synthetic opioid used for tranquilizing elephants, about a hundred times stronger than fentanyl. Possession of forty grams of the substance ranked as a first-degree felony, and Greer was looking at some serious jail time based on that alone. They were hoping to turn up evidence of distribution as their investigation progressed, another first-degree felony. Greer had yet to be charged. In fact, he had been there for little more than an hour, in one of the holding cells.

It was good news for Carrie and Dylan; Greer was going nowhere, which meant they had plenty of time to tie him forensically to the Winslow house. It would take only the tiniest scrap of DNA.

* * *

Dylan watched from behind the one-way mirror with Wallace and Tanner as Carrie entered the interview room. She sat down, then took a slug from one of the two plastic water bottles on the table.

Greer was led into the room by a couple of cops.

'That him, the guy who fired at you?' Wallace asked Dylan.

'I couldn't swear to it in court.'

Greer was tall, good-looking, even more so than the photo they'd seen of him yesterday suggested. He moved with an easy grace for a big man, and his long, dark hair was tucked behind his ears. The cops sat him at the table opposite Carrie. One of them left the room, the other took up a position next to the door.

Carrie unscrewed the cap of the second water bottle and slid it across the table. Greer's hands were cuffed in front of him, but he was still able to take a drink.

'You my lawyer?' he asked.

'I look like a lawyer?'

'No, you look like a dyke.'

'I *am* a dyke.'

Dylan was aware of Wallace and Tanner trading a look.

'I don't have a problem with that,' said Greer. 'My sister's gay.'

'Phew, I can relax.'

Greer smiled, revealing perfect white teeth. 'You must be new. I know most of these assholes by sight.'

'I'm not from around here.'

'No? Where you from?'

'Take a wild guess, Vincent.'

It was almost nothing, the barest flicker in Greer's large dark eyes.

'Paris, Texas?' he ventured.

'Film buff, eh? I'll give you a clue: it's about an hour southeast of here.'

Greer shrugged. 'Don't know that part of the world.'

'Lot of hills.'

'Lot of hills everywhere.'

'Not in the Mississippi delta,' said Carrie.

'Don't know that part of the world neither.'

Carrie leaned forward. 'Well, know this . . . it was us who triggered the arrest warrant, not Albany.'

'Oh?'

'Judges don't hand them out like confetti. They require evidence first . . . hard evidence.'

'If you say so,' said Greer.

'You don't want to know how we were on to you so quick?'

Greer shrugged. 'Couldn't give a rat's ass, 'cause all this talk is bullshit and you know it.'

'Fair enough,' said Carrie.

She pushed back her chair and got to her feet.

'That it?' Greer asked.

Dylan was thinking the same thing.

'You said you didn't want to know. I'm happy to respect that.'

Dylan noted that Greer tracked Carrie with his eyes all the way to the door, where she turned.

'You know, you're a handsome sonofabitch.'

'Gee, thanks.'

'Not much between the ears, though. Word of advice for when you get out of jail, which you will one day, nowhere near as handsome as you are now. Pick your clients more carefully, Vincent — turns out Joe Winslow is a squealer.'

There was a tightening of the jaw muscles beneath the black stubble, and a slight narrowing of the eyes.

'Who's Joe Winslow?'

'See you around,' said Carrie.

She nodded at the cop then left the room.

'What the fuck was that?' muttered Wallace.

'That was genius,' said Dylan.

Carrie had played Greer to perfection, teasing, flattering and ultimately bluffing the truth out of him. If Dylan had detected the momentary giveaway in Greer's expression, then so had she.

It was the confirmation they'd been looking for.

Lyndon Winslow's hunch about his grandson was sound.

SEVENTY-TWO

Carrie was more circumspect; that much became clear as they made their way down the ramp from the South Station building.

'Knowing's not enough. And we can't be sure Joe was acting alone.'

'So, what do we do now?'

'Fuck knows, I'm all out of ideas. What have you got?'

They stopped at the Chevy and talked it through under the cyclopean glare of the sun, the smell of baked asphalt in their nostrils.

If Joe was simply the point of contact with Greer, then the three people who had stood to profit most from Florence's death were all gathered together right now, back at the Winslow house. It was an inviting prospect, leaning hard on them and seeing what gave. In the end, though, Carrie went with Lyndon Winslow's instinct, as spelled out in his letter to her: that none of his three children was involved in the attempt on Florence's life.

'No, let's pay a visit to young Joe. He's not a Greer, not a Truss. This isn't his world. I figure he'll fold without a fight if we surprise him.'

Dylan tried to tamp down the excitement building in his belly. If she was right, all that separated them from solving the case — his first-ever case — was a short drive south to New York City.

* * *

As soon as they were on the move, Carrie turned to her bible: the black notebook where she scribbled, scrawled and doodled her thoughts, and in which all her research was stored away. The latest entry was the stuff she'd dug up on Joe yesterday. He was the editor of an online monthly magazine called *The Stethoscope*.

'"Real Writers Taking the Nation's Pulse Twelve Times a Year,"' she read off.

'Sounds a little self-important.'

'Maybe that's Joe's problem.'

The Stethoscope tackled anything that took its fancy, from current affairs through to the arts. Being subscription-only, there wasn't much more Carrie had been able to discover about it, other than a list of contributors and some glowing accolades.

Carrie pulled up the website on her phone. The head office address turned out to be in Williamsburg, next door to Brooklyn. They didn't want a wasted journey, but neither did they want to alert Joe to their visit, so Carrie called the number listed, ready to hang up if she got put through to him.

It wasn't required. A woman informed her that Joe was out of the office.

'That's not good,' said Carrie. The next issue of *The Stethoscope* was due out in only two days, so why wasn't Joe at work, on the case? 'We need to find out where the hell he is.'

'Where's he going to go?'

'Greer ran. He knew the net was closing. We have to assume they've been in touch.'

They had the cell numbers for the whole Winslow clan; Greg had gotten them yesterday, to check against Hackett's abandoned Samsung and Greer's home phone. Their options were limited, though, when it came to calling Joe. It had to come from someone who could be trusted, and it had to sound natural.

'What about Alice?' Dylan suggested. 'She rode back into the city with him yesterday. Quick call to say see how he's bearing up after his grandfather's death?'

'Maybe.'

'Still not sure about her?'

'No, just struggling to admit I was wrong.' She hesitated. 'I called her father last night, who's also her boss. He persuaded me.'

'How did he manage that?'

'With charm and humor,' she said. 'Interesting man . . . bit of the Lyndon about him. Seems his daughter's not too good to be true, after all.'

'Someone once told me that most of being right is being wrong first.'

Carrie smiled. 'Still sticks in the craw, though.'

Unlike Joe, Alice was back at work in her office.

'Any news?' she asked.

'You sitting down?' said Carrie.

Alice was on speaker, and Dylan heard every incredulous 'Christ . . .' and 'No way . . .' as Carrie spelled out the breakneck developments since Alice had left Connecticut yesterday.

'Did you see it?' Carrie asked, meaning Joe.

'Now you say it. The look in his eye when his guard was down . . . his kindness to Florence . . . his wariness of me.'

'Of you?'

'Nothing obvious, but I could feel it. Or maybe that's just 20/20 hindsight.'

When it came to putting in a call to Joe, Alice didn't feel she was the right person to do it. They hadn't exchanged numbers, and it would come across as strange to him if she suddenly made contact.

'How about Tamsin?' she suggested.

'Florence's mother?'

'They hit it off, her and Joe. He was the only one who gave her a properly warm welcome when she showed up.'

Dylan recalled the heartfelt hug that the pair of them had shared on the front steps of the house yesterday as Joe was leaving.

'I know she has his number,' Alice went on. 'I saw him put it in her phone.'

Carrie turned to Dylan. 'Tamsin could work, no?'

He didn't answer. He was picturing Tamsin's phone in Joe's hands.

'What is it?' asked Carrie.

'I'm wondering what else he might have done with her phone while he had a hold of it.'

Carrie saw it now.

'Alice, we'll call you back.'

SEVENTY-THREE

It had been Abel's idea to show them Peconic Bay in his boat, and her mother couldn't have been happier, especially now that they'd crossed the featureless expanse of water and were meandering along narrow waterways through patches of marshland teeming with birdlife.

Florence's phone started ringing, the sound cutting through the gentle hum of the motor and eliciting an irritable glance from her mother. She was about to reject the call when she saw that it was Carrie Fuller.

'I should take this.'

'Do you absolutely have to?'

She answered the call, but before she could say anything, Carrie demanded urgently: 'Where are you?'

'Abel, where are we?'

'West Neck Creek.'

'West Neck Creek.'

'Shit, you're on a boat?'

'Abel's boat.'

'Tell him to steer well clear of all landings,' said Carrie. 'Better still, put him on.'

Abel listened. He said very little, just the odd 'Got you' and 'Sure' and 'No problem.' He also said, 'Yeah, my gun's down below.'

That was the moment when everything changed.

Abel handed her phone back, and this time Dylan was also on the line, on speaker. She could tell that they were in a car.

'Florence, listen, does your mother have her phone with her?' he asked.

'Mum, do you have your phone?'

'Yes.'

'Give it to me.'

She fished it from her tasseled shoulder bag and passed it to Florence.

'Is it on right now?' asked Dylan.

'Yes.'

'Does she have Google Maps?'

Florence swiped through a couple of screens. 'Yes.'

'Open the app.'

His instructions were very precise, and her hand, she noticed, was trembling slightly as she followed the steps. 'What's this about?'

'Probably nothing. Almost there.' She executed the final step and he asked her what she saw on the screen.

'Joe Winslow.'

It was there in black and white.

'Turn the phone off right now,' said Dylan.

She did as he ordered. 'I don't understand.' 'Joe?'

It was Carrie who replied. 'We're pretty sure he's behind it.'

The words landed like a punch in her gut. She groped for the bench beside her and sat down. It couldn't be. Not Joe. But they had to have their reasons for thinking it.

'Why?' she muttered.

'Let's not worry about that for now,' said Carrie. 'We have to figure out what we're going to do with you.'

'He's coming for me still.'

It wasn't a question, or even a statement. It was a moment of stark realization. The beautiful saltbox house on

293

the water, the calming presence of Abel, the reconciliation with her mother, they had all been a big illusion, a wishful dream. The living nightmare was back. She would never be at peace.

'We don't know that, but we don't want to take any chances,' said Dylan. 'We're coming to find you. Nothing's going to happen. It'll be okay.'

He said it with that voice of his, that languid voice with a touch of reassuring gravel, the one that folded itself around you like a pair of arms.

It helped.

'What do you want us to do?' she asked.

'Get Abel to turn the boat around, head back to the bay,' said Carrie. 'We'll figure something out.'

SEVENTY-FOUR

Hope for the best, plan for the worst. True to the old maxim, they took the bleakest possible view of the situation: that Joe was already there, close by and set on doing harm to Florence. The fact that he had tampered with Tamsin's phone suggested that he'd banked on mother and daughter being reunited. Yes, Lyndon had died in the meantime — his legacy to Florence was assured — but there was no way of knowing if that meant an end of it for Joe, too.

'We presuppose it doesn't, even if it turns out we're wrong,' said Carrie.

Returning to the house on Mattituck Creek was out of the question; they had to assume Joe knew where it was by now, and also that he'd tracked the trio earlier when they'd driven to Strong's Marine — south of Mattituck, on the bayside — where Abel kept his boat.

Carrie had calculated that their quickest route to Peconic Bay was by road all the way; cutting the corner with the Bridgeport–Port Jefferson ferry saved on distance but not time. They were looking at close to three hours according to Satnav — three long hours in which anything could happen.

Carrie proposed a solution: that they get Abel to head back to the marina, where the local cops would be waiting on the dock to take Florence and her mother into protective custody.

'I don't know,' said Dylan. 'Let's say Joe's also there. The second he sees the cops, he knows he's been rumbled, knows the game's up. What if he flips out? I'm not comfortable with a couple of cops we've never met before handling this situation. They don't even know what he looks like.'

'True.'

'Right now he thinks he's in control. Yeah, he lost the trace on Tamsin's phone, but that could be because it's out of juice.'

They continued to discuss the options, narrowing them down until only one remained that met with their joint approval. It would mean Abel and the others killing time out on Peconic Bay, then rendezvousing with them at a different location, not the marina back in Mattituck.

A swift transfer from boat to car. In and out in a couple of minutes.

They phoned Abel, who approved of the idea.

'Let me think of somewhere,' he said. 'I'll call you right back.'

SEVENTY-FIVE

Florence had never been at the wheel of a motorboat before, but it was easy enough to master. You picked a landmark on the distant shoreline and you aimed at it, standing there, or sitting if it took your fancy. Abel's boat had a padded vinyl seat on a post that you could perch on if you wanted to.

Abel appeared from down below and handed her a can of Diet Coke. She relinquished the wheel to him.

'Your mother's quite a woman,' he said.

'You think?'

'I do. She's asleep.'

'You're kidding.'

'Nope, out for the count. I don't know how she does it, I'm a nervous wreck.'

'This is you as a nervous wreck?'

Abel had been as calm as anything since Carrie first called with the news about Joe. Since then, they had followed the southern shoreline of the bay, then cut across to Robins Island, where they had anchored, Abel standing guard while she and her mother had swum in the gin-clear shallows. Killing time. Now they were heading directly west across the bay to the place where they were to meet up with Dylan and Carrie.

'I'm good at hiding that stuff,' said Abel. 'Ask my wife.'

'At least you'll be back with her tonight . . . Tinker, too.'

Tinker was their daughter. She sounded like a blast, and also a handful. Ten going on sixteen.

'Come and see us when this is over,' said Abel.

'I'd like that.'

They continued west for a while, a comfortable silence hanging between them.

'Thanks for stepping in the way you did.'

Abel shrugged. 'Got a life that allows me to. And there's not much I wouldn't do for Carrie.'

'Oh?'

'Life threw me a curveball a while back.'

'Yeah?'

'She caught it.'

'More, please.'

'You're in good hands.'

'God, you're infuriating.'

Abel smiled. 'My wife would have something to say about that, too.'

He tilted up his sunglasses and squinted into the distance.

'Best go wake your mother. We're almost there.'

SEVENTY-SIX

The winding road through the woods petered out at a small parking lot with trees pressing in on the right. It was just as Abel had described it: a remote headland with a long, high spit of sand trailing off to the left, out into the water. Tucked into the lea of the spit, a hundred yards or so from the parking lot, was a crude wooden dock where a couple of sailboats were berthed.

While Carrie put in the call, Dylan got out of the Chevy and arched his back to release the tension. In three hours they had stopped only once, to fill up with gas near Little Neck. He glanced around him. A narrow wooden boardwalk snaked off from the lot, up and over the dune that masked the bay from view. Beside it, a sign spelled out the standard regulations for the beach beyond.

'Two minutes,' said Carrie, appearing beside him. 'They're coming in now.'

'More driving.'

''Fraid so.'

Greg had sorted out another safe house for Florence and her mother near Milford, back in Connecticut.

'We let her down again,' said Dylan.

'We're here, aren't we? Don't beat yourself up, he's a clever little fucker.'

They saw a motorboat round the tip of the spit. Three people. Carrie gave a wave and received one in return. Dylan set off along the boardwalk toward the dune.

'Where are you going?'

'Just curious,' he said.

Clever little fucker. Just how clever? How determined?

He told himself he had nothing to worry about, but he found himself jogging up the boardwalk to the crest of the dune, where the beach grass bowed before the onshore breeze.

Below him, between the tumble of rocks on his right and the far end of the spit, there were people spread out along the sand, enjoying the sunshine and the waning afternoon heat. A couple of skinny young boys were flinging a frisbee around at the water's edge. An idyllic scene. Just one false note, away to his left: a motorboat wallowing in the shallows, beached, abandoned.

He wasn't the only one to have noticed it. A few people nearby were on their feet, staring at the motorboat, and also at the man hurrying up the frontal face of the dune. He was too far off to identify, and Dylan didn't attempt to.

He turned and started running back down the boardwalk.

Halfway along it, instinct told him to bear right, cutting the corner toward the dock, which came into view as he breasted a gentle rise in the sand.

Abel was expertly edging his boat into the space between the two sailboats; Carrie was making her way over from the parking lot; and farther along, the man had cleared the top of the dune and was approaching the dock at an angle down the slope. He was wearing shorts, sneakers, shades and a floppy white sun hat that cast his face in shadow. He was trying to look casual, head bowed, hands in his pockets, no longer hurrying, nothing to draw attention to himself.

Dylan read the scene in a moment and saw how it would unfold. This was his world, the geometry of it: the distances, speeds and angles of approach. The inevitable collision that he was too far off to prevent. Unless . . .

He called Carrie, praying that she had her phone on her. She did. It was in her hand and she answered immediately.

'Don't look. Don't react. You have about ten seconds to get everybody out of sight. Do it now. I'll do the rest.'

He pulled his handgun from its holster and cut back up the dune, picking a path across the sand that would keep him out of the man's eyeline. Carrie was on the dock now, and Abel was tying up the boat. She took him by the elbow and steered him back onboard.

The man must have sensed something in this maneuver, because he hurried ahead, something in his hand now. When Carrie shepherded Florence and her mother back toward the cabin, the man broke into a run. So did Dylan, veering left down the dune, his Sig levelled in case he was spotted.

The man's arm came up and he fired twice when he was some twenty yards shy of the boat. They sounded like harmless pops, but a chunk of wood went flying from the cabin door that Carrie had just hauled shut behind them. Dylan powered forward, narrowing the gap, his thighs burning from the sucking sand.

The man leaped aboard the boat and tried the cabin door. When it wouldn't give, he aimed his gun at the lock and turned his face away.

That's when he saw Dylan. That's when Dylan saw that it was indeed Joe Winslow.

'Police!' he yelled. 'Drop the gun!'

Joe chose to raise it instead. Dylan fired first. Traveling at speed across uneven ground, he was surprised to see Joe jerked to one side and sent sprawling on the deck. He scrabbled off, out of sight, shielded by the high gunwales.

Dylan swept the deck area with his gun before stepping cautiously aboard. Joe's gun had skittered away from him, but it was back in his hand now and he was turning, rising to his feet. He froze when he saw that Dylan had beaten him to the draw.

'Police! Drop your weapon!'

They had been taught to shout it. Shouting had a way of incapacitating a person. Not Joe, though. He was weighing his next move. His left arm hung limp at his side from the wound in his shoulder. Blood dripped from the tips of his fingers onto the deck.

'How?' Joe growled.

'It doesn't matter how, just drop the gun.'

'No.'

Dylan was ready for anything. Joe's presence here was an act of pure recklessness. He had hired a boat and presumably followed them all day around Peconic Bay — biding his time, waiting for an opportunity — before beaching the vessel in full of witnesses. He had come here knowing he would incriminate himself. That made him unpredictable and very dangerous.

'You can't have her, Joe. It's over.'

Joe's eyes flicked past Dylan to the cabin.

'You're a smart guy. What did you think your chances are?'

'What if I don't care?' said Joe.

'Then you die.'

'I'm dead anyway.'

'Is that what Greer told you?' The name struck a visible chord. 'He can't touch you. We have him in custody. That's right. Which means only one person has died so far. What do you say we leave it at that, the lowlife Florence smashed into?'

'It's all her fault,' Joe said with venom.

'If you say so.'

'It's because of her that Valentine went away.'

'That's not what I heard.'

'You don't know!' yelled Joe. 'She turned him against us. She took him away. Then she killed him.'

'Sepsis killed him.'

'She didn't fly him home! He'd be alive if she had. And now this . . . the money, the Winslow Trust! Who does she think she is?'

It wasn't the time to engage with the workings of Joe Winslow's twisted psyche.

'I got to be honest, Joe, I don't give a shit. All I care about is that gun in your hand.'

'What, this one?'

Joe jammed the muzzle under his own chin.

'Don't!' Dylan yelled.

'Not like that!' called Carrie, peering round the cabin window. 'I've seen it. All you'll do is blow off a bit of your tongue, lose some teeth, maybe an eye. Stick it in your mouth, angle it back. Forty-five degrees should do it.'

Like Dylan, Joe couldn't quite believe what he was hearing, and in a fit of irate impulse, he aimed at the cabin and fired.

A brief window of opportunity. Dylan's brain made the calculations, signed off on them and sent the signals to his limbs. He launched himself at Joe, who was turning back when the fist caught him square in the nose, sending him reeling onto the deck.

Dylan had failed to follow up on Bevan a few nights ago, learning a lesson he would never forget. He was on Joe in a moment, wrestling the gun from his hand. He hurled it aside then twisted back and drove his elbow into the side of Joe's head. Then a second time, for good measure.

Joe fell still and limp beneath him.

Dylan was breathing heavily, sucking in air, when Carrie appeared beside him.

He looked up at her. She peered down at Joe and winced.

'Oof, that nose is going to need surgery.'

'I was meant to do that, right?'

'As many perps as possible, alive and in custody, that's what I was taught. Makes all the difference when it comes to court.' Her hand landed briefly on his shoulder. 'Not bad for a beginner. Stay here; I'll go get some rope.'

SEVENTY-SEVEN

Their first night on the road, when Carrie had picked up the tab for dinner in Burlington, she had told Dylan he could return the favor once they'd solved the case. When it came to it, though, Carrie proposed dinner at her and Abby's place in New Haven.

The timing seemed a little premature: just five days since the incident with Joe on Peconic Bay, the press all over the story still, Heather Winslow's arrest two days ago whipping the media frenzy into a firestorm. No one had seen it coming. Well, maybe one person had. Why else had Lyndon asked Bevan to ensure that the camera used by the nurses to monitor him during the day be left on at night? He hadn't explained his reasoning at the time, but when Carrie had heard of it from Bevan, her interest had been piqued enough to pull up the digital recordings.

Carrie and Dylan had been present at Heather's arrest, although for jurisdictional reasons it was the local chief of police who had served the warrant and read her her rights. This had happened in the lobby of Stony Brook Southampton Hospital, when Heather and William showed up there to visit their son, who was still recovering from the damage done to him by Dylan.

Heather had folded immediately under questioning. She had guessed it was Joe; she had confronted him, argued with him; and although he had denied it, she had known it in her marrow, as mothers do. That's why she had smothered Lyndon, or so she claimed: to end it, to put a halt to her son's rampage. There were few who didn't believe Heather's story. As excuses went, it hung together. As excuses went in the eyes of the law, it was an admission of murder. A man's life had been terminated prematurely by her hand. Two hands, in fact, pressing down with force upon a pillow.

The footage was chilling. A brief exchange of words followed by a cursory execution. As Greg had said on seeing it for the first time: 'Pure *Game of Thrones*.' The defense would inevitably plead mitigating circumstances at Heather's trial, possibly with some success, but no one doubted that she was facing a lengthy spell behind bars.

* * *

Florence couldn't make the dinner — she and her mother had flown back to the UK to avoid the press attention — but Alice drove up from the city, lured by the offer of a bed for the night. Dylan headed down there with Ray, who picked him up in Torrington on his way through.

Abby's house was on Granite Bay, just east of New Haven. It was a ramshackle weatherboard affair right on the water, with a small dock at the foot of the garden. She had bought it for a song and done it up herself following her split from Arlo's father, even laying the hardwood boards that ran right through the house and out onto the long deck, where drinks were served on their arrival.

It was a warm evening, windless, and the dying sunlight lay like an orange shawl over the bay. Arlo listened with wide-eyed wonderment as they talked and touched on aspects of the case. He knew that Carrie caught bad men, but he didn't know she was so good at it.

When Carrie asked if Dylan would join her for a stroll on the beach, Arlo demanded to go with them.

Abby stepped in. 'Hey, matey, you said you'd help me make the salad.'

'Mommy . . .' Arlo bleated.

'A promise is a promise. Alice will show you how to chop the tomatoes.'

'Don't bank on it, I have a servant who does it for me.'

'You have a servant?'

'So many I don't even know their names,' said Alice, steering Arlo inside. 'I call them one, two, three, four and five.'

* * *

They took a footpath at the end of the garden, through the rocks to a short crescent of sand. On Carrie's lead, they kicked off their shoes, rolled up their trousers and walked through the gently lapping waves at the water's edge.

Dylan sensed that she had something to tell him, and he had an idea what it might be.

'That was the best, Dyl . . . best ever.'

'I've no way of judging.'

'Believe me, it had everything. Who'd have thought it? Right at the end of my career, I finally land the partner I've been looking for.' She glanced at him. 'It's true.'

'I don't know what to say.'

'It started with you, it ended with you. Man, that was something. You knew he was coming for her; you felt it.'

'I feel a lot of things and I'm usually wrong.'

'No, you knew it, you went to look, and Florence is alive because of it.'

'The only reason she's alive is because of Lyndon's letter to you.'

Carrie nodded. 'True. We'd have got to Joe — we were right there — but not before he got to her.'

'Tiny margins. Creeps me out when I think about it. We got lucky just enough times. I don't suppose it always goes that way.'

'No,' she replied quietly.

'What happened, Carrie? When you were with the FBI?'

She hesitated. 'Like I told you, that's my shit. Maybe one day.'

So, he was wrong. She hadn't brought him here to unburden herself.

Carrie pulled an envelope from her pocket. 'The letter from Lyndon. It was in the Chevy. You should enter it as evidence.'

'Bring it with you on Monday.'

'I'm not coming in on Monday.'

'Careful, my dear,' he joked, 'you'll blow your pension if you don't see out your last couple of weeks.'

'It's all sorted with Greg. And it's not like I have a choice.'

She drew to a halt and turned to face him.

'Dylan, I'm ill.'

He struggled to process the information.

'Ill? What do you mean? What kind of ill?'

'Mammogram ill.'

He stared at her, recalling her mention of mammograms when they'd met up with Mrs. Chiltern at the hospital in Burlington.

'They caught it early, but they need to operate. Soon. Tuesday.'

'How long have you known?'

'Since just before Greg dumped some smartass kid from accident reconstruction on me.' She smiled. 'Sorry if I was a bit crabby that first day.'

'Jesus, Carrie.' He heard the crack in his voice.

'Chin up, buster, I'm going to beat it.'

'Of course you are, of course you fucking are.'

'This old bird is not going down without a fight.'

That did it for him, and she stepped forward to hold him.

'Hey, aren't you the one who's supposed to be comforting me?'

He laughed; they both did, clinging to each other, the water washing around their ankles.

SEVENTY-EIGHT

It was past midnight when Ray dropped him back in Torrington. Ray had chatted incessantly for much of the journey about everything from the a cappella group he sang with to his difficult daughter and his ongoing spat with the North Canaan Beautification Committee. Carrie's illness wasn't discussed; enough had been said about it. She had brought up the subject with the others after dinner, as soon as Arlo had gone to bed. Somehow, it had still been a jolly evening. They had even danced a little at the end to some old eighties tunes.

It was Dylan's first night alone in the house, and he was dreading it. Beth had driven Evie to New York that morning, and tomorrow he would be heading down with another carload of her gear, which now stood neatly stacked in boxes near the front door, ready for him to load.

He stared at the pile then went in search of a bottle of whiskey. He poured himself a big one with ice and put on some Van Morrison, a hero to him and his fellow band members back in the day. A dose of nostalgia seemed appropriate.

Remembering the letter from Lyndon in his jacket pocket, he pulled the pages from the envelope and flopped onto the couch.

Dear Detective Fuller,

If you are reading this, then I am on my way to the furnace. I don't mean the big one down below. I don't believe such a place exists. Rather, I am with Shakespeare, who wrote: 'Hell is empty, and all the devils are here.' I don't suppose there's anything new in that for you, seeing as you have devoted your life to hunting them down.

It now appears there may be one at the heart of my own family. You didn't say as much to me, but you said enough to set me thinking, which I'm guessing was your intention. Am I wrong? I think not. I suspect you knew exactly what you were doing — putting me to work for you.

I have stopped struggling with my conscience. I have accepted that I must bear the blame for triggering the unfortunate events that you are now dealing with. I apologize to you and your handsome young partner for that, but it is what is; the die is cast. I have done what I can to help you. I am too weak to do any more. It wasn't easy, taking up your challenge. The sanctity of family, its protection at all costs and under all circumstances, has been drilled into me since birth. Very late in life, I see the error of that thinking, its self-serving duplicity. It is the hard-nosed preservation of privilege dressed up with noble words. It is a pink ribbon on a sow's ear.

There is nothing noble in what I am about to tell you. I am breaking my word to the man I count as my dearest friend. I said I would do all in my power to protect him if he told me the truth, which he did. Well, now I am denouncing him to you and destroying him in the process. Victor Penfold informed my daughter Olivia of the changes I had instructed him to make to my will. Olivia then shared that information with her husband, Chester, and together they went to William and Heather's house and told them of it too.

One can hardly claim to know oneself, let alone one's children, and certainly not their spouses, but following my questioning of them all I do not believe they are behind the attempt on Florence's life, collectively or individually. A relief to an old and dying man, unless he is unable to persuade himself that the blame lies with your vengeful General Ngomo from Zimbabwe.

I don't have much to offer you, but here it is — a small falsity that maybe speaks of something bigger. The other day, my grandson Joe admitted in front of us all that he had recently met Florence for lunch in New York, at her suggestion. Nothing too unusual in that. She had always got on far better with Joe than any of us. Why wouldn't she call him out of the blue to see how he was doing? The truth is, though, she didn't.

It came out in a conversation with Florence that Joe was the one who had contacted her and suggested lunch. He happened to do this a week after Olivia and Chester had been to see William and Heather and tell them about the changes to the will. He happened to do this while he was still living with his parents, although he has moved out since. Why did he lie? Did he overhear the conversation between the two couples? Did it stir something dark in him, something untapped? Was he ingratiating himself with Florence to assist the plan already taking shape in his head?

Those are some of the questions I asked myself. There is another. Who is Joe Winslow? It's hard to say, given how private he is, how private he has always been. A young man who adored his dead uncle Valentine considerably more than he despises his own father, that much I know. A secretive child, sometimes cruel, usually to animals, that I know too. I am not condemning him, that is for you to do if there happens to be any truth in these observations.

They prove nothing, I know, but they may be of help in your mission. I wish you well with it. There is much at stake, not

310

*least the life of dear Florence, who is destined to do great
things with the opportunities I have handed her. Protect her.
See that she is safe. I beg you both.*

*It was a pleasure to meet you, Detective Fuller. Even if all you
were doing was bending an old, sick man to your own ends, I
would still have liked to know you better. Another regret to
add to the list.
With affection,
Lyndon Winslow*

Dylan laid the letter aside and took a sip of whiskey.

He had been wrong earlier when he'd said to Carrie it
was Lyndon's letter that had saved Florence's life. The letter
had only been written because Carrie had read the situation
early and worked a subtle number on the old boy.

Yes, he had done his bit — some of his insights had
been crucial to the case — but the credit was all Carrie's,
for her vision, for the way she had shaped the investigation:
targeting the henchmen while getting Lyndon Winslow to
play detective from his bed.

Big picture versus nuts-and-bolts. Or rather, both working together, each reliant on the other for the machine to
function as a whole. Could it ever be the same with someone
else? He knew the answer, and he didn't care.

All that mattered now was that Carrie defeated her sick-
ness and survived.

SEVENTY-NINE

Santa Marta's untidy suburban straggle petered out behind them, concrete and dust giving way to lush greenery as the bus climbed into the mountains, its engine laboring against a full load of passengers. Many were young backpackers headed for Tayrona National Park; most were locals going about their business. As ever in Colombia, there was music, loud music: homegrown reggaeton blasting from the driver's Bluetooth speaker.

No one complained. Across the aisle from Dylan and Florence, an old man with a chicken on his lap tapped his foot in time to the beat and gave them a toothless smile. There were no formal stops; the driver simply hit the brakes whenever someone flagged him down. Soon after the road leveled out and the bus began to descend toward the coast, Dylan and Florence gave up their seats to a mother and her young daughter, receiving some slices of melon by way of thanks.

* * *

An ancient pickup from the hotel was waiting for them at the head of the dirt track. Florence chatted away in Spanish to the driver as the vehicle bumped and rolled its way over the potholes, down through the trees. Suddenly there was water all around: a wide river off to their left, and the blue Caribbean ahead, with lines of lazy breakers rolling in.

The hotel, once a private house, was a crazy jumble of pitched, thatched roofs. It stood perched like a giant bird on a high rock, where the river met the sea. The expanse of spongy green lawn out front offered a sweeping view up the river to the slab of jagged mountains beyond, and the eerie silence on the landward side contrasted with the steady thump of waves on the other.

The guts of the building were open to the elements, with crude wooden staircases angling up from the communal area to the rooms aloft. Florence had ensured that they both had rooms facing the sea. They were also open to the elements, with no walls between the rooms proper and the wide wooden balconies thrusting out into the void. Florence had a hammock slung across hers; Dylan's was furnished with a small table and two chairs; and from both there was a forty-foot drop to the water below.

They unpacked, showered and then met up on the lawn. Dylan arrived first, taking a seat and watching the sun go down over the purple mountains. When Florence appeared, she had the gray plastic urn tucked under her arm.

'You want to do it now?' he asked.

'Let's raise a cocktail to him first.'

The thatched bar sat just down the slope. They both opted for caipirinhas, and they toasted Lyndon.

'Thanks for coming,' said Florence.

'It was a tough call . . . a three-day break in Colombia paid for by someone else.'

'Not much of a break, with all the travel either end.'

He spread his hands. 'This feels pretty fucking good right now.'

She smiled. 'Quite a place, no?'

'It's paradise. I can see why Valentine loved it so much, why you both did.'

He hoped he wasn't intruding on her memories.

They finished their drinks and then took a stony path that snaked around the side of rock. The mouth of the river was almost entirely blocked by the jungle-backed beach that extended up the coast, but there was a narrow torrent of fast-flowing water cut into the bank of sand just below the hotel. They waded through it to the beach and strolled down to the water's edge.

'This is where I put Valentine, right here.' She pointed at the mouth of the channel, then stared out to sea. 'I'm still surprised the family agreed to it.'

'It was his dying wish to be with Valentine.'

'Told to Bevan. They could have fought it.'

It was true, they could have. Then again, there were a lot of things the Winslows could have done but hadn't. They could have dropped off the radar or hired a PR company to handle the fallout from Joe and Heather's arrests. Instead, they had behaved with dignity, not ducking the scandal that had ripped their world apart, but embracing it, embracing Lyndon's wishes that had set the whole thing in motion. It was clear already that they wouldn't fight Florence over the family trust. Quite the opposite, in fact.

William, devastated by the destruction of his own family, had disappeared from public view, but Olivia had recently given an interview to *The New York Times* in which she had lauded her father's vision of a new kind of capitalism: one that was more responsible, one that recognized the grave dangers facing the planet and that was willing to take bold steps to mitigate the ill-effects of purely profit-driven investment. Fine words, even if they had been lifted straight from the mouth of her dead brother, Valentine, which must have been pretty galling for Florence, not that she had said anything to Dylan.

It seemed to him, the cynic in him, that the Winslow family was doing what it had always done; it was reacting to its environment, it was adapting in order to survive. Who could say what their thinking really was? Maybe branding themselves as the eco-warriors of Wall Street would not only rinse the family's damaged reputation, but also bring in heaps of new business.

'Goodbye, Lyndon,' said Florence.

The lid of the urn came away with a sucking sound, and she tipped his ashes into the channel.

The gray stain dissolved into nothingness as it was washed out to sea.

* * *

Dinner was served at a long table on the lawn, beneath a sky dirty with stars: fresh grilled fish and plenty of crisp white wine. There were ten hotel guests in all, four of them Danish. One of the Danes asked Florence if it was her first time in Colombia. She gave an honest response, and the table slowly fell silent around her as she continued with her story, which then became their story.

'You are the detective?' asked a young Swiss woman with a mop of corkscrew curls.

'One of them. My partner's too ill to be here, but she's on the mend.'

'The man who saved my life twice,' said Florence, her eyes fixed on Dylan across the dancing candlelight.

'My God.'

'Don't stop.'

'Go on.'

'I probably shouldn't,' said Florence. 'Not before the trial.'

'Hey, *I* will kill if you don't,' declared one of the Danes, which got a big laugh.

EIGHTY

Florence lowered the lid of her laptop and sat there in the darkness, listening to the remorseless crash of the waves.

She could imagine particles of Lyndon swirling around below her balcony, minute grains of gray stirred up by the swell and carried on the currents. She pictured them in permanent motion together, Lyndon and Valentine, their molecules colliding for all of time in this choppy corner of the Caribbean, taking a break together on the beach every so often, before a storm snatched them up and swept them back into the churning soup once more. It was a strangely soothing image, and it struck her that now that Lyndon was finally at rest, so was she.

It was over. She could afford to believe it at last. The evidence against the men who had tried to kill her kept stacking up. Every day seemed to bring yet another piece of good news from Greg about some forensic discovery or other that incriminated them still further. As for Joe, he had not retracted his confession, but neither had he chosen to expand upon it. Her request to visit him at Rikers Island had been granted by the authorities but turned down flat by Joe.

She had wanted to sit before him, to face down the hatred he felt for her, had always felt for her, yet hidden so well. To see him as he really was. It was a curiosity that would never be satisfied, but one that she could cope with. After all, she had lived with the unreasoning hatred of others for much of her life.

* * *

She tugged the leather thong, lifting the wooden latch and entering the room. Dylan stirred as she stepped toward him through the slanting moonlight.

'You okay?' he asked, raising himself from the mattress on one elbow.

'I can't sleep.'

'I know. The damn waves.'

'Not that. I'm feeling bad . . . guilty.'

'Why, what have you done?'

'I just put back our return flights by a few days.'

'Yep, that's bad,' he said.

'I checked with Greg first.'

'He's cool with it?'

'If you are.'

'I was planning to power-wash the driveway, but I guess it can wait.'

She smiled, as she often found herself doing when she was with him. 'Do you mind if I join you? I don't feel like sleeping alone.'

'I don't have anything on.'

'If it makes you feel more comfortable . . .'

She tugged off her T-shirt and stepped up onto the high wooden dais that ringed the bed. He raised the sheet. She laid herself down beside his long, warm body, facing him, almost nose-to-nose.

'I'm on the wrong side.'

'No, you're not,' he said. 'This is my side . . . this has always been my side.'

'I'll fight you for it.'

'You can try.'

'You'll lose.'

'Let's see what you've got.'

She pressed her lips to his: a tentative kiss, the tip of her tongue briefly searching out his.

'That's cheating,' he said, a little breathlessly.

'That's not cheating. This is cheating . . .'

THE END

Thank you for reading this book.

If you enjoyed it, please leave feedback on Amazon or Goodreads, and if there is anything we missed or you have a question about, then please get in touch. We appreciate you choosing our book.

Founded in 2014 in Shoreditch, London, we at Joffe Books pride ourselves on our history of innovative publishing. We were thrilled to be shortlisted for Independent Publisher of the Year at the British Book Awards.

www.joffebooks.com

We're very grateful to eagle-eyed readers who take the time to contact us. Please send any errors you find to corrections@joffebooks.com. We'll get them fixed ASAP.

INTRODUCTION

This Christmas Reflection can be used in various and imaginative ways. Amongst others it is suitable for the Christmastime meeting of a devotional group that meets regularly, for a midweek service or for a group visit to a residential home or use within a Senior School's Christmas Programme.

In this version there are parts for seven people but the script is written in a way that the number needed to read is very flexible. We would remind you of the Copyright obligations set out on page 2 – should you be unable to buy sufficient copies for the number taking part please contact the Publisher for a Copying Licence. Schools registered with PLS (Publishers Licensing Society) can reproduce the script under this Licence providing they record the Title, Author, Publisher and ISBN on their return.

Welcome

Leader: The mince pies are ready and so is the cake
And there's enough turkey to feed 28
The presents are wrapped and the fire burns bright
'Gainst the fine sparkle of the Christmas tree light.

It's very cold outside as the snow lies crisp
Much better to be in on a night like this
Carol singers called, we've invited them in
Come on then ….. let the festivities begin.

But wait, O wait, as the celebration starts
Is Jesus enthroned in the warmth of our hearts
Or is the Christchild to us STILL a stranger
Lying outside in that distant manger?

Reader A: **Isaiah 7 v14** The Lord Himself will give you a sign, the virgin will be with child and will give birth to a Son and will call Him Immanuel.

Suggested Carol: O Little Town of Bethlehem

Leader: It was foretold so long ago
And yes it all came true
One silent night in Bethlehem
The gift of love was born anew.

The world cried out in blindness
No room, there is no room
E'en as the Royal Babe prepared
To leave His mother's womb.

No room was there for the Prince of Peace
In the comfort of the inn
But the humble and lowly gladly received
The Heavenly Babe, the Servant King.

As Mary laid Him in the manger
The world saw from the start
He would dwell in the warmth of a stable
While man cried "There's no room in my heart".

Reader A: **Luke 2 vv1-7** In those days Caesar Augustus issued a decree that a census should be taken of the entire Roman world… etc.

Suggested Carol: Away in a manger

Reader A: **Luke 2 vv8-18** And there were shepherds living in the fields.

Suggested Carol: While Shepherds watched their flocks by night.

Leader: The world was deep in slumber
Save for those who tended sheep
And the wise men who remembered
A watchful eye to keep.

They were the ones who saw the sign
And the first to leave all and follow
They were the chosen ones who'd tell
The world of this wonder tomorrow.

But first they were to bow the knee
In humble adoration
And lay before Him gifts so rare,
A Royal Presentation.

Reader A: **Matt 2 vv1-11** The visit of the Magi

Leader: And Mary (His mother) treasured Him
And pondered these things in her heart
And like the wise men and the shepherds
She and Joseph worshipped Him from the start.

Mary: You are so lovely, such a beautiful child
With eyes of the deepest blue
And I feel the love inside of me rise
As my heart is captured by You......

The shepherds have come to adore You
And wise men come, led by a star
The lowly kneel down and worship
Alongside the rich and the wise from afar.

Joseph: You are the boychild of Mary
God's Son, but born of her womb
Come down to dwell in the hearts of men
But born in a stable, nowhere else was there room.

Yes, You are the Son of the Lord most High
And angels attended Your birth
You are Immanuel, God in the flesh
Our Saviour now with us on earth.

Reader A: I see the shepherds at the manger
And wise men from afar
But look at all those children
I don't know who THEY are.

They have no shoes upon their feet
Not all have clothes to wear
They look so lost and hungry
Why are they standing there?

Where IS everybody?
Why aren't they here to see
The Christchild in the manger
God in humanity?

Reader B: One half are at a party
The other half's asleep
They've handed out the presents
Mince pies, crackers, chocs and sweets.

They've been so busy running round
Preparing for this day

They've missed the Angel and the Star
The gift of Christmas Day.

The children standing over there
Look through the window of the rich
Not for them the turkey and the trimmings
Not for them the trifle dish.

But God gave to THEM an angel
And a star to light their way
The baby in the manger
And a proper Christmas Day.

Next six verses to be read by 2 or 3 readers in unison, or could be sung if desired. Suggested tune: See Him Lying on a Bed of Straw.

Wise men looked up at the bright new star
Silently their hearts said Ah! - Ah! Ah!
That's the foretold long awaited sign
It's crystal clear and bang on time.

Grab your camels and your gifts of gold
And frankincense, myrrh, love untold
It's the Natal Star … go on … be bold
It has a story to be told.

Three wise men set out with real intent
Found the baby that was heaven sent
All the angels sang "Peace on the earth"
For through the Christchild Love is birthed.

Grab your camels and your gifts of gold
And frankincense, myrrh, love untold
It's the Natal Star … go on … be bold
It has a story to be told.

Can a baby save the human race?
Yes, God's radiance shines from His face
Wise men, shepherds and the star knew well
This baby was Immanuel.

Grab your camels and your gifts of gold
And frankincense, myrrh, love untold
It's the Natal Star … go on … be bold
It has a story to be told.

Reader A: **Isaiah 9 v6-7** For to us a child is born. He will be
called Wonderful Counsellor, Mighty God,
Everlasting Father, Prince of Peace …… the zeal of
the Lord will accomplish this.

Leader: How can WE conceive the real wonder
Of God on earth among men
Lying there in all His beauty
Depending upon love from them.

What is the colour of His skin
His eyes, and yet His hair,
WHY 'tis in the BEHOLDER's eye
Because for ALL the Lord lies there.

O what a wondrous thing it is
Confounding time and space

God, the Creator, come to earth
To save in love the human race.
And though it be 2000 years
The angels still sing Peace
As the boychild in the manger
Comes to comfort men in need.

Reader A: We are reminded in the song "It came upon a
midnight clear," of the words "Still through the cloven
skies they come, with peaceful wings unfurled; and
STILL their heavenly music floats o'er all the weary
world."

Suggested Carol: It came upon the midnight clear

Reader A: Yes, more than 2000 years have passed
Since that first Christmas morn
O how much longer will it take
For this great Truth to dawn?

Listen … as the angels sing
Peace to all men on earth
O listen to your whispering heart
As we approach the hour of birth ……….

Reader C: If only peace would truly come
new voice   Into MY situation
if possible   But who's aware and who would care
For it doesn't affect a nation.

Reader D: 'Tis in the cause of love and peace
new voice   the Christchild lies in manger bare
if possible   God in the flesh has come to earth
                  BECAUSE He loves you, and He cares.

                  So would you waste ANOTHER year
                  Immanuel our God is here
                  O how much of suffering
                  Before YOU let the Christchild in?

Reader C: Look at Him lying in the manger
                  And THEN tell me He's still a stranger
                  O look at the Christchild, and let Him be born
                  In the warmth of YOUR heart this Christmas morn.

The following verses could be sung if desired to the tune of One More Step Along the Way I Go.

                  I am looking down on Bethlehem
                  At the shepherds and the three wise men
                  I am showing them the way
                  Leading them to that first Christmas Day
                  For I am the star that shines up in the sky
                  Watching everyone as they pass by.

                  I saw Mary ask the inn keeper
                  If he had a comfy bed for her
                  I saw him turn her away
                  There's no vacancy, no room to stay.
                  For I am the star that shines up in the sky
                  Watching everyone as they pass by.

Mary saw an open stable door
Filled with oxen, ass, manger and straw
Jesus Christ was born therein
Baby Jesus who would be a King.
And I am the star that shines up in the sky
Telling everyone who passes by.

Now there is a brighter star than me
One that many people can't yet see
Born to show mankind the way
Lead them to their first real Christmas Day.
And He is the star that shines by day and night
Beaming, beckoning to all alike.

Suggested Carol: Cradled in a Manger Meanly